Further Praise for *ALSO RISING*

"Amusing portrait of the artist as an earnest schlemiel, leavened with an ironic, Hemingwayesque admiration of its south-of-the-border setting . . . brilliantly executed."

—*Kirkus Reviews*

"(Innis's) balanced yet stirring description of the bullfight becomes the subtext for his sensitive depiction of the life of a dedicated artist."

—*Publishers Weekly*

"Excellent, interesting and engaging novel . . . His pen works like the brush of an impressionist painter."

—*Mario Carrion, Matador*
El Clarin de la Busca

"This dramatic novel is deceptively simple . . . lyrical, touchingly personal."

—*Robert Archibald*
Founder, Taurine Bibliophiles of America

Also Rising

W. Joe Innis

EAKIN PRESS ★ Austin, Texas

FIRST EDITION

Copyright © 1998
By W. Joe Innis

Published in the United States of America
By Eakin Press
A Division of Sunblet Media, Inc.
P.O. Box 90159
Austin, Tx 78709

2 3 4 5 6 7 8 9

ISBN 1-57168-196-5

Portions of this book first appeared as a novella under the title, *THE BETTER TIMES*, in English and Japanese in an exhibition catalogue of the author's paintings published by Kodansha of Tokyo in 1984. Some portions of the text, largely revised, have appeared previously in *THE ARTIST'S MAGAZINE*.

Cover painting, *The Better Times*, by the author. Collection of Dr. and Mrs. José Santos, San Antonio
Pen and Ink drawings by Wallace Burdge
Cover photo by Ansen Seale

Library of Congress Cataloging-in-Publication Data

Innis, W. Joe
    Also rising / W. Joe Innis. — 1st ed.
        p. cm.
    ISBN 1-57168-196-5
    I. Title.
PS3559.N5A79   1998
813'.54 — dc21   97-21668
                                                      CIP

For Suzi and Sunny

Also by W. Joe Innis

How To Become a Famous Artist and Still Paint Pictures

In Pursuit of the Awa Maru
(co-author)

This is wholly a work of fiction. The characters in the story are not real, nor are they fashioned to resemble anyone living or dead. While the events take place in the colonial town of San Miguel de Allende and the artist's colony there circa 1970, liberties have been taken with its geography, its people, its places. The author intends for the truth of the book to lie in its fiction in much the same way a painting, if it's any good, is truer than the thing portrayed.

ACKNOWLEDGMENTS

The author gratefully acknowledges those who have helped get this novel told. In this regard I'm especially grateful to my American Collectors Dr. Noby Hagino, the Drs. Rudy and Blanca Molina, Dr. and Mrs. John Huff and Dr. and Mrs. Jose Santos. A very special thanks to one member of the last-mentioned team, Linda Santos, who served as a fine and gentle editor.

To my tireless amigo, Gil Arruda, a widely known *aficionado* in the country, I owe singular thanks for largely, I hope, saving me from the wrath of those who know the bulls far better than I and for lending me his help in getting to know others who would help get the book out of the barn. Another member of Taurine Bibliophiles of America, Don Conover, a former president, was also kind enough to read the manuscript, offer important suggestions and find a place to excerpt a section in the 1996 issue of La Busca.

And, perhaps most importantly, thanks to the many who suffered my early years in Mexico and made them, for me, so memorable.

Chapter 1

It was the diffused light of the city that made Isaac feel he had arrived. He'd gone by that, how things were lit. It was something he understood only by a kind of trust. Things of importance, he'd learned, had another quality about them, another light that set them off from everything else. Over the years he'd come to question this phenomenon less and less. As an artist, he'd learned some things were best left alone.

He sketched with a camera and came to know the important pieces of landscapes and interiors and the arrangements of the figures he would paint by this light and the curious way it emerged in his view finder.

There was a kind of magic in it. The stone bulwarks of the colonial town that climbed the streets above him took on that magic. He had invested in a good used camera years ago. It allowed him to compose his pictures, the telephoto lens permitting him to withdraw or silently advance across great distances. It was marvelous. The slightest twist of a wrist could sharply delineate a tree branch or the curve of a breast, blurring the color components behind it, rendering the foreground unreadable, save for a brush of color or a darkening form.

The sun, he found, played with this best in the early mornings or late afternoons when it dodged and darted around the lengthening shadows, illuminating, blending, shading until for one split second it lit the art of the thing he'd come to capture. It came, when it did, in a light that seemed to emanate from within the sub-ject. And it had to be gotten down. You needed to click the shutter exactly then and hold still while you did so. It took calming down.

It was the same unworldly light that bathed a piece of the city when he first glimpsed it, stooping down and peering upwards through the sooty train window. Maybe it was San Miguel mount-ed on the plateau above him and lit. Damned if it wasn't lit.

He recognized it — or thought he did — from the black and white photo he'd been carrying around for the past two months in his crumpled guide book. It was place-marked by his slightly soiled letter of appointment to the American-owned school.

Repeatedly for the past two hours, the train had stopped at every wind-blown town along the tracks, some comprised of little more than a cluster of taco stands, or an adobe church pitted against a cantina or two across the square. At each it remained briefly, occasionally less than a minute before jerking to a start. He feared he would not recognize the town in time to get his four cases out of the jammed car. His fellow passengers were families mostly, a ragged clot of primary colors, damp with excitement and too much talk.

His Spanish failed him. Whatever they understood from his recent attempt to learn the language earned him enthusiastic and unequivocal approval. For him, the only gringo on the train, San Miguel was anywhere he'd like it to be. It was a courtesy.

He'd got the glimpse at what he took to be the city and, when the train stopped, got two of his bags out through the crush before the train jerked to a start. Amid jeers, laughter, shouts from those aboard, the remaining two cases were passed through a window as the train moved off in long metallic groans and shrieks. He stood in a swirl of dust as it passed. As the air cleared he exulted. He had been right to get off. Indeed, there was a sizable town outlined against the sun above him. He hoped it was the right one. If it was, he'd have it to himself. He was the only one in sight.

Isaac, in his early thirties, wore the look of a young Lincoln about him, hair combed to one side, big hands holding two of his suitcases, hands he didn't always know what to do with. He crossed the tracks.

He had the loose-jointed walk of a displaced athlete, someone who had come to accommodate his height, but not easily. In this, Mexico would set him back a little. The low lintels of the Mexican doorway would come to remind him that he was taller than most. He would meet them often and just above the bridge of his nose.

A single taxi was pointed uphill, a crumpled Buick. An old man was installed behind the wheel. Isaac crossed to the front and set his cases in its way, should it decide to abandon him.

"*Señor*, this is San Miguel up there? This is San Miguel de Allende?"

"Yes," the driver said after a while. "This is a taxi."

Isaac walked back the seventy-five yards to retrieve his other two cases. When he returned the driver had not moved. He set them down with the others. Isaac's shirt had the smell of the day's heat and anxious travel about it.

He straightened and approached the driver's side. The radio was loud and set deep in the static between at least two stations.

"My cases, *Señor*, they are all together here."

"That's clear," the driver said. He did not have many of his own teeth or those of any one else's. He did not move to get out.

"Shall they to go in the taxi, the cases?" Isaac found the verb form the most trying. He felt safest with the infinitive. Often he'd name it up front and string a trail of approximate nouns behind it. It was the next best thing to competency.

The driver shrugged his shoulders. Isaac opened the trunk. There was a tool case and what looked like a bag of laundry. By sliding the tools to one side he was able to get two of his cases in. The others he wrestled into the back seat with him. He shut the door. The driver said something

"How?" Isaac asked.

"Yes," the driver told him and repeated what he'd said earlier. He spoke to the St. Christopher medal hanging from the rear view mirror and not quite loud enough to compete with the radio.

"I'm sorry, I don't understand," Isaac called forward.

3

"You speak English?" the driver asked.

"Yes," Isaac said, vastly relieved.

The old man listened to the radio for a time, then continued in Spanish: "What is it you want?"

"To go up there," Isaac told him. "I want to go to San Miguel de Allende."

"Up there?"

Here there was only the shack behind them, the building that served as the railroad station. A single road led from it. They were parked on it. There was very little else you could do. Nonetheless, Isaac affirmed his intention. The driver needed a little time to think about it.

"OK," he said finally, but still made no move to start. They listened to the radio for awhile. The driver looked out of the window, then back at the St. Christopher medal.

"When we go," the driver said, "do you want the machine to work or not?"

"The machine?"

He indicated the meter. It was painted over. The glass was broken and there was no flag. It didn't seem possible for it to work.

"Without the meter is a little more money," the driver explained. He told Isaac the price if you used the meter and the price if you didn't. There was a considerable difference.

"Fine. Then let's to go with the meter," Isaac said. "Let's go with it turned on."

"It doesn't work, *Señor*."

"The meter?" Isaac wasn't sure he'd got it right.

"Yes, it's broken. The best thing to do is to go without the meter."

He started the car. It didn't have a muffler. As the car labored up the hill the old man had to turn up the radio.

Where the road had been rutted in the last storm, the taxi hit bottom. The driver raised one hand to reassure him.

Chapter 2

As it turned out, San Miguel in early 1970 did have an other-worldly quality. For Isaac, at least, his first impression lingered. It wasn't that the place was exotic — by then there was little remaining in Mexico that was — but it was different enough from the world he'd left to help him forget what drove him there.

Whatever else the students brought to the place, it remained Old World and suffered them quietly. They were mostly Americans, art and language students and a small population of druggies, exiled flower children who had gotten government policy all wrong. These mostly kept to themselves and to the shadows, drifting, shooting up behind the old market, waiting to borrow bus money home.

Isaac sometimes passed them on the way to his boarding house. They sat at outdoor tables drinking cokes and seeing fear. To be busted is to be locked up for life. It was a policy that assured against recidivism.

Almost all the young American men, whether into drugs or not, were distinguished by long hair and beards; the girls, by what they were willing to wear on the streets. For some Mexicans the long hair was the greater of the problems. For a time, shortly before Isaac had arrived, men with offensive locks were pulled out of the central jardin and into the police station across the street where they were summarily shorn to the scalp. The policy lapsed after the son of visiting U.S. diplomat suffered the shears. He was on his way to Mexico City to hear his father make an important address on human rights. He got off the bus to stretch his legs. He attended the speech in a baseball cap.

When the chief of police was urged to discontinue the practice, he did so, though he could see no good reasons for depriving his men of some harmless amusement. It was never intended to be a foreign policy matter or anything directed against his good neighbors to the north. He was known to like Americans and believed a vast majority supported his belief that men with long hair looked like girls.

That the police were willing to forget the matter was another indication of their tolerance. In this they reflected their countrymen. Despite, or maybe because of, its colorful past, Mexicans — unlike Americans — have come to pretty much accept their lot. Even as they're subjected to exploitive State Department initiatives, they continue to condone the gringo among them. Though the art and language schools filled the hotels and *pensiones* and contributed to a flourishing gallery business among the tourists in town, the tolerance, Isaac felt, went beyond economy.

He couldn't put a name to it, but there seemed to be a genuine affection between the two disparate people. It was a good time to be an American in a country whose people didn't yet want to shoot you.

Isaac took to the town. Set as it was on a hillside some 6,000 feet above the desert, it was lush enough, tropical enough, cheap enough and far enough from Southern California to make a good argument for keeping him there.

The six-hour train ride out of Mexico City was a distance which permitted one to taste Mexico without getting welded to it. In that sense it was a pleasant artifice. Since the town had been declared a national monument — owing to its revolutionary namesake and its considerable tourist potential — the beauty of the colonial architecture obtained and was defended from those who would festoon the place with fast-food franchises and motel chains. Conversely, it legislated against those of its natives who couldn't face opening a business unless every exterior wall is painted in a hideous clash of red, green and electric blue.

Outwardly, at least, it's cobblestone, adobe, jacarandas and enough of a quiet population of colorful and desperate peasants for a gringo to get his laundry done.

As in most Latin towns, life circulated around the central *jardin* and its church. This one, La Parroquia, bore the mark of an inspired brick mason with a penchant for drink who was said to have designed and built it. The church was an ambitious one and, as might be expected, was like nothing you've ever seen. The secularists contend the vision for its faux-Gothic design was a product of ample quantities of *pulque,* a raw, cactus beer that has been blinding natives for centuries. They held that the miracle, if there was one, was in the mason's prodigious intake at that altitude and that the church was merely a product of the manic qualities associated with fermented cactus.

Still, it was hard to discount those with faith. The mason had indeed built a sort of Gothic church without ever seeing one, without, in fact, ever having been beyond Querétero, a town twenty miles distant. It was said he cribbed from a postcard picturing Chartres. If so, this might support the secular version that he'd been blinded by the cactus drink.

Two miracles were implicit in the church: it wasn't as bad to look at as things got, and it still stood.

The morning after he'd arrived, Isaac had been pointed through the streets and across town to the school. It occupied the grounds of an abandoned convent, a cloister that contained elegant patios, lush vegetation and winding walkways that serpentine through inner and outer courtyards, fountains, and several terraces, the best of which is situated to look out across the distant city and its church, a view freely maligned by earnest water color students since the institute opened in 1930.

Formerly the 18th Century home of the Counts of Canal, it had become the heart of an art colony whose popularity ebbed and flowed over the years.

7

Isaac found the office just off the entrance crowded with a bevy of middle-aged women registering for class. He caught the eye of a young secretary, the only one behind the counter who did not seem to be in pain. The owner would not be expected for half an hour.

Beyond the perimeter of the older buildings that contained the central courtyard and its tile fountain were the out-buildings. A newly built life drawing studio was closed to visitors, an ongoing class inside. The gallery offered the usual mix of student excesses, though some of the drawings were well handled. At least one of the faculty was teaching, Isaac noted. Next to the gallery were the sculpture studios, welding, clay and plaster casting. The painting studios were at the far end of the campus, beyond the tree-shaded tennis court and near the new hotel. A watercolor class was being held on the lawn of one of them. Nearby there was a small foundry and a potter's studio and scattered between them a number of out-door sculptures, two of which were heavily indebted to David Smith, another to Giacometti. A fourth, an Arp-like ferro-cement abstract, was apparently being demolished by two Mexican work-ers. It was eight or nine feet tall and stood in a bricked courtyard near the theater building. The workers were taking turns with sledge hammers. A short, wiry man of about sixty-five stood be-hind them.

He wore a flowered short-sleeve shirt and spoke in Spanish to the workers, pointing to where they should strike. He seemed ex-cited. He called Isaac over.

"You gotta remember one thing."

"One thing?" Isaac asked, not quite sure if he had been mis-taken for someone else. The man said something to one of the workers, then turned back to Isaac.

"What am I looking at here? I'll tell you. I'm looking at a Mas-ter's thesis, a student piece some time back, and what you got to remember about this is Importance. They teach you Importance in any of your classes?"

"I'm not —"

"Of course they don't. You know why they don't teach you Im-

8

portance? I'll tell you. Because they don't think about Importance. There's a lesson here and I'm going to tell you about it. You think I like destroying art?" He seemed to be mad at Isaac, almost shouting. The workers had stopped and were watching him.

"Of course not," Isaac assured him.

"Here, look." He was pointing to part of the shattered pedestal, a name and a date had been etched into the polished cement. "You heard of this man? No? Well, yesterday, I asked around. You know what I found? Nobody's heard of this man. Nobody. Is he famous? The hell he is. I'm asking you: Who is this man? You can't tell me, right? And he's had . . . what?" He tipped toward the pedestal and squinted at the date. "He's had ten years, for Christ's sake. And that's why you got to learn Importance. You learn anything about art, you learn that. That's what I'm trying to teach you here. I got to have space for a flower bed, sure. But that's not the point. You think I'd tear down an important piece of sculpture to put in a goddamned flower bed? Whose class are you taking?" he demanded.

"I'm not in class. I'm . . . I just got here. I'm going to teach here. Are you . . . you're maybe Bill Spencer?"

Spencer pumped his hand, all smiles, freckles blanketing his face, his nose peeling badly. His thin red hair was laid down with a waxy, heavily scented substance. A cowlick sought, and was making visible progress toward, liberation.

"You're Dick Welby then," Spencer told him. "Weaving and Indian Jewelry. Damned if I expected you this early."

"No. I'm in your . . . Painting. Shelderval. I'm Isaac Shelderval."

"Shelderval. . ." He seemed to think about it. "No matter. Tell me about your trip?" But he'd turned to the workers, gave them some instructions, turned back. "So when do you start drinking?"

"What?"

Together they looked at his watch. It was almost wider than his freckled wrist, large Roman numerals in black. It was not yet ten.

"Damn," he told Isaac. "Anyway, let's go to the office. Sounds

9

like you had a good trip." He bolted off without looking for company, darted down some steps and headed across the courtyard. He walked on the balls of his feet and as though leaning into a high wind. With each stride he gained on Isaac who had to trot, sometimes, to catch up to him. He had been talking and Isaac missed some of it.

". . . the fundamentals. He asked me that. So I told him, 'Look, I'm talkin' fundamental. Singular.' And he says 'What do you mean?' You know what I told him? I told him exactly what I'm going to tell you: there's only one fundamental. You talk art, you talk business, it's all the same. Get my drift? Tell me the fundamental I'm talking about."

Spencer pushed on across the campus. He acknowledged those who greeted him with a little salute. He did not let up his pace. Together and near the fountain they cleaved through a Japanese tour group, dividing it neatly into two agitated clusters. Just before they got to the office Spencer stopped abruptly. Isaac narrowly avoided colliding into him.

"You understand, I'm talkin' money here!" He glared at Isaac as though an argument was being offered. But just as Isaac was considering how to calm him down, he was off again, this time through the door to the office. Isaac followed.

The secretary with the bright face approached, but Spencer impatiently waved her off. He headed up the stairs, which he took two at a time, Isaac behind him. Spencer seated himself behind a desk cluttered with letters, papers, art books, some open and face down, and an assortment of what looked to be plumbing tools. He pointed Isaac into a chair across from him. Before Isaac could sit he had to move an open can of motor oil which, unaccountably, was on the seat. Isaac did so carefully and set it on the floor next to him. But before he could sit down Spencer was around the desk pulling at his arm.

"I want you to look at these." Against the wall behind Isaac were stacks of canvases of all sizes, stretched, but mostly unframed. They were all turned to the wall. As Spencer paged through them, he explained how he had acquired each over the years. They were

10

the work of former students and teachers, apparently gifts. They were an eclectic lot, some quite good, some terrible. Spencer stayed with each long enough to determine whether Isaac had heard of the artist. Each time he named an artist, Spencer watched his face.

When they came to the last and Isaac failed to recognize the name, Spencer swore quietly, flipped the stack back against the wall and returned to his desk. Immediately he began a search of his desk, frantically rummaging through the middle drawer. He slid it back and cocked his head to one side in order to see into the recesses. None of it stopped him from talking.

"So, you live in New York?" His voice was hollowed and emanated from the well of the desk.

Isaac told him he didn't. Spencer stopped his search and looked at him.

"There you are," he said. "You see?" He returned to the drawer with even more energy. "Did I write you?"

"Yes. I've got. . .You sent me a letter of appointment. I got it here" Isaac found it hard to talk to the top of his head, the whorled hair.

"A letter of appointment," Spencer told him.

Isaac could see he was intent on his search, repeating words as sounds. He was moving the papers with a fury. In the far reaches of the drawer he apparently found what he was looking for. It was a toothpick. He looked at it, then wiped it carefully on a pants leg, tilted back in his chair and immediately began working on a back molar, his blue eyes glazed. He said something.

"What?"

"Read it to me, the letter." He returned to the molar, looking past Isaac, unfocused. Isaac read him the letter, then waited. When Spencer had finished with the tooth, he inspected the end of the toothpick, wiped it off and returned it to the center drawer. He turned his attention to Isaac for the first time.

"What do you do beside paint?

"What do you mean?"

"We got painters. What else do you do?"

11

"But you sent me this letter."

"That's a damn shame and I mean it. Totally my fault. Probably a carbon of it somewhere. I'm betting those damn secretaries put it on my desk. I've told 'em, but I'm guessin' that's what happened.".

"You mean you forgot?" Isaac was incredulous.

"Hired Delphias Stewart. Three weeks ago. Terrible thing. I know what you're going through. I'd fire him in a minute, but he brought his damn family, babies, the lot. You alone?

"Yes."

"Well, there you are. So, what else do you do? All this is a shame and I mean it. You know anything about theater? Yeah, well, nobody does. Listen: you do sculpture?"

"I've done some," Isaac told him.

"Damn Risley anyway. What's he do? Chooses peak season to drive into a herd of Black Angus cattle. Out of Guanajuato. Dark night. They got me out of bed. Got out there and Old Risley's all over the place. Damn shame. Couldn't find some of the parts but got most of him into a box. Cow cost me six thousand pesoes. He taught clay modeling and plaster casting. Wasn't much good at it anyway. A bit assembly line, but Carlos can show you what you don't know. Done some casting?"

"Well, yes. As it happens — "

"Good — Shelderval, isn't it? — that's the stuff. Get it done is how I look at it." Spencer stood and unzipped his pants. He tucked his shirt in, smiled and sat again. "Thanks for coming in," he said.

Struck with the abruptness, Isaac hesitated, then stood. "Aren't I supposed to, you know, sign something? I mean, when do I start? What do —"

"Listen. What do you smoke?" With both hands he'd begun patting the thick layers of papers and old magazines that layered his desk, feeling for something beneath them.

"Huh?"

"Never mind." Spencer retrieved a single, badly crushed cigarette from under some papers near one of the pipe wrenches. He cleared off a corner of the desk and worked at rolling it straight, smoothing it out. When he had it reasonably shaped, he put it in the same drawer he'd stored his toothpick and closed it.

"Go see Angelina downstairs. She'll be the happy one. Tell her you're the new professor of Advanced Sculpture and she'll work up some papers. Tomorrow morning, nine o'clock. Go see Carlos. He knows where the clay is."

Chapter 3

He had not meant to be early. He hated parties. It was not his intention to spend more time than he needed at one. Also, he didn't know Rafael well and certainly wouldn't have burdened him with his untimely arrival if he had.

Isaac couldn't remember where they'd met. In the first months he'd met as many in town as wanted to be met, he figured, and Rafael was one of those. In a small place you see many of the same people. Rafael became one of those who greeted him in the way Mexicans have of making you believe you're close enough to share a wife.

In truth, though, it was a limited exchange of pleasantries, sometimes delivered across a narrow street; or when they met in the hardware store where Isaac came to buy his tobacco, which they weighed and poured into a paper sack; or in the post office which, in the absence of reliable delivery services, acted as sort of a community center; or in one of the grocery stores where Isaac bought some of the packaged American food he'd come to expect in life. He knew him only by sight, but it was certainly not Rafael who swung open the heavy oak door to Sanchez's apartment.

By his own faulty reckoning, Isaac's arrival at the address was well beyond the time he was invited and what he'd guess was proper for this kind of thing. He had kept himself from leaving from his own door early and, when he could wait no longer, had taken special measures to kill time getting there. He took the long way from his pension, walking slowly. It took him through the park and

14

up along the waterworks where the women laundered and caught up on the news. But they were gone, the long line of cement tubs with its stream of water running through them was empty of the talk and laughter and the slapping sound of wet clothes. It was early evening and he was alone and he made himself sit on one of the rock ledges that bordered the long steps leading to the deserted *lavadero*. There he watched some kids play bullfight in the dust street below him. He was determined to be fashionably late and wondered how late that would have to be. He made himself sit there beyond the time it seemed reasonable to leave.

His hope was to pair an innocuous entrance with an equally undistinguished exit. He thought to make it back early enough to continue a drawing he had started, one that might give way to a painting, some assembled crockery against a shuttered window.

He had been in an explosive period of creativity, so prodigious it was embarrassing. He had a stack of finished paintings under his bed. In his studio at school they leaned against the walls. A gallery in town showed a few paintings and two of his sculptures. He had begun re-using his stretchers, stripping finished paintings from them and rolling them up.

He did not believe it was the move alone that brought him to the high productivity, though an environment foreign to him was always stimulating. Nor did the energy derive from his teaching, even if there was a certain amount of invigoration in showing a student something he wanted to learn. He could not account for it, except that it followed the long drought. He had taken the bad time day by day and was surprised that, strung together, it extended for almost eighteen months. And there had been the song writing before that.

These were better times, clearly, and they came after a long, dry march that had begun the morning Abby chose to tell him that she had begun to sleep with men who could better afford her. The plural of the noun particularly rankled him. It was one thing to sleep with a man, another, a group of them. He had been too busy trying to write a song that would bring in some money, and too trusting to notice that she spent a lot less time with the housework then she once did.

She stood in the haze of kitchen smoke that morning — cooking was a special challenge for her — and outlined her priorities. It was an elaborate story. She recited it while welding his two eggs to the frying pan. It amounted to this: her being his wife was getting in the way of her being the singer she always wanted to be. She told him some of the men she had begun with and her need for making the arrangement more permanent. She knew he would understand. He had been in the music business (her use of the past tense did not go unnoticed) and knew how things work. Hadn't he married a singer? What was she expected to do when opportunity knocked as she knew it would? One of her new friends was connected to somebody. Surely he could understand what that might mean to her future. She wanted to know how he could deny her that.

But she wanted him to understand her. There was absolutely nothing personal about this and she, for one, was willing to part amicably. They were grown up people and she knew he would want to stay in touch and be kept abreast of her good news when it came. She would be recording under her new name, Vallinia Free, and he was to look for that if he wanted to follow her career.

By the time she finished, the eggs were a bas relief on the bottom of the aluminum pan, a burnt shadow of their short, happy life.

He truly and stupidly hadn't seen it coming. He had thought her cooking was his greatest trial.

No, he had not meant to be early. But beyond the thick, little Spaniard in the three-piece suit, beyond the dour little man who stepped back to allow him through the door, was silence: absolute, unmistakable, impenetrable. Either he had the wrong door, the wrong day or was, once again, the first to arrive.

It could be said — as it no doubt was — that Isaac was not good at parties. He guessed that being early contributed to the assessment. Lately at these things, so punctual was he that by the time the second guest arrived, he was part of the family. Already

16

he would have been introduced to the children, sampled what looked edible in the hors d'oevre tray and made a studied tour of everything remotely interesting in the way of art, craft and literature that appeared open to inspection in anything but the bedrooms. Already he would have complimented the hostess on her choice of parrots.

All of which took at least two drinks.

But however strong his intentions, he could not seem to overcome the power of heredity. His father, it was said, (by him to everyone) never missed a train. It was one of several social defects which, mitigating as they did against his own success, he thought to pass along to his son.

Isaac had learned well. It took the two drinks to convince himself that an art teacher ought to be offered a few perquisites, that a certain amount of social gaucherie was forgivable, that he was not, as some undoubtedly had it, a crashing clod, however it may appear.

If Spencer hadn't forcefully insisted, he would not have been there at all, to the Sanchezes' or to any of the other functions he'd been obliged to attend lately.

A few weeks after his first meeting at school, during which he found himself warming to the monastic life of a teacher, Spencer caught him between classes. He invited him for coffee, which they took at a back table in the school cafe.

Spencer didn't talk until he had drained about a quarter of his cup. He brought it back to rim level with a long, steady stream of sugar from a jar on the table. Fearing a spill, he brought his lips down to the rim and vacuumed its edge. He was wearing another Hawaiian shirt, this one featuring the repeated image of a badly rendered hula dancer. With it, his red hair, freckles and the open grin he offered Isaac as he looked up from his coffee, he was a condensed version of Arthur Godfrey.

"Ah, there you are then. So, getting along are you? Carlos giving you trouble? Good man, that one. Needs keeping it in his pants a little more, but essentially solid. Held the fort, so to speak." Carlos was a somewhat off-handed Mexican from Dolores Hidalgo who had served as a co-teacher with Risley. Even before Risley's crash, he had done most the teaching. Risley, could remain incandescently drunk for months on end, a condition that Carlos could no longer keep from Risley's students after the day he was found sleeping in the plaster bin. That was shortly before he met the cow that permanently sobered him.

Carlos's legendary loyalty to Risley concerned Isaac. He had worried that Carlos might resent his coming to replace him. He needn't have.

"I like Carlos, works hard," Isaac told Spencer. "He's developed quite a following." His romances around town were legendary, involving convoluted plot twists with all the narrow escapes usually associated with bedroom comedy.

Spencer said: "Students tell me you got the makings of a teacher, though I can't guess how they would know. How do you find them? Is Rodin in any danger?" Spencer added some more sugar to his coffee. He stirred it. It was now the consistency of maple syrup. He held the upturned cup to his lips for the last of it to drain.

"It's a mix, I'm sure you know," Isaac said. "Some serious students, but mostly you got the . . . you know, the students who are not so keen on the work, on the labor of it."

"The labor of it." Spencer pulled a thick wad of napkins from a tightly packed dispenser, folded it and slid it into his trouser pocket. He looked again at Isaac and waited.

"Of course," Isaac continued, "Carlos and I are up to handling the heavy stuff, but it's just . . . well, not the same. Without the labor, the heavy work, it becomes a different thing, sculpture. I guess I feel it's important that they know that. It's part of the product, what sculpture is. When I try to put them to work — "

"You talking about the old broads?"

"Pardon?" Isaac was sure he hadn't heard him right.

"The little ladies. The dabblers in their tidy smocks and funny hats"

"Well, I suppose —"

"Those," Spencer continued, "who've come down for their af-

18

ternoon pitcher of *margaritas*, who've given themselves three months to become modern masters."

"Well, yeah. I think that . . . you could say that."

"Of course I can say that." Spencer picked up the check and studied both sides of it. He returned it to the table. Some graduate students Isaac recognized from his classes came in, took a table by the window and fell to a loud and heated discussion on the merits of remaining true to the picture plane.

Spencer listened to them, then turned back to Isaac. "Shelderval, this is not a new business for me. I've been at it since the caves. Remember this: it is a large bunch of shit to be young and to simultaneously believe you're an artist." He nodded to the students. "It is an equal piece of shit to believe this and to be old. I know what you're saying about the old ladies, exactly. What do you think we ought to do about it?"

"I'm not sure there's anything —"

"Right. Shelderval, you've hit on it. I understand how you feel, and you're absolutely on the money. Understand my position and you'll understand what constitutes the backbone of this — hell, any — art school." Spencer slid his coffee cup and saucer to one side. He licked the spoon and put it in his shirt pocket.

"I didn't mean to sound like I was registering a complaint. I only meant to respond —"

But Spencer was standing, looking at the check again.

"This appears to be all right." He handed it to Isaac. "But watch them. Sometimes they pad it, charge you for things you didn't eat or drink. It's a concession — art supplies, junk food and bad coffee. I'm not happy about how they run it. They're not bad people, but always check the tab. You can pay up there." He started for the door, then came back.

"Listen, go to the parties, will you?"

"Pardon?"

"Those invitations you get? Use 'em. Go to all the damn things if you can."

"The parties?" Isaac remembered some invitations stuffed into his in-box. Most of them were addressed to Risley.

19

"We're here at the behest of the Mexican government. Those invitations are from influential townies. You're one of six full-time gringos on the teaching staff. You need to go where you're invited. Politics, old man. I play it; you play it. Fair enough?"

"I didn't —"

"No problem at all. Just wanted to have you understand, old man. It's a small town; the school, a cultural part of it. It's best not to offend anyone. We play by the rules or we're closed. Am I right? Also it's a dead town, as you no doubt discovered. Night life, I remind you, is a counter-clockwise walk around the *jardin*. So people have parties. So go. Go to the damn things. Get your name around. You think Billingstein made it because he could paint? The old fart was color blind. Couldn't tell ultramarine from ox piss."

Reggie Billingstein was former chairman of the art department and remained listed on the board of directors. Over the years he had published a series of slick volumes on watercolor techniques featuring endless renditions of Mexican markets. He retired to Taos, Isaac had read recently, where he painted Pueblo Indian life. His palette, style and subject matter remain strikingly unaffected by his move.

Spencer was shaking his hand. "Damn shame, I know. Keeps you from your own time. I know what you mean. But get used to getting out among 'em. We got the Guerber lecture in a few weeks. Need to get the word out. Absolute crap and a damn shame, but there you are."

Isaac had seen the posters and swore to miss the event. It had been ballyhooed since he'd come. Heinrich Guerber was a SoHo dandy who, together with Warhol, Rauchenberg and some others, was proving you could get very rich pleasing New York's cognoscente.

"Why here?" Isaac asked. "What brings him down here?"

"Spent some weeks in a painting class one winter, long before he began remaking the world in his own image. We're his alma mater, such as it is. Anyway, we're all he's got. Was hopeless, as I recall. Possibly blind. It was marketing or nothing.

Isaac began to take on the parties. He noticed Spencer most often made a showing. Isaac would spot him across the room. He'd be grinning, pumping a hand with both of his, leaning in, laughing. He'd dart in his stutter step from group to group. When he'd look again, Spencer would be gone. The school owner was abrupt, maddening, self centered and, for a reason Isaac could not fathom, wholly likable.

Since the old Spaniard who ushered him into the Sanchezes' offered neither his name or position, Isaac avoided any further awkwardness that may arise from wrongly guessing whether he was hired help or family. He did so by lavishing his attention on whatever was around. Luckily, there was a marvelous clutter of fine old things that filled the living room.

Though small, the room carried a sense of space through its vaulted ceiling and the pair of elongated Moorish windows that occupied one wall. They had been shuttered against the noise and lights from the central *jardin* below. The furniture, some of which was hand-carved and stately, was an eclectic collection, each piece chosen for itself, not to complement some central theme. For the most part, good, livable stuff.

The art, too, was a bountiful find of good taste, a time- less sampling of that which was good to look at, displayed without concern for school or period.

On a table just off the foyer amid a clutter of books and papers rose an exquisite, Olmec-inspired piece of erotic sculpture. On a dimly lit wall behind it was a small, early Jasper Johns. Somehow they worked together. As near as he could tell, there wasn't a parrot in the place.

The old man tracked him quietly. His identity was finally revealed when Rafael called out to his father from a back room.

Still, he said little in response to Isaac's questions. It allowed him to make an uninterrupted study of what he could find. When the *criada* handed him his second drink, Rafael and Maria emerged, greeted him with effusive apologies for not meeting him at the door and disappeared again, leaving Isaac, once more, with the old man.

They took seats facing each other, finally. Isaac set himself the chore of finding common grounds, if any.

Old Man Sanchez had the look of Picasso about him, owing in part to the full mouth and wide, slightly lidded eyes and in part to an athletic physique the years had only managed to thicken. He boasted a tan pate and had neatly laid some white hair across it. The mutuality Isaac sought was not immediately forthcoming. The responses, when they came at all, were slow, considered. He did not, or would not, speak English.

Yes, he was Spanish, born in a small village near Valencia, or someplace that sounded like it. No, he did not like Barcelona and did not evidently care that Isaac did. No, he did not understand about art, artists or art teachers, but was not averse to those who could make a living from the field, if that was how they wanted to spend their lives.

Yes, he did not live with Rafael and Maria. It was a city, this, and he did not live in cities. He lived where his animals lived. No, he had not been misunderstood about the animals. He was the owner of Los Valiontes, a ranch in the far hills, and he lived with his bulls, and they were a thing Americans would not be expected to understand. Yes, they were fighting bulls. Yes, they were compared favorably with La Puntas; in some respects they were more honored, if he may say, and how was it an American would know about such things?

By the time the fashionable hour had arrived, and as though the guests had been queuing at the door waiting for it to be declared, they began to percolate into the living room. They were compelled to talk around and over Sr. Sanchez and Isaac.

The two were paging slowly through an old leather-bound volume on bull raising the old man had given his son years ago.

Occasionally Sanchez would pause to relate a story of a classic fight. Knowing the terminology of the fights, together with his near total immersion in the language in recent months, enabled

22

Isaac to follow the old man easily. Loosened by the drinks, he was able to respond in kind.

He told the old man of a fight he'd seen in Pomplona where the last bull shattered a horn on the *barrera* on his initial charge out of the *toril*, and how the crowd, angered that the bull was not immediately replaced, threatened to storm the Presidente's box. It did not matter to them whether the horn had been badly shaved or that the bull was blind or that there were complicated jurisdictional questions about who would pay for a replacement. They wanted to tell the Presidente where he could put his one-horned bull.

The old man said that in Madrid that would not have happened. There, they would not have taken the time to explain to the Presidente what he might do with the crippled animal. If another bull wasn't forthcoming, the crowd would have shown him, then gone out and burned the city.

When Isaac turned in response to the hand that lightly touched his shoulders, he faced the Mayan-like profile of Maria Sanchez, the old man's daughter in law. She was trying to extract a tall, square-jawed man from the group he was talking to. Isaac stood and together they waited for the man to finish with his appreciative audience. With some reluctance he turned from the laughter he'd generated, yielding to the gentle touch of his hostess. The humor he had stirred was still in his face as he leaned toward Maria for the introduction.

Whatever Maria may have known of Heinrich Guerber's reputation in contemporary art, and Isaac's lack of one, she chose to introduce them as equals, two established figures in the art world. Though they both knew Maria was only half right, Isaac was startled to see the color wash from Heinrich's face. Clearly, he was stung by the slight.

Chapter 4

It took Heinrich only a moment to recover. You had to have been watching him carefully to notice that he had done so with some effort.

"Oh, I'm sorry, Maria. The name. Please forgive me. I did not recognize. Foolish. It is Isaac then?" Heinrich's years in SoHo had not yet corrupted his heavy German accent. He turned to Isaac. "You are some sculptor, yes?"

"One of many, I'm afraid."

"You're too modest; and a professor you say, Maria? It is good to be among the intellectuals. It is the professors who will save us from all the talk of art, no? Someday we will spend an afternoon, Isaac. You can teach me the sculpture. You can teach me what it is and why you have chosen to honor us by working in such a medium."

His voice was pitched high and a little too loud for comfort, and he had the habit loud people have of favoring his listener by leaning toward him.

Isaac tried to ignore the sarcasm. He played it straight. "I'd enjoy discussing sculpture with you. How long will you be in town?"

"Not long, I'm afraid. With all the attention on you, I'll be obliged to sneak away within a blanket of darkness, yes?

Heinrich had recovered his humor, could barely, in fact, control himself. His face colored with suppressed laughter as he sought and apparently won approval from those around him.

"Yes, one day it will be a great pleasure, Isaac. We will visit, you and I. You can tell me how it is I've missed all the things that are said about your work. I admire you. You've maintained great privacy in the face of fame, Isaac. Marvelous. Ah, that's the secret, yes? That's what I must learn: How to be at the same time famous and unknown."

Heinrich contained himself no longer, but before Isaac could get his words together and be heard above others who had joined in the laughter, he was being embraced.

"Please, Isaac, it is only a joke." Heinrich pulled back, tears in his eyes, a hand still on Isaac's shoulder. He was looking beyond Isaac as he spoke, still searching for someone. "Such bad jokes. Means nothing. I want you to know it means not a thing."

If anything, Heinrich Guerber was too handsome. Like Isaac he was in his early thirties. Unlike him he carried the outdoor look of the rich about him, of country clubs, spas and heat lamps. It did not look like he'd ever been to SoHo, let alone earned his iconoclastic reputation there. Isaac remembered some of what he'd read about him.

Heinrich was the heir to a steel magnate who owned a sizable chunk of Cologne, or was it Stutgardt? Family sent him to Yale where he majored in Sixties politics and American coeds. Was relieved of the burden of study early by flunking out. With the opening salvos of the sexual revolution it was no time to be in school.

Like Whistler, who traded on his brief stay at West Point, Heinrich was the Yale man who threw it all away for art. They also shared a fondness for spritely attire and knew how to use people and the press. But decidedly unlike Whistler, Heinrich had not been issued discernible talent. Fortunately, New York's SoHo was neither like Paris or London a century before. The absence of artistic ability wasn't considered an impediment.

When he'd first come to SoHo, Heinrich had begun with pallid little geometries, a dim echo of Mondrian, who pre-dated him by 40 years. He began to win an audience when he turned performer, which he did by painting over established works of art. His notoriety rose in direct proportion to the market value of the works he destroyed. He won his first real distinction when he over-painted some noted American Impressionists and some second tier French ones. He did so with heavily layered vertical stripes. His infamy became negotiable the day he revised the family's Cezanne. That the ghost of this master bled through the newly laid oil only enhanced the effect.

"Ah," he said. "You must . . . There. There she is. Please for-give." He was signaling to a dark-haired girl across the room in a group which included Rafael. When he caught her eye, they wait-ed in silence for her to make her way through the crowd. She held her wine glass at the stem with the tips of her fingers. She followed it, moving around and through the crowd in a continuous serpen-tining movement that terminated at Heinrich.

When the German pulled her against his suede jacket, she folded the drink to her chest. It was filled to the brim. She had nei-ther looked at the glass nor spilled a drop. Heinrich pressed his face into her hair and spoke loudly enough for those around him to hear.

"Mem, you are so beautiful. Like a deer, sometimes. The way you walk is like that. Marvelous. Sometimes so marvelous."

When he looked to Isaac, he was the beaming proprietor invit-ing a comment in kind, and grinning, he was prepared to wait for it. Isaac looked at the girl.

She had the thin, fragile look of hollow beauty one would find on the cover of women's magazines, the kind of beauty one could normally and quite easily dismiss. There was a vanity about it, about the way she carried it, heightened it. To be sure, there was vanity, but there was something else, something beyond it. Some-thing, maybe, in the way she moved her eyes away from Isaac's. There was something beyond beauty in the look of her, and it took him a moment to discover it: the thin, hairline scar that lay across the corner of her upper lip provided it. It worked to give a curious set to the mouth, a faint lopsidedness about her when she was smil-ing and a slightly pinched air of determination when she was not. There was a sensitivity about it that worked behind her eyes. It was a slight wound, an old wound, but she still carried the schoolgirl concern about it. There was a timidity to her look.

"Mem, I am most pleased to have you meet an esteemed professor of Sculpture from the Instituto here. Isaac, Memori. My dear Memori. How she has been interested in sculpture. She'll monitor a class with you, Isaac. How will that be? Has a certain flair, I think. Marvelous hands. Look at these."

He held forward one of her hands for inspection. Isaac thought he'd glimpsed a flicker of impatience in her eyes, but it was gone too soon to be certain. The three of them looked down at her fine, thin hand. Isaac could think of nothing to say about it. Instead, he turned and introduced Sr. Sanchez, who had risen at the girl's approach. Heinrich spotted the book left open on the table.

"So, then, we have a man of letters here," he said. He craned his neck to better see the book. It lay open to an illustration of the testing of a calf against the *pic*. He reached down and picked it up. "Ah, this is very nice. This is not a bullfight, Sr. Sanchez?"

At first it appeared the old man had not heard or, having heard, did not intend to answer. When he finally spoke, Heinrich was forced to lean toward him to hear.

"Yes," the old man said in English, "it is not a bullfight."

Since the old man was clearly going to leave it there, Isaac felt obliged to offer the explanation.

"I see." Heinrich replied to the short lecture without looking at Isaac. "And this, this testing. It is to determine exactly what? That this is a brave bull? That it is a bull worthy of fighting? Is that the reason it is being poked by the pole?" The German celebrity wanted the old man to answer.

"Heiny," Memori implored. "Please, don't start up on this."

Because Heinrich was still searching the Spaniard, he missed the intensity of Memori's request. Either she was working at an intuitive level to head off a social gaffe, or, more likely, she had spoken to Rafael of his father or overheard Isaac talking with him about his bull ranch.

"But, Mem. You see I'm interested. Truly. I'm interested to

27

learn about this testing. Is it a scientific testing, this? It is some kind of preparation?" Heinrich continued to play to the crowd, which had drawn inward like a breath.

Isaac saw that the old man had been right from the beginning He had sensed being baited from the first, whereas Isaac, stupidly compelled to move the conversation along, had not. Now Isaac was further obligated to defend himself.

"Yes," he answered. "You could say it is some kind of preparation. The testing determines how . . . what kind of animal it is."

"What kind of animal," Heinrich repeated, still addressing the old man. "But that puzzles me. Is it important, what kind of animal is it? This little bull will grow into a bigger bull. Is that not right? And in the name of bullfighting it will be tortured and killed. Whatever kind of animal, won't it be dead in the name of bullfighting? Yes? And is it not a curious name to attach to what isn't a fight at all? The outcome does not favor the animal. What does it matter, the kind of animal? What does it matter about this testing?"

Memori shifted were she stood. She had developed some color in the hollow of her cheeks.

"Heiny has a tendency to speak a little too forcefully sometimes," she said quietly, insistently. She, too, was addressing the old man. "I think what he means is he does not understand the bullfights. I'm afraid I have trouble here myself, but —"

"But, Memori, what you say is not right," Heinrich proclaimed. "It is something I understand very much." He did not look at her, did not break his smile, did not look away from the old man. "I'm afraid all too well. In Juarez I have seen one such thing. And I would be blind if I did not understand it. With all due apologies to you and your country, Sr. Sanchez, it is one of the customs I cannot abide. I find it despicable, I'm sorry to say."

The rest of what Heinrich had to say had apparently been readied from the beginning:

"I am told I should see the pageantry of it, that it is a kind of ballet. I'm told these things, that it is like seeing Memori on stage, that it is a beautiful dance. But I don't see it. I see nothing in the beauty. I see nothing more than what it is.

"I see what is the bull and he is humiliated. I see that he is tortured. And, if my stomach is not upturned, I see in the end of it, that the bull is finally and quite irrevocably murdered.

"And I have watched those who have an interest in this, this pageantry. I have noticed that they applaud this animal only when it is dragged out by its horns by a team of mules. I have watched all this, but there must be something I am missing. Perhaps, Sr. Sanchez, you can tell me what it is I do not understand."

"Heiny," Memori touched him lightly on the arm. "I think Mr. Sanchez is being —"

"I'm sure Sr. Sanchez can understand that there are those who may differ with the customs of his country. Are there not your own countrymen, Mexicans who protest this . . . this bullfight of yours? Are there not those of your own people who share my view?"

Heinrich was enjoying himself. From the beginning he had not lost his smile.

Isaac started to say something, but took a sip of his drink instead. Heinrich was right, of course. The bullfight was indefensible. It had been a long time since Hemingway, Conrad, Fulton and some others had made bullfighting permissible for Americans, before it fell from favor. It had been an exotic import. Painters like Manet forgot what they were good at and traded in it. Later it became fashionable to sit among movie stars on the shady side of rings in Spain and Mexico and recite Hemingway as though you wrote it yourself.

For a while it was fine to attend the fights and sit where you could be seen and be close enough to the *barrera* so that one of the matadors you have befriended could dedicate a bull to you.

Then, for a while, it didn't matter much whether you went to the bullfights or not. Isaac had started to go to them then. It was a good time to study them. You didn't have to worry about the fashion of it. If you chose to take the *corrida* seriously, you could learn about it from the only standpoint that mattered. You could learn to see the fight as a piece of cultural history, a core part of the countries from which they derive. And you could learn what that culture and its special history had to do with you.

Later, when fashion exerted itself against them, it mattered very much that you did not attend bullfights. Fashion stripped them clean of their beauty and laid bare their cruelty. If one continued to attend the fights, as Isaac did, it was best not to talk about it. The things you learned about art, life and how death came were things you still learned in the bullfight. The only difference was you didn't talk about it.

The bullfight was like a painting. And, like a painting, it could not be divided into its parts without losing itself to the study. When you took a painting apart, what you see were all the dabs of pigment, the brush strokes, the imperfect weave of the linen support, the mistakes in the underpainting, the hesitations. You no longer see the whole of it. You don't see how it was intended.

Not long out of high school, and in Tijuana, Isaac saw his first fight. He had gone with a girl who knew about the fights. At least she knew what her father — an economics professor and *aficionado* — had told her. Throughout, she explained what was to happen in each act, what the mechanics of the fight were, and the difference between a good pass and one which looked like a good pass. They drank dark wine that ran from her father's *bota* in a warm stream and sat in the sunny side amid a crowd of boisterous Mexican laborers who had scrambled over the fence to ringside. The laborers had waited for the entrance of the first bull and came all at once into the empty seats, climbing down, pressing in on Isaac and his girl, smelling of sweat. When the *bota* was passed into the crowd, it was drunk from and passed along. It came back much lightened.

It was one of the worst fights he would ever see. The animals were badly disgraced by clumsy, fearful matadors. The kills were bloody, cowardly, and meaningless. She apologized for the fight then and later, after they tried to make love on the floor of her father's study beneath a marvelously glowering photo of Hemingway and a collection of old *cartels*. They had drunk too much wine and there was the prolonged awkward intensity of their efforts and it made him ache when he left her, when he walked to his car.

Later, and mostly, he remembered the fight. Something about

the potential of it drew him back. He came alone two Sundays later and every Sunday thereafter for the balance of the season. He remembered the first time the potential was realized, the first time it came together. He remembered fighting back the tears of it.

A young Indian, Luis Olivera, drew the third and sixth bull. He was superstitious and would not fight the *colorado* he drew for his third. He did not like the color of it and moved it quickly to the *picador*. He ignored the shouts and whistles he drew and those who stamped their feet in disgust. He did not place his own *banderillas*, which he often did, and killed it clumsily.

The crowd was angry, but they would wait to hurl their cushions. There were other fights to see and the concrete was hard. They would wait for when he would appear again for the sixth bull.

The sixth was a marvelous animal. The Indian had believed what he'd been told about the bull after the draw and had not been afraid to discard the *colorado*. He worked it as though he were someone else, as though he were outside himself. He drew the bull close to him and took the blood of it on his suit with each pass. He did things with the animal that were impossible to do and did them without trickery and beyond the time the crowd pleaded for him to stop, pleaded, lest he ruin it with a mistake. And he carried it beyond that, even beyond the crowd. When he was ready, there were only he and the animal and they spoke to one another. Face to face.

Isaac was not alone in believing that they spoke. The crowd leaned forward to listen. Olivera did not move his *muleta*, but spoke to the bull with his eyes. The bull shifted its forelegs, moved them together in order to expose the small spot at the base of the neck and between the shoulders that would take the sword. Incredibly, he lowered his head to receive it.

Olivera killed over the horns without skirting them, and the bull dropped instantly and there was a moment for the crowd to absorb what it had seen.

That was the first time he had seen it come together. It had never happened for the fighter again. Three Sundays later there was a wind and his cape had not been weighted enough. Olivera

31

took the horn of his first bull up the rectum. Impaled there, he was paraded around the circumference of the ring. The *bandilleros* threw capes in front of the bull but it could not be persuaded to give up its prize. Head up, the bull trotted briskly along the *barrera* ignoring those who shouted, pounded on the wood, or ran in front of it. The Indian had not passed out, but was trying to work himself off one horn by gripping the other. But either the pain was too great or he could not get the leverage he needed. It took the bull stopping. It took for the bull to lower his head.

He had seen Olivera twice, maybe three times after that. It had taken him nearly a year to recover. But it was never the same. He fought, this Indian, always as though he remembered where the horn had been and how the bull had carried him. He never put the art of it together again.

To explain any of it, you had to start with the fighting bull, and how it had been bred since the Cretans to behave like no other animal on the face of the earth. But Isaac knew that all of the explanations would sound lame against those, like Heinrich, who had made up their minds before opening them. It was deeper than the mechanics of it but nobody wanted to get beyond them. Isaac was on the wrong side of public righteousness. It was a collective opinion and drew its strength from its numbers. Arguing the bullfight's virtues in the face of it was next to impossible. You couldn't even get a hearing. It was best left alone. And alone was exactly where Sanchez intended to leave it, a piece of prudence he had learned, no doubt, before Isaac was born.

But the German wanted to chew on it some more. He did not know about Sanchez's profession, and would not leave it. Stung by what he considered Memori's defection, he was committed to get an answer from the old man. Heinrich saw the Spaniard's reticence as a running wound he was trying to conceal. The German, smelling blood, sought to open it further before calling in the flock.

"Is it not so? Are there not those here in your own country who view this, this bullfight of yours, as — how do you say — barbaric, as an excuse for cruel and sadistic excesses?"

At last when the old man spoke he did so clearly, in full control of his English.

"Mr. Guerber, this is a good country, but it is not mine. Like you, I am something of a guest here. But I have lived here long enough to know of some similarities, some things that are the same with this country and my own. There is even one unfortunate parallel one can make about your own country. The cruel and sadistic excesses you speak of. They're no strangers to your homeland. Would not recent history bear me out?"

Heinrich started to speak, his face reddened, but Sanchez held up his hand against it.

"Please," the old man said, "I know that is unfair. It is selective. My own country, sadly, has its own history. You are anxious for me to defend the bullfight. You want to hear my side of it. But I fear that would be impossible. If I told you what you do not believe, you would not hear my argument. It would go into the stone of your ears. Even as I talked you would be preparing your next speech. With your permission, Sir, I would rather not do that.

"Instead," Sanchez continued evenly, "I would rather tell you about a custom my country and this one share. It is this: because this is the house of my son and his wife, the custom allows me to tell you that this is your house as well. Since you are the master of your own house, here you can say and believe what you please.

"So, Mr. Guerber, you can see how unimportant it is that you are wrong. In your own house it only matters that you enjoy yourself."

It was perfectly said. Cool, deliberate, without a trace of rancor. It should have ended it. Memori had started to pull discretely away, her hand still resting on Heinrich's arm. Sr. Sanchez had turned to retrieve his drink from the table. Maria had relieved Heinrich of the book. She replaced it on the table. On the far side of the room there was laughter about something.

Chapter 5

But two things worked against it ending there. Heinrich had been clearly diminished by Sanchez's brittle comment, and that, in the eyes of Memori. She was the second thing. He had not fully recovered from her apparent defection. Since he still could not have known that Sanchez was a bull breeder, a profession that had probably occupied his family for generations — something Memori knew or surmised — he could only look at her comment as an affront to his masculinity, an abridgment of his male prerogative. No. It was clear to Isaac that what this German needed — did she really call him Heiny? — what he needed was an uncompromising victory, a surrender of steel. It would have to be unconditional. If the old man would not provide it — and it was clear that he would not — then it would have to come from Herr Professor, the unknown sculptor.

For the first time since they met, Heinrich faced his adversary.

Normally Isaac would have been quick to declare a no-contest. He wasn't inclined toward heavy discussions. Even with those who understood and felt as he about a subject, he wasn't good at skirmishes with words. His was a world of shapes and colors and textures. When he used words, he wrote them. That gave him the time he needed to arrive at the right ones.

But discussions were another thing. In them he found himself groping in a fog of language, the perfect expression, a name, a fact just out of reach. When words wouldn't come, when he couldn't define their shape, he'd move his big hands in ways that he hoped would compensate. He had been told about the habit and had watched himself as he'd shaped things in the air. Those who told him about it were right. It was a curious phenomenon. What he did with his hands were not gestures. They couldn't be called that. A gesture would strengthen what he'd said. Instead, there was no sense to what his hands would do. If he were building things with them, it was nothing he could recognize.

Sometimes the words would come to him while he was shaping the idea. It was always a disappointment. He hoped that what he'd done with his hands would prove that he'd meant something more.

So, had it not been for the other thing, the argument that Heinrich wanted to win, so badly needed to win, would have fallen of its own weight. In a sense Isaac could attribute all that was to follow, beginning with that night, to his father's penchant for meeting trains. If it hadn't been for Isaac's consummate punctuality, he would not have been two drinks up on everyone else. The two drinks would make the difference. Or was it three?

Had it not been for the drinks, he'd have held in check his innate desire to overturn Heinrich's perfect cart of apples. He'd have quietly disliked the German as he had for years disliked the work he was doing in the name of art. Maybe he'd have been charitable and would have considered what must be a host of redeeming qualities he was hiding, that time would come to reveal. Instead he acted on what he knew:

— Heinrich Guerber was German. Though this was a condition of birth and sometimes remedial, it was enough to arouse recollections of the time Isaac spent in Frankfurt.

— Heinrich was a member of the Post-modern art establishment, the shock and squeal set that was turning art from its considerable history to a faintly sensational exercise in sociology and politics. SoHo and a dozen or so American and ex-pat artists like Heinrich were at its center. They had captured academia, the press and were tied to the tail of the contemporary museum boom. Together they made the strictures of the 19th Century French salon system seem like a call for entries in a clothesline show to artists on the outside, and Isaac was very much that.

— The German traded in pure, uncut self-assurance, an arrogance that might be tolerated as a requirement in a competitive profession had it not so clearly excluded Isaac as an artist and living being.

— He wore his girlfriend as a badge. Doing so diminished both of them. Public displays of affection had a good deal more to do with public, in Isaac's mind, than affection.

— He allowed himself to by called "Heiny" and had bastardized his girl's perfectly attractive name to "Mem." Isaac would have difficulty liking a couple he needed to address as Mem and Heiny. He couldn't imagine it.

— Isaac didn't like men with camel coats and glossy fingernails who could pose for cigarette ads on the back cover of Life Magazine.

— Finally, if the truth be told, Isaac was attracted to his girlfriend and, as impossible as it may seem, sought reciprocity.

Still, all this he might have held in check — the things he did not like about Heinrich, the things he liked about his girlfriend — had not the drinks loosened him.

When Heinrich turned to Isaac and invited him to respond to the question he had asked Sr. Sanchez — to tell him why he'd found so many contemporary Mexicans against bullfighting — Isaac was ready. He was sort of ready.

"OK, sure, well, maybe," Isaac declared. "Maybe what you're saying is right. There are Mexicans, a lot of Mexicans, who are against the bullfights. They feel, more or less, as you do."

"So," Heinrich returned, "what does that tell you?" Heinrich was lining up for the kill, the edge of his ubiquitous smile had lost some definition.

"It tells me how things get, you know, corrupted, I guess," Isaac said. "It tells me that there are those here, as anywhere else, who are persuaded by money. They believe that being rich is be-

36

ing right. So they listen to people. They listen to rich people from rich counties in order to find out what they should do."

"And this," Heinrich said, "this has something to do with the bullfights?"

"I think so. It's a new, sort of, morality, this thing. It's a government of the rich, and those who get their power from it or who don't know better sign on. They're ashamed of their own history, who they are. They worry when something isn't endorsed by the international set. The worry comes from guilt, I think." Isaac hoped he was making sense. "The middle class feels most of it. When people who haven't had money begin to make some they leave a lot of their friends behind. It's better for them if they don't remember where they came from. If they believe, for example, that they are not Mexicans at all, but somebody else, it's a lot better. It's easier to forget."

"And we're going to learn soon," Heinrich said, "what all this has to do with the thing we've chosen to talk about."

"What I'm saying is some here believe more in fashion than their own heritage, their values, traditions. Bullfighting is a throwback and they're embarrassed by it."

"So," Heinrich had all of his smile back. "If it is a tradition, even one as ugly as this, it should be continued. This is what you're saying?"

"Ugly is a word you use," Isaac said. "I wonder if you understand it. There are some very ugly traditions here which are fashionable. Like the tradition for peasants to dress their starving children in Indian costumes so they can dance for pesos in front of the church. This is internationally acceptable. Those who come in tour buses think it's cute."

"At least it's not bloody; it's not murder."

"Isn't it?" Isaac asked.

"If this, my good friend, if this, as you say, is evil; aren't you defending one evil on the basis of another?"

"Maybe," said Isaac. "But you and I disagree on what is evil, what is ugly. I don't think you'll understand me when I tell you what you believe is ugly, evil, is not that at all, but beautiful."

37

As Heinrich laughed, the color rose in his face He turned to Memori.

"He is saying this fight with the bull is beautiful. Can you tell me the beauty in killing animals?" He turned back to Isaac. "I'd like to know where the beauty is when an animal is tortured and mercilessly slaughtered. Is there some beauty in an animal vomiting blood because it suffers a sword wound in the lung. There is beauty in that?"

When Isaac noticed his free hand begin to move in reply, begin to shape the thought he wanted to express, he took a sip from his drink and brought the offending hand to his side, hooking his thumb inside his belt. He felt he was on the verge of something and to test it he had to get it right. He didn't want to fumble with it.

"It's how we come to see the world, I guess. We, you and I, don't see it in the same way. Maybe it's because we've arrived from vastly different places. I don't know. I do know we see things differently. It's important to know that, to understand there is more than one way to look at the same thing, to acknowledge the difference, maybe. I doubt there's hope for more. You say the bullfight is ugly. I see it as beauty. We could talk forever and nothing would change.

"But," Isaac went on, "what's important is that I'm willing to accept your view of the thing. I can understand the ugliness about it and why it's not popular. I can see what you're talking about. I can even see why you don't see *beyond* what you're talking about. I'm asking you to be equally generous."

The proprietary hand encircled Memori's waist. This time, if she did lean toward Heinrich, the move was imperceptible. Smiling, looking down at her, he spoke:

"You see how it is? I talk of the bullfights to the American professor and he gives me philosophy. I pluck a note and I get an entire cantata. Is it that you are going to speak to me of art, professor? Is that what this will come to?"

"I don't think I've ever left the subject, Heinrich."

"Here it comes: the bullfight as art. Are we going to read from

38

Death in the Afternoon? Are we going to get Hemingway's romantic drivel? Wake up, Isaac. The earth doesn't move when you make love. Romance is dead. Art, as you know it, died with it. It died with Beuys, with Oldenburg, with Warhol when he silkscreened his first soup can. And now it dies with me. It died the day your friend Ernest put his big toe inside the trigger guard of his shotgun and blew his face away.

"Isaac, if I'm the first to bring you the news, I'm sorry. All of it is gone. Music, literature with its nice little stories, theater, and sadly — as I've so often and so patiently reminded my sweet Memori here — the dance. It's gone too, the leggy little girls standing *sur les pointes*." He tried to draw her closer. She may have resisted or she may only have wanted to speak:

"You know I won't believe that, Heinrich," she said sharply. She started to say something more, but held it back. Apparently, this was an open wound between them; it had been probed, Isaac guessed, many times before. "You prefer," she said finally, "that things you didn't understand, didn't exist."

For the first time Isaac noticed her slight lisp. It was a thing she must work at controlling. It accounted for the careful way she formed her words. Her anger revealed the flaw.

"Ah, so that is it, Memori," Heinrich said. "The professor has won a convert, or is it that all this time you are a lover of the things that are done to a bull, a lover who chooses to hide in the closet."

"You know that's not true as well." She had control of her lisp again; only the tonelessness remained.

"But clearly I don't know. Are you not arguing on the side of the professor when you tell me I don't understand? You must favor, dear Memori, what's done to these animals. Do you also see the torture, the murder as art."

"In life there are these things," Isaac said. "Maybe art's a reflection of that, a putting together of things, you know, both good and bad."

"But this, this is ridiculous." Heinrich had lost his cool arrogance to the flush of anger that swept his face. "You're saying that because there are these things in life, we should inflict them on animals. And do this for the sake of art?" This last he directed toward the girl.

"I agree," said Isaac. "That would make a poor case for torture and murder."

"But is that not what a bullfight offers?"

"No. Death need not be murder, and what's done to a bull before it dies is not torture," Isaac said.

"Tell me," Heinrich leaned in toward Isaac. "Tell me what you would call it if I were to place barbed sticks in your side, if I were to prod you in the neck with a sharpened pole, and if I were to do this until you could not hold your head up?"

There was a little too much conviction for it to be a simple analogy. The threat of it was in the tone, the fading smile.

"If it were done to me," Isaac said, matching the tone, "and if I were unable to defend myself, it would be torture. And if in the end you killed me — provided, of course, I was still defenseless or you were very lucky — it would be murder. But if these things were done to a fighting bull —"

"—It would be art!" Heinrich's laugh was explosive. It was as loud as it was humorless. It was for an audience and, looking around him, he was pleased it earned one.

"No," Isaac said. "It wouldn't be art. But if it were done with truthfulness and done well it might contain things that comprise art. It would depend on a lot of things. I think you've got to understand the fighting bull. It's not a cowardly animal. Our host, Sr. Sanchez here, can tell you that."

"Yes?" Heinrich waited for the old man's corroboration, eager to engage all three if need be.

The Spaniard did not answer at first. He had been following the argument with his eyes. He had made no move to voice his own views, but had been watching, first one, then the other. Now, invited to speak, he took his time.

Isaac remembered how skillfully he used the pause for effect and his advanced age to excuse it. The old man would have made a fine actor.

"Yes," he said at last, "it is true what is being said. The fight-

40

ing bull is not a coward. It is many things, but it is not that. But this talk is no good. You must see. The bull is something you must see to understand. I would be very much honored, Mr. Guerber, if you would come to my ranch so that I can show you such an animal. It would be my great honor if all of you would come."

"You have such an animal at your ranch?" Heinrich asked.

"I have many more than one, Mr. Guerber. The raising of the *toros bravos* is what I do. It is the job of my family since early times in Spain."

"Oh, I . . . I can see now," Heinrich said. "I'm afraid . . . Well, if I've insulted you, please forgive. It is something I did not realize."

The old man worked the pause again.

"You need not be afraid of an insult unless it is intended. I would only feel an insult if you would not honor my invitation. On Sunday, this Sunday, we have what is called a *tienta*. It is in part a celebration and a way in which we who raise bulls can judge the quality of the stock. I hasten to tell you that there will be no torture, as you call it, or murder, as you also call it. But you will see some of the lesser animals as they work against the cape. From those we can judge the line, how those we will send to the *corrida* will likely perform.

"Normally, those we test are the cows, for, as every woman knows and every man denies, it is in the female that valor lies. Still, here I feel a need to modify that slightly in deference to what you may not know and in honor of keeping the line of argument pure and the instruction simple. It will not be young fighting cows you'll see, Mr. Guerber, but young fighting bulls, though, to be honest, the difference at their age is largely only a semantic one.

The old man turned to Isaac: "You have a good understanding of the bull. Have you worked something other than your tongue? Have you worked with the cape?"

"Not in front of anything with horns."

"Excellent. Then it would be a good thing for your education, professor, a good thing for Mr. Guerber to watch." He turned to Heinrich. "I apologize that I cannot offer the same opportunity to you, sir. But without understanding, it would be dangerous. For the animals, I mean. I'm sure you can appreciate that. It will be quite enough, I think, for you and your attractive lady to watch."

"That's very kind, Sr. Sanchez. While I'll be in town, I'm afraid that we —"

Memori cut him off. "We would very much like to visit your ranch, Señor. It would be something I'd like very much." Her eyes met then slipped away from Isaac's.

Heinrich was startled, then tried not to look it. He spoke through a mechanical smile. "Yes, yes of course. I do have some business . . . but I would be honored, most honored. Perhaps if I can dispense with my appointments . . ."

"Good. Then it shall be Sunday." Sanchez said. He turned again to Isaac. "Those horns, the ones you have not worked against . . ."

Sanchez must have read something in his face. Though the drinks and Memori had worked on him, had made him believe that facing a bull on Sunday was an excellent idea, Isaac was having trouble stifling another part of himself which knew him best. This part was having trouble calling him anything but a damn fool.

" . . . These horns," the old man continued, "should not overly concern you. There will be others who will help you. There is that, and there is the other thing: the horns are the horns of small animals. Should you forget the things you know, the mistake will not be costly. Small animals deliver only small wounds, as a rule."

Something worked against the corners of his mouth as he continued: "They are hardly ever fatal. The wounds should not gravely concern you. They'll heal long before your ego."

"That's a comfort," Isaac told him.

"And feel free, Isaac, please, to bring a guest. Unless, of course . . ." the pause again. "Unless you would rather not be seen by a friend. Unless what you will do on Sunday is something you will not want a friend to remember."

Chapter 6

Had he been in better spirits, had he not opened and closed the Sanchezes' party, and had his mouth not tasted like the inside of a basketball, he probably would not have taken on the Señora that morning.

But he woke to the bells, to an ear-splitting dawn of bells, the godawful, perpetually clanging church bells, the cacophony of which was, he guessed dimly, heralding still another of what must be an infinite procession of saints born to Catholicism and thereafter resurrected at 6 A.M., regardless.

Isaac had intended to celebrate nothing more than a hangover. He had a class at nine and could have slept till eight. He could have slipped down after the Madras and all the others had headed their various ways. He could have talked Fat Tina into coffee, some pineapple and a fresh roll, maybe. With a little luck the dining room would be otherwise unoccupied, the glowering Señora off somewhere counting her money, feeding her parrots or fussing with her pots. Or out buying another padlock.

Instead there were the bells, only slightly muffled by the pillows he crushed to his head. That night there would be firecrackers. The resulting din would stir every dog in town and for miles beyond it, a vast population of flea-bitten, bone-chested strays that no doubt could, with any kind of leadership, collectively devour mankind and bury the left-overs.

Isaac cursed the bells and the saint that gave rise to them. He cursed the Catholic church and its resistance to Gutenberg and movable type. He cursed Mexico, the brilliance of the morning sun, those on the street below who started their day with it and who had no regard for those who didn't. He cursed the peasants who sold firewood from the back of mules. He cursed the fruit farmers who would not submit to the marketplace and hawked their products from the street, and the peddlers with towering cages of shrieking birds nobody ever bought. He cursed little boys who could not find their way to school without finger whistling, and the schools themselves for their insistence that educational emancipation for their ragged charges would come through an eight-hour day of drum and bugle studies.

He cursed the shudder of tin trucks on cobblestone streets and a second story room on the Calle de los Insurgentes that took all of it in.

Particularly did he curse himself when he recalled what was really bothering him that morning: his foolish agreement to stand in front of a fighting bull on Sunday.

Remembering how the drinks and Heinrich's girlfriend had made him a willing candidate for the lunacy, Isaac groaned, dropped two long legs over the edge of the bed and sat up. There, he was forced to wait for the return of blood that drained from his face. It was a while coming back.

He found his way across the cold tile floor, turned on the shower, brushed the moss from his teeth with tap water and hoped it was not over-colonized with amoebas. A part of him at least. This part made him work his mouth and spit several more times than was necessary, taking care not to swallow. The other part didn't give a shit.

The mirror revealed the face of a drowning victim, speckled by spots of toothpaste. It was an astonishing image, and he studied it for signs of life. When there appeared to be none, he turned away. He dropped the lid of the toilet, sat down and began to wait the five minutes it would take for the shower to warm if the heater were working. If it were, it would take another three to cool again. If he showered in two, he'd have enough water to shave.

44

Outside there was the strangulated sound of a donkey. It began in a hoarse series of inhaling-exhaling noises, building to a herniated shriek. Just as it reached a hysterical frenzy, it ended. There was the hacking sound of loose phlegm, a violent spit, then a long, audible fart.

"Noose," it yelled. "Wanna noose? Gringo noose?"

Isaac rose slowly, crossed into the bedroom and pulled on his trousers. He fished in the change on the dresser for 50 *centavos*, pulled back the curtains and stepped into the blinding sun on the balcony. He faltered, grabbed for the rail.

Below him in the shade of the street, toothlessly grinning, was the newsboy, a middle-age peddler with one crooked leg that did not quite seem to belong to him, a leg he had to drag after him as he walked. It lent to his stance a considerable list, a defect he sought to counter by carrying his sack of newspapers on his up-hill shoulder. He sold the English language daily out of Mexico City and sold it sometimes only a day or so after its publication.

That he could imitate a donkey and break wind on command served him well. He was colorful enough and bore enough of a resemblance to what he was imitating to earn a place as one of the town's least likely tourist attractions. And, if you were looking for old news, he was noisy enough to be placed in any part of town at any time, even if the wind were not right.

In the afternoon, when he sold as many newspapers as he was going to, his thing would begin. He would hang around the *jardin* for the tour bus out of Celaya. When it deposited anything feminine he'd get excited. That's when he'd launch his special act.

He would approach the woman from behind. He would stand innocently until she was occupied with her camera or was gathering her luggage or was bent over fussing with her children. He would drag his leg, his near-empty sack flapping at his side. He would come like that until he was inches from her. Then he would start the donkey noise. But he would not build it to a crescendo as he would do on the streets in the morning. He would start at the agitated, hysterical part, and those who had seen his approach

45

would watch, those who were not shopkeepers and had seen it too many times.

The high-pitched shriek of a donkey inches away would spin the woman in her tracks. She would not know whether she was being attacked or witnessing an epileptic seizure. She would want to run but would not be able to work it out right away, how to make her exit and whether running from an epileptic was appropriate.

Horrified, she would stand transfixed, waiting, maybe, for the vile creature to fall to the ground and swallow his tongue. Abruptly, then, he'd stop the noise and smile. Even with the horsey look of it, it was not a bad smile and the woman would see that it was a joke, that he meant no harm, that this unfortunate man was certainly not going to attack her in front of the crowded Tres Estrellas bus that brought her. And it no longer seemed likely that he would convulse and die.

But if she turned from him then, if she started to move away, he would start up again with the raking noise he made through his nose and throat, shuffling after her, dragging that leg, until she turned again. Then he would stop and smile as before. He would keep this up until, perplexed, uncertain, she returned the smile.

Even if her smile was uneasy, was a product of her considerable embarrassment at all the commotion centered around her, even if it was to appease those who were watching the pageant from the bus, it would be enough for the peddler. And grinning, he would answer her smile. He would not say a word but would answer with a fart loud enough to echo off the facing wall of La Parroquia, the cobbled Gothic church.

And he would stand, much as he stood now on the street below Isaac's balcony, inordinately pleased with himself.

He arched the paper over the balustrade to Isaac and waited, looking up, grinning, his hands cupped together. Isaac checked the dateline. It was three days old, but a paper he hadn't seen. He dropped the centavos piece into the stubby hands. The newsboy checked the coin and buried it in his leather pouch. He looked up shaking his head, still grinning.

"One peso," he said, holding a finger in the air. "Gringo noose is one peso today."

It was the same game. He hadn't varied it. If Isaac didn't play, he'd start the braying again and there'd be another fart.

"No," Isaac called down, "it is 50 centavos like before."

"One peso," he called back. He was still holding up his index finger. Isaac's head hurt. He did not like to start his morning with this thing. He did not like being the straight man for this cretin of a newsboy. But, it was easier to go along, to play his part.

"But last time it was 50 centavos," Isaac told him wearily. The sun hurt his eyes. It would be better if he were inside.

"*Señor*. That was last time. Last time there was no big noose. It was 50 centavos."

"And this time there is big news?" Isaac had finished his lines. He only had to wait for the newsboy to finish his part and he could go inside.

"Yes, there is big noose this time," the peddler said. He was excited and took two short hops on his good leg. "Big noose this time is this!" He replaced his index finger with an upraised middle finger and the humor of it consumed him. He could not believe the comedy of what he'd done and wagged his head with it. He couldn't get over it and carried it with him up the block. It was another block before he had himself under control enough to begin the braying noise again.

By that time Isaac discovered that his shower was cold.

Isaac had stayed at La Valencia since the first day off the train, when the toothless taxi driver dropped him in front of it. He hadn't NOT liked it enough to move.

It was an old colonial building converted from a single- family mansion into a boarding house. It was clean, thick walled, airy and just enough off the *jardin* to be half as expensive as anything on or near it. And it had Fat Tina, an Indian out of Tabasco with an insuppressible need to giggle, an ability to quietly suffer the Señora and a facility for making *tamales russos* and garlic soup.

When he entered the dining room, she was taking a breakfast order from a small woman contained within the folds of a great striped madras. He caught Tina's eye, but before the Madras could spot him and wave him over to the central table she occupied, he took a place at the last remaining small table. He nodded to George and Harry, retired Canadian school teachers who carried on a manic over-the-hill romance that would dissolve, sometimes for days, into petulant silence. They wisely sat at another small table. The third table was occupied by two of Isaac's students. They were bent to their meal.

Those who had not timed breakfast right would be compelled to sit with the Madras, a fate that usually befell the unwary overnighter.

Isaac opened the paper to determine what had happened last week. Reading history in this way — *Time* magazine arrived three weeks late — softened the news and furthered the distance between him and the rest of the world. If an urgent international problem needed attention, it was comforting to believe that by the time he read about it, another problem, no doubt, had already replaced it. A domestic revolution was another thing. But that wouldn't be in the paper anyway. Whoever won would no doubt show up at the door.

The Madras was trying to work up enough Spanish to complain about the way her breakfast had been delivered. It was either something about the eggs or how the *tortillas* were done. Either way, Fat Tina was agreeing not to do it again, nodding her head as though she understood, giggling behind some fluttering fingers. They had gone over the subject, or variations of it, for the months he'd been there.

The Madras was living from the government pension of Rest His Soul, which Isaac took to be her long dead husband, a lower level foreign service officer out of Liverpool. They had spent enough time in India for her to have supplied herself with a lifetime wardrobe of every color madras one could imagine. It was well known that she took, and only paid for, two meals a day. The third, lunch, she made on her hot plate in her room. Invariably it was an odorous curry concoction strong enough to permeate foot-thick walls. If you were sensitive to the smell of the pungent spice, you could identify a hotel guest on the street with your eyes closed, even days after he checked out.

She wore an array of brass bracelets, a ring on every finger and smoked Mexican cigarettes in a short plastic holder. Her flair for dramatic costuming carried over to her paintings. He had been trapped into seeing them his second night.

She had lived long enough at the hotel to warrant one of the interior rooms and it was wall-to-wall paintings. Though it was early evening, it was pitch dark inside. Her windows had been draped with heavy cloth, and there was the cloying smell of incense that fought in vain to overcome the curry.

She told him that she thought of her room as a museum. One by one she turned on a tangle of key lights she had gerrymandered from two outlets. As an artist, she would have made a better electrician.

Her thing, as she put it, was German Expressionism. It was something he had to take her word for. In her paintings he could neither see the German of it nor the expressionism. Each of the paintings was at a loaded-brush war with itself. There seemed little hope for a cease fire. Her ideas were stolen and worked to death and each carried with them a little story that kept reminding her of a larger story. At the end of the seemingly endless tour she asked him which he liked best. It was a question he was not prepared for.

"Well, I . . . just don't know. There . . . there are so many."

"Don't be silly," she said. "You must, absolutely must, choose just one. Just one, mind you, out of all these." She was in the center of the room and with her brass encircled arm extended toward the wealth of her work, she tried for a pirouette, as Loretta Young might have done. But her age and the fact that Loretta Young did not wear what looked to be a tent worked against her. It was not on the whole a smooth effort and for a moment she was visibly off balance. To save her from toppling, he started toward her, but she recovered nicely.

"Please, of all my little babies, choose one." She may have been smiling, but it was too dark to tell.

He sought and then pointed to the least repulsive piece. It was not easy. He settled on a muddy watercolor. It had been pasted to a board, the edge of which had been sprinkled with glue and rhinestones. If one overlooked how it was displayed, a difficult task, and focused only on the watercolor, it was merely aimless and heavy handed. In fact there was, in one corner, a mildly interesting passage, though it may have been that she spilled something there.

She pulled the painting from the wall. It was heavy. The board on which it had been pasted looked like a piece of hardwood she had found somewhere, maybe a desktop or a piece cut from a headboard. She had trouble turning it around. The title was on the back and she turned it into the light so that she could read it.

"*Sunset of My Dreams*," she told him.

"I see," he replied.

"It's for 650 pesos."

She handed it to him. It weighed a ton. Some of the rhinestones came off on his fingers.

"Well," he said. "That's a good, you know . . . price. Considering. When you think of . . . it." He was going to say "of the weight alone", but caught himself. What he had taken for an interesting passage had only been a shadow of a tangled cord. It was projected on the wall where the picture had been.

"Now, let me warn you," she said. "It will not, absolutely not, take a hint of direct sunlight. Sun is the worst for watercolors. And for these — well, you can see, with any fading, how you'd loose the subtlety. And that's the point, isn't it."

He agreed, if only because he was looking for a place to put the painting. There were two heavy nails and a tangle of rusted wire on the back. He doubted he'd get it to hang on the wall again. It worried him that it might pull part of the wall down. Gingerly he set it on the floor and leaned it against a heavy brass samovar that stood against the wall. He stepped away as though to admire it from a distance, easing toward the door.

"Squint your eyes," she said. "Real tight, like this."

She faced the painting. He guessed she was squinting her eyes.

"See what I mean?" she said. "That's how you can tell a good painting. If you squint your eyes — look at what I'm doing — you see basic shapes. The simple beauty of it. Watch me walk back now. Do you see how it works when you move away?"

He had by then gotten to the door, his hand on the knob. "Listen," he said. "This has been great. I appreciate seeing, you know, everything."

"*My Enchanted Spring*," she told him.

"What?"

"A companion piece. I've been thinking of doing a companion piece, but I will not — I absolutely refuse — to diminish this. I use to tell my late husband, rest his soul, how they're like children, my paintings. Oh, how like children! You suffer the birth, you nurture, but how they can blossom. But bring another into the world? Oh, they don't like that a bit."

"That's certainly true," Isaac said. "That sure is something you got to think about. Anyway, I really enjoyed —"

"You might as well take it with you. You might as well have it to enjoy straight off. And I certainly trust you to pay me whenever you can. Don't think I'm going to worry about that for a second." She had her back to the door, her hand resting on his sleeve. To open the door he'd have to slide her away. Though she could not have weighed much, her gold slippers seemed firmly planted.

"I'm sorry that this, you know, has gotten this far," Isaac said as gently as he could. "But I don't . . . I really didn't have buying this painting in mind. You asked me to choose the one I liked best and I did that. It was kind of you, but I don't want to have it, to buy the thing."

He had opened the door. In the light that streamed through he could see that she looked hurt, then brightened.

"Listen," Her hand tightened on his arm. "Don't you worry about the paying. Heavens, I know how things can get on top of us, if that's all you're worrying about. We'll make a schedule. Little payments each week. A little something now, of course."

"No. Thanks. I don't think I want to buy this thing."

"Without the frame, then. We're talkin' 400 pesos without the frame." There was an edge to her voice, a rattle of brass each time she moved.

She followed him into the hall.

"Tomorrow night, then," she said. "Another look won't cost a thing. Promise me. Maybe you could bring some wine."

He had made it down the stairs. Her voice followed him:

"Three hundred then. I can't go lower."

He was outside, crossing the interior patio. Some of the guests were finishing their coffee in the quiet of the fading light. They had stopped talking and watched Isaac as he hurried across to the alcove leading to his part of the hotel. Some of them were smiling. He had nearly made it before the Madras found an open window from which to shout down to him:

"Two hundred and fifty, then. And you can have the God-damned frame!"

There was nothing on the front page of the three-day old paper that could compete with how his head felt, so he laid it aside and took down the tall, cool glass of orange juice Fat Tina had served him. Freshly squeezed, it went down in one tilt. It washed against the walls of his stomach and was instantly absorbed. When he turned to call her back, he faced the Señora. She planted herself like a little monument behind him.

She was hefty, but compressed. Her eyes were as heavy as lead shot. She was able to move them only with difficulty and they weighed against the creased flesh of the sockets that contained them. She wore black, as was her custom, and for the first time since he'd come, she was smiling. It was an ominous sign.

The *Señora* had inherited the hotel from her husband at his death a decade before. She ran a tight ship and took pride in it. Severe, tight-lipped, she had been an old woman, he guessed, all her adult life and a good part of her childhood. Her husband had brought her home as a bride to his family in Tarantula. Even then, Isaac guessed, she would have worn black — black stockings, black skirt and sweater. On Sundays she wore a matching black veil when she made her pilgrimage to La Parroquia. Even when he roused her once in the middle of the night by pounding on the front gate, she had opened it fully clothed — black stockings, black skirt and sweater. It could have been that she slept that way. It had been his third night in town and he'd been talking to a Puerto Rican ex-pat and some of his girl friends at La Cucaracha, an expat watering hole.

She had opened the gate for him to pass, but clearly she was not pleased to see him. She told him that it wasn't done.

He was not sure he understood.

"The door, *Señor*. It is closed." She spoke to him only in Spanish. He guessed it was to train him, for he had heard her speak English to other lodgers. Beyond this concession, she didn't truck with the foreign.

"Yes. I'm sorry, but I only have the key to the room."

"Yes," she said, "that is so." She turned, re-locked the gate behind them and crossed the patio into the main entrance. The light in the hall had been turned off. A small light burned from her room, a tiny closet of a place just under the stairs. It once could have been a pantry. He could see a small, unmade bed, a crucifix above it. She headed directly toward the room, stooped, shuffling on stiffened legs.

"*Señora*, permit me. If I do not have a key to the gate, I shall have to wake you again when I come in late."

"That isn't done, *Señor*."

He wondered if there were some other entrance that he overlooked. When he asked, she shook her head and turned toward her room again.

"But if I'm not to wake you and I do not have a key, how am I to get to my room?"

At the door to the room, she turned again. With the light behind her she stood in silhouette, a little pyramid of a woman who would not, he guessed, easily topple in a high wind.

"The lateness, *Señor*," she said. "What isn't done is the lateness. When you come before twelve, *Señor*, the gate is open."

Incredulous then, he had confirmed it the next morning with George. It was a kind of morality she imposed on her guests. She

53

didn't see any good reason for lodgers to be outside beyond midnight. More importantly, she probably could not stay up beyond that time. Her day over, she would lie on her cot until then, watching her lodgers for any lapse of impropriety.

She had to make sure none of the girls from the town were brought in by her men guests. While there were only a few Mexican girls who did not care about how their behavior reflected on the church and family, there were many American girls from the art school. She had heard about the school and did not like what she heard. She knew, for example, that some of the girls earned money by shamelessly taking off their clothes and subjecting themselves to other students who sat in a circle and drew pictures of them. She had seen some of the drawings that the students who were staying with her had brought to their rooms and left. They were shameful. They did not belong in such a hotel as hers.

Unless there was a midnight mass, there was no reason to expect the gate to be open.

After the first time, Isaac didn't bother with the *Señora*. He scaled the gate. It was a tall gate, perhaps 16 feet high and it rose, together with the walls on each side of it, from the narrow sidewalk off the street. It was made of rough hewn planks, and with his weight on it the gate moved perilously within the slack of the chain and the padlock that contained it.

There were a few toe holds, but it took all of his physical faculties to climb it. At the top he had to edge under some branches of a laurel tree that lay across it, then hang and drop to the inside patio, carefully, so he wouldn't land in one of the potted ferns or otherwise wake the *Señora*. He had performed this gymnastic stunt several times in the months he'd been there and was getting quite good at it.

But being drunk was quite another thing. After Heinrich and Memori had left the Sanchezes' party, he had remained talking to Rafael and a group of his Mexican friends visiting from Morelia. The men, by then, had separated themselves from the women so that they could tell their stories in the crude way that made them funny and so that they could drink without someone counting the glasses.

Isaac had not tried to scale the gate under the conditions in which he found himself. He had not remembered he needed to until he stood face to face with his problem.

He had almost made it over. He had reached the top of it, had swung one ankle over the edge and was pulling himself up when someone called to him from the street. Two uniformed police stood under a street lamp. The one who spoke, did so quietly, respectfully.

"*Señor*, with your permission. I am sorry to disturb you, but maybe it would be better if you came down. It would be good, I think, if you would come down and talk to us."

Isaac, suspended as he was like a tree sloth, hesitated. He did not want to climb it all over again.

"*Señores*," he called down. "It is permitted, what I am doing. It is where I live. Inside is my room and I live there."

The two policeman talked between themselves. They talked for what to Isaac seemed a long time. The same one called up to him again.

"*Señor*. Of course you live here. Clearly. We would not question that. We honor your word. If you say you live here, that is the end of it. But, if you live here, would it not be easier to use your key and to open the gate? We understand that it is your home and you can do what you like here, but would it not be easier to open the gate than climb over it?"

Isaac tried to get his Spanish together. "It is true what you say," he called down over his shoulder. "But it is that I do not have a key. It is because of the *Señora* inside."

"Your wife," the policeman said, "she will not give you the key?"

"No, it is not what you think." Isaac was beginning to tire. Suspended as he was made the alcohol pound in his head. He was already into his hangover and dangling there was making him dizzy. He was beginning to mix up the Spanish words. "My wife is not the problem. It is the key that is the problem. The *Señora* will not give

55

me the key when it is late. The key to the big wooden door." He was sounding like a Berlitz course.

The two talked together some more.

"*Señor?*"

"Yes?"

"If your wife will not give you the key, perhaps she can come to the gate and let you inside."

Isaac was fading rapidly. He did not know how all this started about his wife. He couldn't seem to shake them of the idea. Hanging there, he considered his options. It would take longer than he could possibly maintain his position to explain to them that he had no wife and that he was talking about the morality of the old lady who owned the hotel. The second option was an improvement over the first.

He would simply climb over the fence, drop to the other side and to hell with them. He doubted he would be shot. Few of the local police carried pistols. Those who patrolled the streets carried only truncheons. They worked the *pulquerias* in town and would use the clubs only for self protection and when they didn't like the person they were arresting. They were mostly drunks who needed attending to, but then only when they had lost control and began to tear things apart. Drunks could not be taken seriously, and even if they were brought in, they were allowed to work off their fines by sweeping the streets the following day. If they were shot, that would not be possible. Partly, it was on behalf of a clean city that the police were unarmed.

Of course, sometimes the argument in the *pulqueria* involved a drunk with a loaded pistol. This could be a problem, particularly when the argument got heated and the drunk, not knowing how else to conclude it, shot his friend off the bar stool. It would not be wise for policemen carrying only a club to arrest such a man. And it would be equally unwise to arm the policeman and provide him with the potential for a two-way shoot out.

It was best to come up with an equitable policy, which the police, in due course drew up. They took the informed position that any argument in a *pulqueria* was no doubt started out of town, out

56

in the fields and ranches where hard work and long days created tension between men. And when the argument was not resolved then and there with a hoe, shovel or maybe an ax, only then was it brought to town. Since the town only inherited an argument that should have been settled earlier, well beyond the town boundaries, any shooting that resulted from it was not the responsibility of the local police.

It was only a technicality that the deed was committed in a *pulqueria* in town. It could have been anywhere. Since this was a jurisdictional matter, policy limited the police to asking the one who did the shooting to kindly dump the body outside the city limits on his way home. The policy was not harsh and permitted the offender to finish his drink first.

So Isaac knew the police probably didn't carry weapons. Over and above the *pulqueria* problem, it was not a good idea. There was very little for a policeman to do in the long hours before dawn and they, too, had a tendency toward drink. Having a pistol strapped to his side was a temptation. It was like firecrackers which badly needed to be shot off. At night a policeman would shoot at anything just to hear the noise.

To go over the gate, Isaac thought, would probably not earn gunfire. But the solution was only temporary. Having nothing better to do, the policemen would persist. They would pound on the gate until they woke the Señora. And she would not be pleased. She would show them to his room. There would be a lot of talk and he would end up paying more money than the incident warranted.

Instead, Isaac eased his foot off the top of the gate, hung and dropped to the sidewalk. The blood had drained from the leg that had lain over edge of the gate and he stumbled. He caught his balance, straightened, tucked in his shirt, and started toward the two. But he had forgotten about the curb and stumbled again. This time he could not recover easily on the uneven cobblestones. It took both policemen to keep him from sprawling headlong. They were polite and tried not to smile. They held him straight until he could stand on his own.

"It is better," the shorter of the two said, "that you came down.

57

It is dangerous to be climbing in the dark. Here it is easier to talk. Here you can tell us again about your wife and why she won't let you in." He was the one who had done the talking before. He wore a brown service cap with a black leather strap. It did not fit very well. It seemed a size or two larger than it should have been and hung just below the tops of policeman's eyes. But his partner did not have a cap at all.

The one with the cap seemed sympathetic and, of the two, most in control.

To expedite the matter, Isaac stayed with the story about his wife, how she would lock the gate when he was out drinking. The policeman with the large cap nodded his head. The cap was not quite in sync with the movements his head made, but there was understanding in his eyes, what he could see of them. His eyes told him that he, too, had a wife and knew how they were, how they'd send the oldest boy to lead him from the *cantina* just when the arguments and the fights were going nicely, and how, in her anger over the money he spent there, or the job he would lose when he didn't show up the following morning, she would say things that were not in keeping with what women are supposed to say to men.

It would be worse if children were involved. It would not do to have children around to hear a wife talk to her husband that way. The boy children, particularly, would learn bad ways. The boy had to see how it was with such women and how they needed to be trained.

So the man with the over-large cap understood about Isaac's wife — had he had one — and the second man, who looked younger and who did not, apparently carry the authority of his partner, solemnly nodded in agreement.

Isaac's was a good story, and it saved him a good 50 pesos. The 20 pesos he handed the short policeman was accepted only reluctantly. And neither one would take the extra ten he offered if they would break the padlock for him. This, the older policeman said gravely, would be done as a service.

The younger man was dispatched to find some equipment. The other talked to Isaac of his own wife until he returned. He car-

ried a long iron stake. The older man took over then. He slid the
rod through the gate and tried to pry the chain apart, but there
was too much slack in the chain and he couldn't get leverage. Some
of the dogs started up.

The younger man found a rock and suggested they break the
lock, since he believed the lock would break before the chain
would.

The older man would have none of what the young man was
suggesting. Breaking a chain was a serious matter and it took experience. The older policeman waved his partner off. The younger
one retreated, set his rock down, and returned to watch his partner worry the chain. He worked at it a long time. Two other men
appeared out of the night and joined Isaac and the young policeman. All of them watched the experienced policeman work. His
knuckles were bleeding badly. Still, he could not get enough leverage. After a while he stopped and pulled the rod out from the gate.

"Listen," he told the younger man. "It's easier if I break the
lock. It would be better than breaking the chain. See if you can find
a large rock somewhere."

The younger man nodded, got the rock again and handed it
to his partner. The older policeman held one end of the rod on the
padlock and hit the other end with the rock. The lock snapped and
clattered to the patio inside. He pushed the gate open for Isaac.

"This thing about the key," he reminded Isaac. "It is not good
for a man to be climbing around at night. A woman must be told.
One woman talks to another and you know how thing can get."

The group behind him on the sidewalk agreed.

Isaac told him he knew how things could get.

"It is your choice, of course, but it is best to get them out of
bed on a thing as serious as this," he told Isaac. "Tomorrow your
head will hurt and you will not feel like it."

Isaac promised he would see to his wife immediately and
thanked them for their help.

"It is a service," the older policeman said, retrieving his cap.

"It is nothing," said his younger partner.

Isaac had never seen the Señora smile before and he suspected the worst. When she laid the broken padlock on the breakfast table, his suspicions were confirmed.

"Good morning," he told her.

"*Señor*, this," she said pushing the lock toward him, "this is not done." The smile remained ominous.

Isaac sought a conciliatory tone: "Please, *Señora*. It is a problem and I'm the cause of it. I am sorry that I have made it break, the lock. This is not as it should be. But it is a small thing. I shall buy you another lock before this night." It would be an investment. He could get a lock for ten pesos. It had cost him thirty to climb the gate last night, and he'd been lucky. There were no medical bills.

"This is very bad, *Señor*. It is my property and it is broken, the lock."

"Yes, *Señora*. But it is not a permanent loss. It is something that can be made right. I shall have another lock for you. I will buy it and bring it to you this afternoon."

But it was not enough. She wanted penitence: "To break the property of another is a serious crime, *Señor*."

"Yes," he said.

"It is something I could discuss with the police."

"You could. But I doubt they'd be interested."

"This is not done."

"True, *Señora*. It is not a good thing. But neither is locking a paying guest out of your hotel. Neither is that done."

His head was still pulsating from the bells that woke him. Had it not been for that, he'd probably let it go. She would chew and worry the thing for a while longer, he guessed, but in the end she'd leave him to replace the lock. But he had a raging thirst and wanted to get on with breakfast. He didn't feel like stringing out his apologies, though he knew well enough the custom. He didn't feel like spending the time the *Señora* felt the lock was worth.

"I don't like this thing you have done," she said.

"*Señora*, what is done is done. The life has these things. I will

60

buy you a lock. Right now I want to finish my breakfast. Then I go to work."

"These things have to be paid for," she told him.

So that was it. She wanted her contrition in pesos. She wanted the new lock and a little something more. She was passing the plate.

This, Isaac knew, also was perfectly in keeping with custom. He was living in her country, not his own, and he needed to submit to the practices that prevailed. He needed to give her something for the inconvenience. It wasn't worth arguing about. But she had chosen a bad morning for Isaac, who was usually generous in these matters. There was something about her perfect righteousness, her moral indignation that pricked him. He pitted her black-cloaked piety and Catholic good taste against his pressing need for a second orange juice. She came in second. Wars were waged for less.

"Then go find the police, *Señora*. Maybe they will fix your lock. Maybe they will pay you a few extra pesos for your troubles. They will know a good deal about your lock as it is!"

The dining room had grown quiet. The students had stopped eating. George and Harry, who had just risen from their table, didn't immediately move from it. They were accidental witnesses. Only the Madras, alone as she was at the long table, had taken it all in from the beginning.

She would no doubt talk to the *Señora* about it when he'd left. They would talk in English and spend the morning with it, clucking, shaking their heads. The Madras would tell the *Señora* about the feeling she had since first laying eyes on Isaac. She wouldn't be able to explain it, she would tell her, but she had intuitive feelings about people that almost always were right. Everyone who knew her marveled at this, she said. Take it from her: this new art teacher was not to be trusted. Between her and the *Señora*, the Madras doubted he knew much about art. She had it first hand that he had absolutely no taste in paintings.

When the *Señora* went into town that day, she would carry the broken lock in her black apron. She would show it to her friends.

61

She and two or three of them would sit on a cast-iron bench in the plaza and talk about Americans, the things they were capable of doing. The years had been kind to the *Señora* and she had been able to collect lots of stories about these rich and thankless people from the north and the things they did. She would have stories about those who skipped out on their bill, had stolen towels and soap, and about liquor parties that were held in their rooms and how the rooms had been left.

In the shadow of the great church and in a hushed voice she would again tell them about the dirty pictures the students drew and about those who taught them to do so. She would spend a lot of time describing the details of the drawings she had seen. She would tell her friends that there were men as well as women who posed for such things. As her friends leaned closer to hear more, she would pull her cheeks into hollows and shake her head. She had lived too long. Seen too much.

"Perhaps, *Señor*," she told Isaac, using her English for the first time, "this is not the hotel that you should stay in. There are other hotels for your kind. Perhaps by the end of the week you will find a place where it doesn't matter what you do. Perhaps that would suit you better."

"*Señora*: I'll have your lock this afternoon. I'll be out of her tonight. Now will you bring me one Goddamned glass of orange juice!"

Still smiling, she returned the lock to her apron and shuffled off. When Fat Tina came back to the table she had another glass of orange juice, a toasted roll and some fresh pineapple. He would miss Fat Tina. Altogether it was not how he would have chosen to start the week.

Chapter 7

The school was across town from his boarding house, a good half-mile walk. It was one Isaac enjoyed.

It took him through the market place and the long neat rows of fresh fruit and vegetables and where the fish was hung open to the flies. It took him past the open door of the carpentry shops and the leather shop that measured and tooled his sandals from a paper tracing he made of his feet, past the warm, thick smell from the bakery to the big open store that sold film and sacks of grain and the long steel reinforcing rods he'd bought for use as armatures, then on into the central *jardin*.

Here he passed the several hotels and art galleries, including the one which displayed his work, and the shops that offered primitive crafts and polished furniture, and a store that sold only ceremonial masks.

Under the arcade were two open air cafes and a pharmacy and a book store that carried used paperbacks, tourist junk and sold tickets to the buses to Mexico City and to Toboada, the hot springs resort about ten miles out.

Opposite the plaza and in the shade of the arcade just off the church, peasants and their children waited in line for the best food in town. They waited in the drifting smoke of the cooking fire, shot through with slanting sunlight and vertical shadows, for the woman on the low stool to parcel out her hot tortillas and beans and spit-roasted chicken. She sold beer and Coke from a rusted cooler.

It was an interesting walk and colorful and the radios the shopkeeper had were all tuned to the music of the local station and most everybody greeted one another.

Nearer the school there were two lesser galleries, a grocery, a dealer in scrap metal, a garage that pumped gas from a rusted machine and a store that sold art supplies and leather goods and picture postcards of Taxco and the Virgin of Guadalupe.

Across the walled Instituto was an empty field that was used for dumping trash and for the circus when it was in town.

When it was early in the week, as it was then, Isaac had to thread through five or six Indian families who camped on the stone steps leading into the school. They and others who stood on the sidewalk on either side of the portal waited for the painting instructors who would choose some of them to pose for the week. They did not know whether Isaac was one who would do the choosing, and the men rose and doffed their sombreros, and the women and children smiled and greeted him.

Those who were selected would earn five pesos a day and would work the week. They had learned to dress more colorfully than they would normally, bringing out their bright serapes and most vividly striped rebozos. Some of the women carried flowers and baskets of colorful fruit and some of them suckled their babies. If they were not chosen they would spend the week in the square waiting for the tourists who would want to take their photograph. Some of them would charge a peso or nothing at all if there was resistance.

By the end of the week when their flowers had wilted and they had eaten the fruit, they would wait in the plaza anyway. They would wait for Sunday when they could go to mass and put some of the money they earned into a tray. It was a payment plan that assured them steady work, boy babies and a better life the next time around. The money was missed, of course, but a ticket to heaven — even when arriving at the gates in a second class bus — didn't come cheap.

The bulletin board outside Administration was used by students and anyone who wanted to communicate with the English speaking population. There were offers to share rides to Brownsville, the East and West Coast, easels and stretchers for sale, *criadas* wanted, Spanish tutoring, theater productions and musical announcements, those seeking tennis partners and automobile parts and steady shack-ups. Mostly there were houses and apartments to share. One neatly lettered announcement caught Isaac's eye:

"Art instructor offers to rent a quasi-luxurious flat (flush toilet) and studio space (stove and refrigerator aren't worth keeping anyway) near *jardin* to a serious, independent male who can mind his own bleeding business. Private entrance. Dopers, drifters and social reformers need search elsewhere. 28 Avenida Pico. No parrots." It was signed "S. Boswell."

The sculpture studio was already humming when Isaac entered. Before he could get his apron on and cinched, he was called over by a student waiting for his help in casting.

Carlos had already opened the bins and tool closet. He was pounding the recycled clay into bricks on the far side of the studio. The model was in place on the throne. She was dressed in a coarse cotton shift and sat with her head cupped in her hand. Sunlight from windows over the plaster bin puddled at her feet. A second source of illumination streamed down from the sky light high in the vaulted ceiling. The shaft, thick with plaster dust, painted a piece of her shoulder and the side of her face and set them against the dark figures working beyond her. She could have been posing for a Rembrandt, maybe *Jeramiah Lamenting the Destruction of Jerusalem*. She was snoring, a glint of spittle at the corner of her mouth.

The model, a carry-over from last week, was one of Carlos's girlfriends, a bored young Indian with a flat nose and vacant eyes. She had spent the preceding week fighting off sleep. She had begun this week surrendering to it. She stirred when Isaac moved the dais a quarter turn.

The Rembrandt chiaroscuro was a waste. She was to be the

65

subject of a portrait bust for those who had begun classes and were not working on their own projects. Her head and the placid face that went with it were her least compelling features.

"I'm ready to cast, I think," the student told Isaac. "I just need a little help with the eyes, maybe. I'm not certain I have them right, the eyes." He was a businessman out of Chicago and had come the week before to learn about art for the first time. He managed to deliver the message about the eyes in a tone that made it sound like he was quite sure they were perfect.

He was a balding, heavy-set man who had been a good natured novice until that morning. He had been on a three-week vacation and enrolled out of boredom. Now his eyes, dark beneath a thicket of brows, defied Isaac to find anything wrong with the masterpiece before them. The twenty hours of labor on the piece had transformed him. He had become a neglected genius. The subject for this miracle was a clay modeling of the head of a man of uncertain origins. It was bad, Isaac noted, but not nearly as bad as these things get.

"Maybe it's the left eye," the businessman said. "What do you think?" He could not hide the emotion in his voice. It could have been a study for Donatello's David. Isaac had heard that he owned three apartment buildings on the Outer Drive and had bought and sold a National League baseball team.

He was in the bloom of his first creation and didn't yet understand the trick of the eyes, his own. He'd been too close to the work and didn't know how convincingly they could lie to him. Since the modeling was an improvement over some first efforts, Isaac felt inclined to help him. He wanted to show him now rather than have him learn later, as he was sure he would, why the life-size head mounted on the armature before them was a mistake.

Though the criticism would come in place of what he'd wholeheartedly expected to hear, Isaac thought the businessman could take it. He asked for his modeling tool. Isaac cleared the dry clay from the curved edge with his thumbnail. He positioned it at the left ear, then drew a deep line in the clay that ran through the careful modeling of the eyes to the same point on the right ear. It revealed the positioning error, one the businessman would have easily seen once he got away from the sculpture for a day or so. The critique in intaglio provided another favor. It erased the niggling detail his student felt the eyes warranted over the other shapes in the head. Sadly, he very nearly would need to start again.

"Jesus Christ!" he told Isaac and those in the rest of the studio. "I mean, what the hell!"

Isaac explained about the favor, that he could really not show him another way, that he could not, in honesty, tell him it was wonderful or that if he niggled a little here and there he'd have an Epstein.

"I mean, come on!" Isaac's student had stepped back, eyes burning with outrage. "Look at what you've done here!" Holding out both hands to the desecration, he sought solace from his fellow students. But they were returning to their own work.

Isaac explained how everything in art was built from the beginning and ended in the end, that if anything was wrong along the way — as it certainly was in the piece they were discussing — than all of it, or almost all of it, had to be done again.

"Sure. But I mean, my God!"

Isaac could see what he meant, that it would be easier if he had not drawn a line through his sculpture. But, he argued, that wouldn't make it right, that he would only end up with a portrait with something wrong about the eyes.

"To hell with it!" the businessman pointed out. He took off his apron and threw it over the bust. He stormed out past the sleeping model.

When he came back, as surely he would, they'd argue some more, Isaac reasoned. In the end he'd repair the damage and after some more hours he would have a better piece. It would still not be as good as the stockbroker believed, but Isaac would show him how to cast it. When it was in the plaster and could no longer be seen, it would improve some more. When the student would chip it out the next day with a mallet and chisel, the piece would emerge. It would be a vast disappointment. Not as great as his disappointment had he cast the first rendition Isaac had criticized, but a disappointment nonetheless. He wouldn't believe it was the same piece he had worked on and wondered if Isaac had switched it with the work of one of the inferior students he had been compelled to work with.

In the clay, after he had repaired the damage resulting from his teacher's jealous rage, it looked so much better than it did in the plaster. The Chicago businessman did not know that the long hours working on it had mesmerized him, had made him think the piece was somehow important.

But Isaac felt sure his student would finish just the same. His three weeks were running out and he had nothing to show his wife. Under the running water he'd sand the roughness from the plaster. He would repair the airholes and the parts of the face damaged by the chisel. And with all the work it would seem better, and he'd put some concoction of patina on it and would mount it on a piece of mesquite.

The concentrated hours of work would again make him believe it was something it was not. But this time he would remember how he had been tricked. He had not used his eyes before and did not know all the tricks they could play. But he had grown wary. And this was the first sign of learning. Sadly, it was a confusing stage. Now he was not certain his teacher had been as jealous as he first thought. Still, he would not ask for a critique, fearing it would remain negative. Not trusting Isaac to lavish praise on his work, he was forced to turn to the wholly inferior students he worked with. But, while more circumspect, they also revealed a jealous streak, as it turned out.

Now, with his first piece waxed and finished, he did not know what he had. Sometimes when he looked at it, it was good and worth preserving. At other times it looked like something the former owner of a baseball team would make.

Still, he'd take it home with him on the plane. Not trusting it to his luggage, he'd carry it on his lap, but wrapped up.

At home he'd show it to his wife, in part to prove that he hadn't spent all his time in bed with his secretary and in part because he wanted it praised. When she exclaimed its greatness — she also

68

may have been fooling around in his absence — he'd display it on the mantle.

He would stop and study it sometimes in passing. When his friends visited he would joke about it, about a businessman trying to be a sculptor in three weeks. But he would watch his friends when he joked. He would try to read their faces. After a while, he'd put it in the attic.

After the businessman stormed out, Isaac turned the dais again. The Mexican girl stirred herself into a yawn, then settled back. She had a half-hour before break, before she could rest.

Carlos had finished with the bricks.

"He is not a happy man, that one," he told Isaac.

"He's been in a fight with his ego," Isaac told him. "It will be all right for him later. I think he wants to learn."

Isaac lectured the new students briefly, got them each an armature and two bricks of clay, found them each a stand near the dais and started them off, showing them how the clay from the beginning must be pressed tightly against the armature, how you should begin to look for, and feel for, the form from the start.

He cast a piece for a middle-aged woman who was afraid to get plaster on her shoes. She had a hooked nose and very little in the way of an upper lip and leaned a breast against his arm as he tried to explain the process. She pretended not to understand. He showed her how to place the shims, the thin brass sheets that would serve to divide the cast in two once it was hit sharply with a mallet. He showed her how to mix the plaster into a pan of water and how, when it was stirred to the right consistency, it could be thrown on the clay with a back hand flip of a cupped hand and how you needed to work against the time the plaster would begin to set up and could not be worked anymore. But she would not take the pan from him. She was afraid she would ruin something.

She had a ring that would not come off, she said, and was afraid to dip her hand into the plaster. She had worked on the clay part of it for a long time and was afraid she would damage what she'd done in the casting. She stood in her embroidered pink smock and watched Isaac work. She stepped back when he broke the two-piece mold away.

Later, she would have other reasons for not cleaning the mold and, when Isaac had done so, she would watch him coat the inside of each piece with clay slip and wire the two pieces together and pour a new batch of plaster into the neck of the mold. She would continue to entertain him with compliments, the least she could do in payment for his labors.

When the mold had set, she would not want to chip it out. She didn't want to get dry pieces of plaster in her hair. Even when Isaac or Carlos would show her how, if she handled the mallet and chisel correctly, the mold would break away evenly, cleanly and if she did it properly there would be no cause for concern, and the surface of the piece would be spared. But she would tell him that she was more into the creative part of sculpture.

On the first break for the model, Isaac asked Carlos if there was an S. Boswell on the staff.

"There are those who come only sometimes. They do not teach all the time. Maybe he is one of those," Carlos said.

"Part time?"

"There are many who come and go like that." He was scraping some dry plaster from the spatula.

"Your girlfriend," Isaac said. "She seems tired."

"She is always tired, that one."

"Perhaps she does not sleep at night. Maybe you should let her get some rest, this one."

"No. That is not the problem. It is not because of my demands on her. She does not sleep at night because she is young and has discovered that she likes the making of love. She likes this more than anything. She is young and not very smart."

The model stood by the door. She had no interest in looking at the dozen or so clay portraits of her that were in progress. She did not think the work in clay had anything to do with her. What she knew is that in a few minutes she would again have to sit in the turning chair and be still for a long time. Occasionally she would

70

look to Carlos. She was chewing gum and the cracking of it carried to where they stood.

"She is not smart in the way she makes love?"

"No," Carlos said. "She is smart in that. She is dumb in almost everything else. She is going to have a baby."

"Yours?"

"Who knows. Her family is in Guadalajara. I'm sending her back there at the end of the week."

"They will be delighted," Isaac told him.

"Yes."

"Will her father or brothers come looking for you?"

"I don't think they have enough for the bus fare."

Throughout the morning he found himself glancing toward the door. Each time a student would come in, he expected it to be Memori. Once Spencer came in with some students from Hermosillo.

"Isaac! Good man! Hell of a job you're doing here. Where is — there! There's the one. Carlos!" He turned to the group crowding at the door behind him. "Two of the best instructors in the business. Wonderful job. Look. Look at some of this work! Look at what we're turning out here. See this? Museum piece. Look at the power of some of the work over here." He swept out, the group trailing.

"It was better this time," Carlos told Isaac.

"What do you mean?"

"Last time he took me for one of the students."

On the second break Isaac crossed the patio to Life Drawing.

Hoffstedder had a class in progress. The model, a fleshy Rubenesque blonde with enormously thick legs, stood on the throne, her torso twisted, her head turned so she faced the door. She carried a long silk scarf that bridged the distance between the hand at her side and the one upraised. She had seen the pose somewhere. Her flat colorless eyes moved down to Isaac as he entered. She was in visible pain.

Hoffstedder was an Austrian and the only instructor to wear a tie. Though he had been a dance teacher in Palm Beach during some lean years, it hadn't corrupted his bearing. He had the studied reserve of an exiled count or a family butler. He could have sold art on 57th Street, had he not known something about it.

He bore a stick of charcoal and threaded his way through the benches. He'd stop occasionally, bend stiffly from the waist and make notations on a student's drawing. He was a good draftsman and more. He showed with Isaac in the same downtown gallery. There had been a one-man show of his in the campus gallery a month after Isaac had come. He had a Picasso sense of reduction and was able to bring forward the character of the subject within a few deliberate lines.

There was the feel of Matisse in his drawing. He was as good at his art as he was bad at teaching it. He could not imagine how others saw or didn't see things. Or how anyone could be without talent. He would want to do their drawings for them. Though he fought the impulse, more often than not he'd yield to it.

Sometimes, sitting astride the drawing bench, he'd forget the student behind him. Back straight, beginning with long sweeping movements of his arm, he took what he saw and played out a series of strokes and counter strokes, leaping from one part of the large sheet of drawing paper to another. Meaningless, at first, he wove the drawing together in a kind of Bachian progression of stabbing, straight lines which seemed in keeping with the construction of his own very linear profile, his long nose and angled jaw. He saw himself in everything he drew.

But when the teacher re-emerged, it was to wonder where he was and what the student wanted. Brusquely, he'd hand the student the charcoal stick and walk away. Whatever diplomacy he may have applied to the Palm Beach matrons and their cratered faces, was lost in his classroom.

As Isaac waited, Hoffstedder descended on a student he had been standing behind, a graying man with wire glasses, a pointed beard and a black beret. The student, Isaac knew, was in the master's program. He had been in it longer than anyone could remember. He wore a Levi jacket. On the back of it was a silkscreened drawing combining several Parisian landmarks. Black letters beneath bore the inscription: *voulez-vous couchez avec moi?*

"So!" Hoffstedder said. The student, startled, turned on his bench awkwardly to face the instructor. He tried for a smile. It did little to melt his teacher.

"This is the model you are drawing?" Hoffstedder asked him. Though not loud, his voice carried the room. "This is why you've chosen to come?"

"Oh, this? Oh, nothing serious. No, nothing serious at all." The student rose to take his place next to his instructor. "A little trouble getting it down this time. Lost concentration, I think." He spoke quietly hoping his instructor would see the value in a private conference.

"It's clear you lost something," Hoffstedder told him.

"What do you think?" the student said. "Something here, I believe. Maybe it's the negative space in this passage."

Isaac had him for one of his classes. He should have mastered in terminology. It was well known that he had accumulated some 600 hours toward his master's thesis, a project that involved, he'd heard, landscaping a Giverny-like garden and painting a series of pictures from it. He had consumed a good deal of the time in the design and construction of a pond and bridge.

It was a good design, one that would have made Monet proud. Sadly, though he purchased a lot just south of town that held promise, he could get nothing to grow on it, except a very low lying species of barrel cactus and, on the water, a two-inch thick blanket of a brown algae. The real estate broker had failed to tell him that at one time the land had been the site of a kerosene storage facility. Isaac heard he was waiting out a response to queries he'd made to several nurseries in the States seeking a hardy water lily.

"I think you're right," Hoffstedder told him, his voice as resonant as before. "There is something wrong. But I think your trouble is more with positive space. If you cannot see the model, move the bench."

"You see, I'm trying for a linear presence here that I hope to translate —"

"Try for the model. If you look, you'll see one in front of you. You'll see that she is standing on her feet. Do you think, maybe, that she has wings? That she is floating from the gas of an undigested taco?"

"*Well*, I didn't *want* to get tied to a sense of reality. I wanted to get a — I don't know — a freer line here. I wanted to discover . . ." His voice trailed off.

"But this is real. It's in front of you. The model stands there, you see? If you don't start from that you won't finish anything. Here is a woman. Here is not a ball of papier mache'."

"Well . . . of course, but I wanted to go beyond —"

"Tell me," the instructor bent and indicated something on his paper. "What do all these things mean?"

"I don't know. It's something, you know, experimental. I wanted to heighten this area, to make it stand out."

"Ah, this is a success," Hoffstedder told him. "I can see that it stands out. It hurts my eyes, it stands out so. It is good you are not a conductor of a major orchestra. You would place an enormous burden on the man who bangs the cymbals."

"I see what you mean. You're saying the purity is diminished, the passage is not quite —"

"What I'm saying is that your drawing is nothing. If you have to pay for your paper it is worse than that. Draw the model. That's why she troubles herself to stand there."

A girl with long dark hair, who was thin enough to be Memori, sat with her back to Isaac a few benches from the master's student. She was making hesitant moves with her charcoal vine. But when she reached down for something in her drawing box, he could see she wore bangs and a face full of acne.

Isaac caught Hoffstedder's eye and he began to work his way over, pausing at a drawing, leaning in over a student's shoulder, making his swift, clarifying strokes and moving on. He walked on the balls of his feet, gliding like a ballroom dancer, barking like a drill instructor.

"They are burdened, the lot of them," he told Isaac, his voice thankfully modulated.

"Negative space," Isaac said.

"Ah."

"Got him in one of my classes. He's no better at sculpture."

"Everyone's got him in one of his classes," Hoffstedder said. "He takes art as religion. He's memorized the psalms. Been trying to drive him out for years. Make a splendid art teacher, I suspect."

"They who can't, teach."

"They who can't teach, teach."

Isaac agreed, then thought how the description could be turned against both of them.

Hoffstedder started toward the model:

"This is a twenty minute pose!"

The model, beginning to sag, straightened noticeably, but the flesh behind her upraised arm was trembling. There was the agony of it in her face. He asked about Boswell.

"S. Boswell? Not here. No. No teacher like that. Perhaps . . . wait. It could be Sturgeon. I'm not sure of the last name. Maybe it's Boswell. Been in town for a while. Exhibits some. I think he's — excuse me." He turned again to the model: "All right, rest!"

There was a groan from some of the students as the model collapsed, sinking to the edge of the stage, deflated. She rubbed her arm and flexed life back into her fingers.

"You are five minutes too weak."

"I just couldn't hold it. I was getting a cramp in my arm."

"I asked you for twenty minutes. I did not ask you to stand in that ridiculous pose, did not ask you to look like something you've seen on a French postcard."

"I'm sorry. I thought I could hold it."

"You will rest for five minutes and take something you can hold, or you'll buy the paper that's been wasted on you."

"Do you want me to stand?"

"I don't care that you are flat on your ass, if you can stay there for twenty minutes."

The students were rising, moving back off the benches away

from their drawing. Some turned immediately to a new page of drawing paper in order to conceal what they'd done. The more confident continued to study their drawings, tilting the head, moving forward, changing a line, deepening something, shading something else. Some moved around the room to see how and what others saw.

"She's a good one, this model," Hoffstedder told Isaac. "When she doesn't have cause to think, she's good. Look at her now."

She was leaning back on the throne, her feet flat on the floor, legs apart. A gigantic breast swung down and lay across the folds of her stomach, the other fell free with the twist of her torso. She was exhausted and the colors just beneath her flesh drove a deep-running current, a liquid pattern of lights and darks and subtle blues. She was picking at something in her ear.

"He's the second coming," Hoffstedder said.

"Boswell?"

"If that's his name. Check with Duckworth. He keeps files on everything. Ought to be in the C.I.A. He'll no doubt have something on this guy, if he's the one I'm thinking about." Lester Duckworth had taken on the title of department chairman when Billingstein retired to Taos.

"What kind of work does this Boswell do?"

"His work," Hoffstedder said, "you won't have to ask about. Taught natives in the jungles outside Palenque somewhere. Joint Mexican-American program for the uplifting of cannibals. Bring them a taste of art, when it's flesh they crave."

"He's got an apartment to rent and I'm being evicted," Isaac told him. "What do you think?"

"You like, maybe, monologues?"

"Why'd he leave the jungles?"

"At the polite request of the government. The Indians thought he was Cortez, the white savior. It was happening all over again. Natives gave him their maidens and everything they valued. They made songs about him. Would follow him anywhere. Some of the local politicians got nervous, fearing he'd lead a *coup d'etat* and deed another chunk of Mexico to the States. The program was abandoned. That's his story, anyway. More likely he planted a seed in the chief's daughter, or contracted clap, or both."

"Where does he show?"

"Some gallery in Texas, I understand; Houston, maybe. Abstract colorist, or something. He'll tell you about it."

"Have you seen his work?" Isaac asked.

"Only heard about it. From him and from others who have heard about it. If he doesn't come clean and reveal what he's been doing, he'll be famous some day. It's the way with some, and this one particularly."

Hoffstedder called across the room to a group of students standing by the sinks: "If you smoke outside, you can maybe draw better inside."

Isaac caught Chairman Duckworth just after his class broke for the three hour siesta. He was standing outside his studio with two students, both young women, each carrying a stretched canvas. The three were watching Isaac as he came up the path from the tennis court.

"Just the man I want to see. I was going to shake this," he indicated the two students, "and see if I could pry you out of the clay."

Had Duckworth been proportional, he would have been a balding, handsome man of about fifty. Sadly, his upper body did not match that of the lower. It was as though he were parts of two separate people joined at the waist. The thick, short legs did not at all belong to the elongated — even elegant — torso. It was as though God began to shape the fellow from the head down, and ran short of clay. The result was his knuckles were not as far off the ground as they might have been.

He'd also been a disappointment for Spencer who took him on as a comer from the eminent Academy of Cultural Studies in Chicago fifteen years before, an heir-apparent to Billingstein, who was then into his third how-to book and showing signs of restlessness.

But unlike Billingstein's Mexican market scenes, which, if nothing else, were easily recognizable as such, Duckworth's paintings were more amorphous. They all wore the look and coloration of a very bad shin bruise. His first and subsequent shows in Chicago and New York did little for his reputation and less for his dwindling bank account, since he'd paid for them. Sadly, however much his Bruise Series — as they became known to a small circle of friends — meant to him, they did not ignite the enthusiasm of the buying public.

Since he was plugged into the cultural scene, good at organization and had been around longer than most, he was appointed chairman of the department anyway, shortly after Billingstein left for New Mexico. At the time there were still plenty of students on the GI Bill, and they would come to Mexico whoever taught. For GI students the advantages of studying in Mexico were many. The place was cheap, the *cantinas* were open for as long as you could still convey your intentions of ordering another round, and it bore absolutely no resemblance to life in the U.S. Army.

Spencer had hoped for more from Duckworth. When it became clear that he wasn't going to get it, that Duckworth would not likely get famous, he resigned himself to using the old Billingstein brochures in the promotional mailings. That it became a cost saving measure took a little of the sting off his disappointment. Duckworth's paintings never improved. Spencer and almost everybody else quietly suffered his yearly exhibition in the school's gallery.

"I want you to help me on Friday's program," he told Isaac as he approached. He introduced him to the two students, both in mini-skirts, sandals and beads. The pretty one was young enough to wear braces. She tried her best not to smile. The painting she carried at her side contained little cellular bubbles of various colors. They defied any obvious organization. He thought he might be able to read a hidden number within them, like a color blind test.

When she saw Isaac tilting his head to see it, she proudly held it upright for him. It didn't help.

"What program is that?" he asked Duckworth.

"Isaac, you may be the last uninformed artist in Mexico. The lecture. Heinrich Guerber. The New York Times' answer to art in

78

America. You don't get out much?" The two girls appropriately giggled, one with a hand to her mouth.

"That's right. I'd forgotten." Isaac did not like it when a lecture was called a program. He did not like anything when it was called a program. He liked it still less when he got invited to work on one.

"He's already in town," the girl without the braces said. "I've seen him at the Bugambilia. He was with some Mexican actors and some dancers from the Ballet Folklorico and the mayor, I think. He's a dream."

"The mayor?" Duckworth asked.

This caused the girl with braces to abandon her habit of withholding them from view. Together the two girls dissolved into laughter.

"He was with his wife." The girl without braces was the first of the two to regain control. She added wistfully, "Looks like a fashion model, or something."

"I don't think he's married, is he?" Duckworth asked. "I should mention it if he is, in my introduction Friday. That's why I wanted to see you, Isaac."

"I never heard he was married," the girl with braces said tentatively. When that was met with silence, she confirmed it: "I'm sure of it. I'd have read it somewhere. No. He's not married."

"There you are," Duckworth said. "There's still hope, ladies." This set the girls off again. Still giggling, they excused themselves with little waves and set off. The two men watched the young girls in their short skirts move down the winding path. They watched them tip toward each other and laugh. They watched as one ran ahead of the other. They watched until the two were out of sight behind the weaving studio.

"Need your help, Isaac. I know what I want to say in the introductory notes. Just need the right words. Get it straightened out." Duckworth handed Isaac a folded piece of drawing paper. He watched Isaac open it and read some of the penciled notes that filled the page. "None of it is chiseled in rock, Isaac. You can cut and paste to suit. I don't want to put people to sleep before the main man gets a whack at it."

"Sure. I'll look at it; get it back to you," Isaac said, relieved he wasn't to be further involved.

"Good. Was having my problems with it when I remembered your application. Figured you might be the solitary figure aboard who could execute a complete sentence. You've done some journalism."

"That might mitigate against writing a complete sentence. I confess to journalism, but only when I've been hungry," Isaac told him.

"Wrote some songs, didn't you?"

"Lyrics. It was a bad period. You shouldn't hold it against me."

"Isaac. This is interesting. Spencer didn't know, and I didn't know until I got to reading your file in detail. 'Arrested Development.' Didn't you write for them? You didn't write that song . . . what's is it? The one you're always hearing?"

"No. If you're always hearing it, it's not one of mine. I didn't remember putting all that in the application. Must have been drunk."

"Please, Isaac. This is a help to us. We need to understand our resources so that we can draw on them." Duckworth had reverted to a tone appropriate to a department chair, then lost it again. "Imagine. Married to Vallinia Free. You old devil. Great songs. What's that slow ballad? You know, the sultry, moody thing she does . . . what is it? Va-boom, va-boom . . . I can hear it. What the hell is that song? She's still very popular, isn't she?"

"I guess, but when I was married to her she was Abby Shelderval. As wives go, she wasn't so popular. With me, frankly, she wasn't popular at all." Isaac, for the life of him, couldn't remember putting all this in a letter of application. But it had been a while back. Doubtless, he had been in one of his black states. Probably didn't intend to mail it. Certainly hadn't expected to hear back from it.

"This is an important time for us, Isaac. And I'm pleased you're aboard. Spencer seems to like you and I'm getting some

80

feedback from your students. All to the good. I know you're more interested in teaching painting, and between you and me, I'd not give up on that. I'd expect some changes in a little time."

"Good," Isaac said. "Perversely, I'm enjoying the factory. Stoop labor is always good for the soul, but I'd expect it will wear thin in time. I like painting and was disappointed when Spencer had filled the slot. But I've been a little out of fashion, you know. Nobody paints pictures anymore."

"Isaac, I've seen your slides and some paintings downtown. You've got a good sense of color. I mean that. You only need to loosen up some. Free yourself. Shed the yoke, so to speak. Only an opinion here, you understand. And I mean nothing by it, Isaac. But what I'm saying is do we have to know — I mean, do we really have to know — that this is a landscape, a tree here, a person standing there, some sky. I mean, do we need that? My opinion, you understand."

Isaac nodded, as though he were thinking about it. What came to his mind was Duckworth's series of shin bruises. He let it go.

"Looks like Heinrich's going to play a part in that future of ours, Isaac."

"Heinrich?"

"Looks that way. Maybe you've heard. The Heinrich Guerber Foundation is planning to endow an off-campus extension down here, a spin off from his College of New Art in the Hudson Valley. The foundation's got more money than God and it looks pretty good."

"New Art?" Isaac could see Guerber buying up and painting over the Italian Renaissance.

"It's exciting. We need an infusion of new blood. We need to get serious. Need to be seen as a force in the avant garde, part of the cutting edge. Got one or two students now who look pretty strong. It will mean some building, new studios, an extension to the hotel and, as I was saying, some key people in some key places. A little more money to go around. That won't hurt, right? Heinrich's visit is preliminary to all of it. Be here maybe ten days, and

81

head back. The bean counters will come down to dot the 'i's. The money and building plans will follow."

"Looks like this is set to go," Isaac said.

"Not completely. But I hear he likes what he sees. He was a student down here years back. Wants to bring us on-board. Has a real feel for Mexico, the soul of the peasant. I hope you're free Monday. He wants to meet the staff."

Monday, Isaac remembered, would be the day after he died, tragically, in a bull ring. Fortunately, Heinrich would be in the audience. He wouldn't expect Isaac at the meeting.

Chapter 8

In what remained of the mid-day break Isaac set off to find the address.

According to Duckworth, Sturgeon Boswell had been a popular teacher at the Instituto some years back and had attracted a number of students from Mexico City to the school. When it became known that he maintained a rather spotty correspondence with the revolutionary painter, David Siqueiros, the local authorities grew uneasy. What had begun as a cursory check of the American's mail for anything worth keeping — a democratic practice embracing anyone mailing letters — took on greater significance. Letters were read instead of shaken out for spendable currency. Interpretations were made. One was that a meeting was being arranged between the two in Cuba, where the exiled painter lived.

It wasn't much, but in the Cold War of the mid-sixties, you didn't need a lot. A government functionary was sent to urge Spencer to consider whether maintaining such a politically active teacher in the face of land reform and other Communist plots was a good idea. Spencer allowed as how it wasn't. The American was offered the job in the dank jungles of Palenque, believing he wouldn't take it and go home.

The rest Duckworth offered Isaac was advice. If he were Isaac, he would avoid Sturgeon Boswell. He remained politically unpopular. He could do no one any good, particularly one being groomed for a sensitive position in what would soon be a new age school of the fine arts. It would be a mistake to look up Boswell. But Duckworth wanted Isaac to know this was just an opinion and didn't mean a thing. He, Isaac, could do whatever he liked. If he wanted to side with the damned Communists, that was his right.

There was no number for 28 Avenida Pico, at least none he could find. There was 64, a pair of doors without any discernible number, then a number 2. The next door was 127. Isaac interpolated, factored in where he was and who may have done the mathematics, subtrahended his own problems there, and picked an unnumbered door. When no one answered he tried the latch. The door swung inward.

He stepped over the footboard into a small courtyard. On the adobe wall to his right was an incomplete fresco. Dominating it was a violent sweep of sienna that arched downward from the tile overhang of the adjacent roof, nearly to the brick deck. There were several splashes of red ochre in the middle distance which could be taken for figures. A pastel blue underpainting was well absorbed into the plaster. Its chalky coloration bled through and linked the colors. A cartoon had been pounced and some other colors laid down.

All of it seemed tentative, uncertain. If it were to be a landscape, the artist had made a start. But that had been some time ago. It had not been worked on since.

Suspended from the staircase leading to a closed door on the second level were perhaps twenty hanging plants. These and all those occupying the dozen or so large ceramic pots scattered in the enclosure were quite clearly and irreversibly dead.

Beneath the stairway another door, this one open, beckoned. He had to reach into the room to knock on it. In doing so he stepped on half of a very old carrot. No one answered. Tentatively, he moved inside.

The apartment was dark against the sun outside. What lighting there was, was indirect. It came from a low window on the far side of the room. It faced a wall of bricks maybe three feet away. There was the smell of turpentine and varnish overlaid with the smell of stale beer and something that resembled burnt popcorn.

On a wrought-iron coffee table surfaced with mosaic tile were a stack of books, some open and face down. Most of them were on Mayan Civilization, ancient pottery and pre-Columbian sculpture. On the far corner was a three-inch stack of Tarzan comics.

In an adjoining room to the right was a dining room table. On it was a clutter of dirty dishes, the ravages of an uneaten dinner. Where a centerpiece might have been, stood a pair of well-worn climbing boots. Gessoed canvases were propped against this table, its chairs and the credenza behind it. Drawings in every stage of incompletion were scattered everywhere. On a braided throw rug between the rooms lay an upturned serving dish. It was crawling to his left.

When Isaac looked more carefully he saw it was a tortoise. The shell had been painted like a Rouault in some of the colors of the mural outside, but heavily leaded in black paint. It was eating some lettuce that had been scattered on the rug and the tile floor next to it. It moved watchfully, its pale neck extended.

Off the main room and from the back there was some light and the sound of a radio. The station it had been set on had the tunneling sound of far-off Europe in World War II. Instead of Churchill, waves of a decidedly Spanish version of "Twist and Shout" washed the room.

A young woman materialized. She was in a cut-off tee shirt and what were meant to be white shorts. She picked her way barefooted through the clutter of drawings and canvases and lettuce. Isaac thought he recognized her from school, but when he began to introduce himself, she held up her hand. Frowning, she shook her head, nodded to the lighted room in the back. She continued as though crossing a shallow stream on flat rocks. Gracefully, she stepped over the tortoise.

The creature followed her with his eyes, a lettuce leaf dangling from its jaws. She exited through a door to his left and closed it with a gentle, if decidedly final, click. The tortoise blinked once, stared at the closed door, then turned its head to Isaac. After a while it began to chew the lettuce leaf again.

He crossed to the room from which the radio played. The

lights emanated from a string of flood lamps that spanned the ceiling on two walls. Some had been painted in primary colors. Shirtless, and with his back to Isaac, a man stood working at a baroque easel, rich in size and timber. It held a large, mostly horizontal canvas in its jaws. On a tall wooden stool next to it sat a large porcelain enamel tray. Piled on it was an assortment of rotting fruit, cheese and vegetables. All were coated with a thick layer of varicolored fur. To the right of the tray on an elongated dish rested a bloated and badly decomposed carp.

"Excuse me. I'm looking for an S. Boswell. I'm an art teacher. That be you?"

The figure shifted perceptibly, and was still again. Isaac wondered if he had been heard. Gradually it raised one hand and the brush that was held in it to the height of the shoulder. The brush returned to the hand-held palette to drag some colors together. It could have been a signal or that he was measuring something. Isaac waited for the man to turn. Instead he bent to what Isaac took to be a fresh canvas. On closer inspection he could see that there was a faint bloom of coloration on its gessoed surface, a highly diluted version of the sienna he'd seen outside. Along the edges were thousands of tiny strokes which worked their way around its perimeter, faintly blue. One stroke was colored and valued very much like another, though there may have been barely discernible differences.

Scores of tubes of paint lay open on the work table next to him. One of them, a large tube of Titanium white had fallen and split open on the paint-spattered tile beneath him. The radio in the room was loud. The group on it sang deep from within the tunnel. They made no effort to give up twisting as they did last summer.

He was a big man with a tangle of black hair that had worked its way down across his shoulders tapering to a single line that traced his spinal column. He took his sable brush loaded with the color he'd been mixing and lay a long, thin line of blue from left to right across the lower third of his canvas. He straightened and stood back, exactly on the tube of paint. It gushed a stream of brilliant white that arched upward, curled and folded neatly across the toe of his boot.

He studied his painting. When he spoke, he spoke to the colored line on his canvas:

"You son of a bitch," he told it. "Would you look at that son of a bitch!" He signaled for Isaac to approach. "Look at that. Tell me if you've ever seen anything like it. Tell me what you think."

Isaac, believing he had missed something, approached. There was only the thin cool line on the warmish tint of the underpainting. As he leaned in to look, he caught, full force, the smell of the rotten fish and ripe cheese that had lain dormant in the still air. Blinking, the rotted still-life gripping the back of his throat, Isaac answered the man. He truthfully did no know what to think.

"Are you kidding, for Christ sake?" He was still speaking to the canvas, shouting above the radio. The Beatles' tune had ended and an announcer was winding up a hard sell pitch for a brand of dish soap. He was standing much closer to the tunnel opening than the singing group had been.

"You can't hear this? Listen. I'll be Goddamned. Listen to this thing. Hear those vibrations? How those colors sing? It's a symphony, for Christ sake!"

Isaac tried. All he could hear now was a commercial jingle exhorting the qualities of Dos Equis beer. The painter listened to his colors a while longer, then placed his palette on the table, his brush in a jar of turp. He turned to Isaac for the fist time.

"You're not a painter, then."

"Sculpture. I teach Sculpture." Isaac thought it best not to mention painting.

"I'm sorry," the man said, as though consoling him for the loss of a close relative.

"I'm looking for S. Boswell."

"Sturge. Sturgeon Boswell. The kind of name you get if you've got a fisherman father and a compliant mother. If you're interested in buying art, you've come at the right time. Catch me now, I'm affordable. Expensive, but affordable. Another six months you'll need a letter from Peggy Guggenheim and a waiver from Leo

Castelli. If you're looking to collect rent or taxes, or know some-body who is, you got it all wrong. I'm not making a nickel, which is why I need a job, if you've come to offer one. But I'll be damned if I'm going to help you teach sculpture. Do people still do that?"

He enclosed Isaac's big hand with a matching one. Grimly, he pumped it twice. He would be in his mid-forties and wore a full beard. It was trimmed back neatly from his lips. The beard and his dark eyes lightened the skin around them. He had the pale, pleas-ant look of a man leaning to fat, one who would look good in it, once it overtook him, as it was certain to do someday.

"I saw your notice on the bulletin board," Isaac explained. "About the apartment. You're renting an apartment."

"You a fag?"

"I don't think so."

"Last guy was. Wrote poetry and fell in love with my garden-er."

"That's hard to believe," Isaac said.

"That he was a fag or that he wrote poetry."

"That you have a gardener."

"Well, it's true," Sturge said. "Been with me for years. When he's not drunk, he waters the plants on the patio."

"But they're all dead."

"Yes." He seemed to think about that. "I don't pay him much."

"I see," Isaac told him.

"Anyway, guy was a poet. Had a good sense for words, but a bad sense for the Mexican macho. Paco did not take kindly to his offer."

"The gardener?"

"Yes. The police report had it that the poet had fallen from his car just out of town and that was why he was dead. Figured falling from a car was the only thing that could account for how his head looked. You may have read about it."

"No."

"The American consulate protested the event. The office questioned how the poet could have fallen out of his car at high speed when it was parked neatly at the side of the road near where they found him. The Mexican authorities thought about that. They agreed that there may be something in what they said.

"They decided to appoint a board of inquiry from Mexico City. But it was a long way to come for one dead poet, so the board wrote to the American consulate and told them that they had been wrong about the poet falling out of his car. This, they agreed, was impossible. He had fallen out of someone else's car. Further, they could not account for how the poet's car was parked at the side of the road like it was, but felt it didn't matter anyway since the poet was dead and would have no further use for it.

"There was some more paperwork back and forth, but basically the explanation seemed to satisfy everyone, everyone but me. I not only lost a guy to pay rent, I had to buy the box for him."

"You had to bury him?"

"No one in the States would claim him or pay the two thousand pesos it would cost to ship him to the border. He was a poet, remember. It wasn't like he contributed to the economy or would be of any lasting value. Also, of course, he was queer. So Paco and I planted him on a Tuesday afternoon on the side of a hill near the electric generators."

"Paco said some 'Hail Marys' and I read him parts of the last poem he'd been working on. We had gathered a crowd by then. It had started with some kids who had followed us up the hill to watch us dig the hole. You know how doing anything earns an audience here. By the time we had him planted and covered over we had a respectable funeral, maybe thirty or forty people standing around.

"One guy said he knew a *mariachi* band that would play for him, so we waited while he ran to town to bring them back. Well, he couldn't find them, but he did come back with his brother who carried a trumpet. His brother said he'd like to play something appropriate to the occasion, but he only knew 'Guadalajara.' Since no one knew the poet any better than I, who was going to say 'Guadalajara' was not what he wanted to hear? To me it seemed fitting. I asked the guy with the trumpet if he could play it slow like

89

a dirge. He told me he was new to the trumpet and slow was the only way he knew how to play it.

"The end of it was that it was kind of moving, with everyone feeling bad about the way the trumpeter could not seem to get the notes in the right order and how whoever it was being buried outside a Catholic cemetery would surely spend the rest of eternity burning in hell anyway.

"Like I say, it was sad. All the women appropriately cried and most of the men looked down and shook their heads a lot. A couple of them looked about to lose control, though it may have been that they were wincing at the high notes the trumpeter tried for. I looked at Paco. He was truly remorseful. By this time he had come to like the poet. He was genuinely sorry that he had beaten his head in. It's $75 a month, American."

"What?"

"The apartment. Want to see it?"

"Does it smell better up there?"

"If you take it, you can make it smell any way you want."

"I'm curious," Isaac said. "That still life you're working on. Doesn't it bother you? The smell, I mean."

"Sure does."

"Then why?"

"You mean this? He drew the ferrule of his brush across the decaying apple. The green fuzz of the molding cheese had crawled up onto the brown, wrinkled skin. "See this color here?" He turned the brush and poked at the spot where the apple and cheese intersected. "Know any other way I can get a color like that?"

Chapter 9

Following his afternoon classes, Isaac moved from his hotel. He gathered his clothes from chairs, door knobs and the floor of his closet and stuffed them into his four battered suitcases and strapped them shut. He took his recent paintings off the stretchers and rolled them up. He lashed the roll to one of the suitcases.

The cases had served him well. Over the years they had seen several countries and a half-dozen moves. They had earned a rest. Instead he toted them down the stairs and set them just inside the front gate.

He had to pass through the dining room where the Madras, this time in gold lame', was presiding over a cup of tea. She concentrated on not noticing his passing. He had not seen the *Señora* and had left the new lock by the table near the door to her little room. He waited at the gate for the cab driver.

Isaac had approached the driver in the *jardin* not more than twenty minutes before. Four taxis were waiting under the shade of the laurel trees just off the stone steps leading up to the plaza. The first in line had been the old man without teeth, the one with the broken meter. He went to the next, a young man with slickened hair. He gave him 10 pesos and told him to be in front of his hotel in as many minutes. The driver told him that Isaac could count on it. He could ask anyone about his reliability.

"There are other drivers you can not be sure of," he said, conspiratorially.

"Fine," Isaac told him.

"They will tell you they will be somewhere and they will disappoint you." He frowned his deep concern.

"And you will not?"

He looked hurt. "*Señor*, you have my word."

When it became clear the driver was not going to show, Isaac decided to make the move on foot. Sturge's place was not all that far from La Valencia. It was only a mater of juggling the luggage so that he could make it in one trip. He didn't want to risk leaving some of the bags unattended while making two. Clearly he could not involve the Señora or any of her staff to watch them for him. It would be best just to clear out.

It wasn't far, but he could only make half a block at a time. He'd have to set the load down and shake the blood back into his hands and arms.

It was muggy and at first the streets were crowded. When he set everything down, people would have to step around it, sometimes moving off the narrow sidewalk. But in a few blocks it got better. The crowd thinned and those who passed him did so at a run.

What happened then could have been anticipated.

The rainy season in San Miguel is a wholly tolerable, sometimes spectacular event. Almost daily for three months, a clear flawless sky would blacken within minutes as thick wet clouds rolled in over the high plateau above town. Since the city was built on the lee side of weather, you couldn't see it coming.

There would be a moment of still, then — and at once — lightning would split the air, bolts that would come in threes and fours from everywhere, and nearly simultaneously the thunder would sound, one crack of it swallowing another, tumbling downward like a wall of steel barrels cascading along the near vertical cobblestone streets on the upper reaches of town. And the rain would follow. It would come, not in drops, but at once. The swollen sky would split and there would be water, lots of it. It would fall with force and instantly there would be rivers where streets had been.

They would be rivers for the hour the rain would fall and afterwards. They would be that way even when the clouds rolled off and the sun reappeared. But they would soon drain and the cobblestones would emerge bright and crisply colored in mottled browns and grays and greens and reds, like stones rolled and washed smooth on a beach.

It was spectacular and wholly tolerable, the rains, and afterwards there would be the clean smell of the electrically charged air. Wholly tolerable because it came almost like clockwork. If it were the rainy season, one could almost count on the late afternoon cloudburst. It would come between five and six o'clock and last an hour. It flushed the town and was a small imposition, as long as one remembered the phenomenon and was not caught walking the streets or moving everything he owned from one place to another.

Isaac had not thought about the time of day. Even when it grew dark and the streets began to clear, he only thought of how much easier it was to carry the cases in the deserted streets. He was a block from the jardin when he was reminded. The first crack of lightning exploded behind him. Thunder recoiled behind that. He made another half a block before the rain hit.

There was shelter under the arcades facing the plaza, but it was where everyone had gathered. There, it seemed, everyone on the streets — anticipating what he had not — had found a place to stand. It was a wall of people and it did not yield readily to the American and his clumsy load. The people were dry and stood talking and smoking and looking beyond him at the deluge. It did not occur to them to make way, and with all the luggage, he could not push through them. He tried several times at several places. Finally he found a spot where he was able to take his load partially under the arcade.

It was a place that had opened up a little because of the splash of a rain spout that gushed from a roof top gargoyle. He had taken the full force of the spout to get to it, and the water ran down his face and into his shirt. The woman who stood in his way had rotted teeth and drank from a large bottle of Coke. She did not yield to the urgent way he nudged her with his cases. He was taking water down the back of his neck.

He was able to drive her back a few feet against the crowd behind her. Her reluctance to move was not an act of hostility. It was nothing overt at all. She shuffled backward only because she had to. She did not take the Coke from her mouth but sucked on it like a sugar tit, as she gave him an inch at a time. Moving back was a small inconvenience and she did not hold it against Isaac. Three children appended to her long skirt. Each drank from a smaller bottle of Coke and held to her clothes with knotted, dirty fists. It was easier for all of them to move rather than to sustain the insistent pressure of Isaac's cases. But they did not move far or willingly. They gave him the foot or two he needed in order to set his cases down on the toes of those near him.

The straps on one of the cases had given way and it had opened slightly. It was the case that contained his art books, some drawings, his visa and teaching papers and the only shirts he owned that would otherwise have been dry.

The straps were wet and swollen and they would not slide within the metal binding, so he left it and straightened.

"Whatever you have in there is going to be wet, I'm afraid."

The girl who stood before him was not. Memori stood smiling at him, her hair done upwards, high on the back of her head. She wore Levi's and a light jacket opening to a simple cotton blouse. She was still as thin as he remembered, but not nearly as tall. What she was, mostly, was dry.

"Well, it's not like there's anything important in there," Isaac said.

He was suddenly and conspicuously wet and conscious of how he must look, hair flattened to his head, shirt, pants drenched, water still running down his face.

"Does it always rain like this?" she asked. "I've never seen it rain so hard. It's a little frightening."

"Only when I'm out with my suitcases," he told her.

"It does look a little suspicious," she said.

"What do you mean?"

"Only last night you promised to fight a bull for us. And here you stand with your luggage as though waiting for the next bus out of town. And in the rain."

"Not a bad idea," Isaac said, "the leaving. It would be indefensible, cowardly and the perfect thing to do. But instead, I'm trying to move households, believe it or not."

Somebody was pushing something into his back. It was a cage of chickens and the man who carried it pushed it out ahead of him. He was in a hurry and drove the cage past them into the crowd. The chickens were quiet, clutching for balance on the heaving floor of the crate, bone thin, features flat and dampened. Their eyes stared out at Isaac in silent panic.

"What brings you out in all this?" he asked. "Is . . . is Heinrich, is he with you?"

"He has a meeting at the house." she said. He had been told that they had been staying at Casa Blanca, the house of a well-known Mexican writer. The gleaming white house stood high above the city on Piedra Chinas, a narrow, rain-rutted alley, a sheer ascent.

"You walked?" he asked.

"It's easy coming down. Walking up is another thing. I thought to have a look at the galleries. Got here just before the rain. Saw your paintings. They're beautiful. I thought —"

She was jostled violently. Her head snapped back. He reached out and caught her by the arm.

"Are you OK?"

"Yes. I think so. It's getting awfully crowded, isn't it."

If anything, the rain was coming down with still more force and the crowd was being compressed by the late-comers, those who continued to seek shelter under the arcades. He was losing his suitcases behind him and had to reach back and slide them along. The air was thick with a damp smell of *cigarillos* and garlic.

"I'd like to get you out of this, but it looks like we're stuck. It's going to get worse before it gets better."

A boy of about nine wormed his way around Isaac's suitcases and slid between Memori and him. He crossed over Isaac's toes.

He was pulling someone along with him by the hand. It was an old man and he stumbled over the cases and fell into Isaac. Isaac was able to steady him, to jam him upright in the crowd. He was blind and his eyes were sewn shut. He had a stubble of a beard and smelled of tequila and urine. The boy urged him along and the crowd surged into the space they vacated.

Inch by inch the crowd closed in against Memori and him and they were pressed to stand close to one another. She was uncomfortable, embarrassed with the proximity and kept her head averted. He could smell the fragrance of her sometimes, mixed as it was with the rain and the smell of things around him.

It was a soft light she stood against and her hair had deepened to blue-black. The pale slope of her forehead curved away into darkness and lost its edge to shadow and the hair that framed it. A straight and foreshortened nose cut an outline against the dark behind it. Where a cheekbone rose nearly to the surface, her skin blushed faintly. He looked over her, beyond the crowd, and out through one of the arches to the wet of the world beyond. One of her legs lay against his own.

"I expected to see you in class," he said.

"I expected to come. He thought it might be better if I didn't."

"Heinrich?"

"He thought it would be better if I took in some lectures in the theatre arts while we're here." He could detect the faint lisp again. When she looked up to him, there was the pale thrust of the neck, but she buried it quickly.

"Do you always do what Heinrich says?"

"Yes. Mostly. Mostly I do that." He bent to hear her. She spoke to him in a whisper. "But not always."

There was something he wanted to remember, but it would not come forward.

Rain was an inch-thick sheet of wavy glass and he could hardly make out the trees in the *jardin*. They had been groomed like umbrellas and, when it wasn't raining, would stand out starkly against the lighted sky. Now they were there only in waves of blue and green, a vertical sea. Wet on wet.

There was a brilliant flash, darkness and the renting sound of a taut, bone-dry canvas, ripping slowly at first and building, tumbling into a swelling of thunder that rolled through the arcade. The crowd tightened in reflex and Memori was pressed against the length of him and tried not to notice.

"You're wet," she said, but he could see the pale in the hollow of her throat and the color that moved across the porcelain face. And all of it triggered him back to the shadows of that other time, to the thing he wanted to remember. It was a song. One of many he hadn't sold. This one he hadn't tried to. It was another life and he had written the song alone in a restaurant with rain washing the windows outside. He had written it for the girl he slept with the night before, and now he could only remember a part of it, a single stanza, and he wasn't sure he had that right. Not at all sure. He had written it for her to sing. It was a love letter and thinking about it revived the promise of those days.

Articulated limbs that face the morning
Through the window lace.

It was a sad and exciting time. There were songs that he had sold and they were playing them back to him on radios wherever he went, for a while playing outward the things he had privately written. There didn't seem to be a stop to it, and each day the songs climbed higher on the charts.

Though the words and melodies escaped him now, they seemed important to him at the time. Now, he could only remember the way things felt. The times were a narcotic and he carried the scar of them. He had lain aside his life and for a while thought he'd done the right thing. There was a certainty of where he was going. How it would be. There'd been lots of phone calls.

Performing in the warming of my mind.

But it ended there, or should have. Though there were many things, good and bad, it never mattered, never grew beyond the promise. Believing she would come to love him, he had married her, and not long after that it ended. It ended with a hollow ache and songs he could no longer remember. Only one song came back to him. Out of all the other, only this.

97

This willowy girl of mine.

And when it was all over, when the phone calls stopped, she left him. But not right away. She stayed to tell him how sorry she was about the marriage. She wanted him to know that it had nothing to do with him. It was the being a singer, she said. And as an artist, he was sure to understand her. She couldn't shake the need to be in front of an audience, to sing, to be loved.

He told her he understood the last part. She knew that, and was sorry. But she was talking about the importance of her career. She was sure he could understand how much she needed to see people, needed to find work.

Both of them knew what she meant. Seeing people was a code for sleeping around. It was part of the business, she said, and told him how sorry she was. She wanted to be honest. She wanted him to know what her career meant to her and how impossible it would be to wait for his songs to get popular again. She was still young and the waiting would make her older. She talked again about her honesty. But it was a strange kind of honesty and it came only after the phone calls stopped.

This willowy girl
Who tastes of fragile wine.

And it was an honesty she didn't act on right away. After the morning she told him she was leaving him for other men, she stayed around to prove it. Or maybe it was he who stayed around long enough to believe it.

Memori had said something about the rain.

"What?"

"It's slowing a little, beginning to clear."

"It's like that," he said. "Sometimes it doesn't last long at all, the rain. The sun will be out in a few minutes, maybe."

"I was beginning to like it here," she said.

Some of those on the fringe of the arcade were moving out, breaking across the plaza at a dead run, jackets, shirts over their heads.

"But theater?" he asked.

"He thought it would be easier, the short time we're here. He

98

thought it would be better than sculpture, then taking a class with you."

"Sure. It's a lot of work, sculpture."

"I don't think that's what he meant," she said.

"What do you think he meant?"

"He didn't like it that I seemed to side with you last night, that I wanted to see the ranch on Sunday when he didn't. This morning we were talking about it. He wanted me to think of a reason for not going. We were talking about what he'd have me say. We were talking about that when Sr. Sanchez called. He's very persuasive. Heinrich tried to beg off, but couldn't. He had to assure the old man we were going, that we wouldn't miss it. It seemed important to him. He's sending a car."

"Good. I want you there when I die."

Her laugh came all at once and pleased Isaac much more than it ought to have. It made him laugh and want to think of other things she'd find funny. She waited for this, watching his face, smiling. But he could think of nothing that would make her laugh again or keep her watching his face. After a while he asked her about her dancing.

"It's ballet. I was still in school when Heinrich came, when we began to date."

"And you quit?"

"It was really time I did. It had always come easily, dancing. I grew up in Wisconsin, a small town girl. Dancing is what separated me from others girls. They all wanted to marry well or be movie stars. For me there was no doubt in anyone I've known since I was ten. I would be a professional dancer. Nobody was pushing me. I don't mean that. It was just that if you had the talent for such a thing, you did it."

"You were good?"

"I auditioned in New York for the School of American Ballet. They thought I was special. What was funny was that I hadn't considered otherwise. It wasn't conceit, though it sounds like it. It was just that I hadn't thought about my not being special. I mean when it came to dancing. The talent was always there."

The crowd had eased, but she made no move to step away.

"So what happened to change your mind?"

"At school I looked around," she said. "Something was missing. I had as much talent as the other girls, maybe more. What I didn't have was the thing that would lead a few of them to excel. I didn't have the drive, the inward thing. I didn't want it enough. One teacher kept after me: 'Where's the grit? she'd say. 'You're waltzing. I want to feel the grit. I want to feel it between my teeth.' It made the teachers very mad. The struggle to the top had broken them in a way. They were teaching, which was what was left if you're too old to dance anymore or had otherwise lost the fight."

"They were hard on you?"

"Yes. But that was all right. I could understand it, how they felt. I'd been given this talent and I didn't care enough about it. I could see why they were mad."

"Then Heinrich came," he said.

"You can imagine. He makes a big stir wherever he goes. He'd come to the school to speak. Half the student body would have followed him anywhere."

"And you did."

She did not look up. He waited for a reaction, for her body to tense against his. Instead she spoke evenly, looking into his wet shirt.

"If this is anywhere, maybe so."

"Maybe this is where you belong." It was a reach, but he tried for it. He waited for her to pull back, to end it there. She chose not to speak to it.

"Last night I was watching you" she said. "And listening, of course. I can't tell you why I did so. I don't like the bullfights. I don't pretend to understand them. But watching you, I could see what would be a difference, I guess. The difference between you and Heinrich. I couldn't get that difference out of my mind. And the other one: the difference between you and me."

"This difference," he said, "the one between you and me. This is bad?"

"Yes," she said, but she did not move away.

100

The rain had stopped and people were walking by the couple who stood together under the arcade. The two Americans could have been lovers, if they weren't so incongruous. If the tall man with the big hands had not been so wet or if the young woman, who could have been a fashion model, had not been so cool and elegant beside him. They stood as close as lovers, and maybe they were.

Standing together, the two Americans made it difficult for people to walk around them. In New York or in any other one of their cities, they would have been jostled. They would have had to find somewhere else to go where they could be alone. Here they were deferred to, not so much because they were Americans, though that mattered, but because they were lovers, or appeared to be. People left them alone and tried not to bump into them.

One of them was surely to take one of the buses out of town, to Mexico City or beyond. It would not be unexpected that they would embrace, there under the arcade, or kiss, before that one would leave the other and board the bus.

Even with the incongruity it could be imagined that they were lovers.

When she did step away, the intimacy was over and there was no further reference to it. The porcelain quality returned to her face and she extended her hand.

"Isaac, I'm glad we met. I'm sorry for all the talk. I think it was seeing your paintings. Or maybe the rain. I'm sure it was something."

"Yes," Isaac told her. "I suppose it was."

She started away, stopped.

"On Sunday. I'll see you on Sunday?" He waited, but she did not say anything else.

"Yes," Isaac said.

He watched her move off through the crowd. She waited at the corner for a bus to pass. It was crowded and painted in an uneven blue and silver, and those by the window looked out without seeing.

Behind it a man pushed a cart through the exhaust smoke, and Memori had to wait for him. Then she moved across the street. Much of the street was running water and she had to dance. She did it very well.

On the other side she did not look back.

Chapter 10

The dress code in San Miguel was not a rigorous one. If you liked, you never needed to get beyond your hand-tooled sandals. Even for the more formal affairs, dinner at a restaurant in one of the better hotels or attendance at a catered affair, you could still show up walking on your Goodyear retreads, though decorum had it that you paid some attention to the state of your toenails. You'd want them clean and, if they'd grown some since the last time you were invited anywhere, you'd want them pared back.

The equivalent of black-tie in town was another thing. You wanted to make sure your khaki trousers and flea market shirt were washed and pressed and, if you were a teacher, you needed a faded corduroy jacket to prove it. Naturally, you wore socks with your sandals.

Isaac had bought a bundle of white socks at the market for just such occasions. Sadly, they had undergone a rather startling transition when the criada had washed them with a yellow, color-fast shirt. Though a lot of sock shows through a leather sandal, the yellow, once the color intensity had been calmed by the dust in the streets, was not altogether unpleasing. If Isaac could get used to it, he figured, others could.

Though it was not clear that Heinrich Guerber's lecture and reception at the Instituto would constitute a black tie affair, with all the hoopla attending it, Isaac felt he would not be out of place wearing socks. Sturge, he noticed as they set off walking the middle of Calle de Quebrada toward the school that early Saturday evening, had paid a similar tribute to formality. He hadn't let up talking since they'd left the house.

"Look. You can put it on Picasso. You can put a lot of it on him. And he bloody well wanted it that way. A clever son of a bitch, you know that?"

"Yeah, but I don't know," Isaac explained. "I mean, I like his work, most of it. He gets a bad rap, but it's not—"

"Of course you like his work!" Sturge had a large voice which he used effectively on his opposition. "Everybody likes his work. That's what I'm talking about. Listen. This guy took it all. Never mind what he stole from Braque. He took drawing, painting — try to get *Weeping Woman* out of your mind — ceramics, performance, assembledge, the works. What's that story? Remember? He's eating fish, a fish dinner. His mansion in the south of France. Some guests. He's quiet, not saying much, pulling away the flesh from the bones of his sea perch, stripping the fish clean.

"His guests notice his concentration. The conversation fades, the room silent. All eyes are on the stubby little Spaniard at the head of the table. When he's finished, he holds the fish carcass up off the plate by the tail. Only the tail and the head are in place. The rest, bones. He's got that ear-to-ear grin and the guests applaud lovingly. They're drinking his wine and they're sitting with God. Wait. I got to go in here."

Sturge dipped his head under the lintel of an open door to a carpentry shop they were passing. He filled the doorway and than moved through it into the gloom of the place, the dust slanting in diagonal stripes. An old man with weepy eyes had been at a sander. He pitched it to one side, clapped Sturge on the shoulder. Shaking hands, they double pumped, once as friends then, regripping, as *compadres*. Another man emerged from the back, crossing a mound of sawdust. His yellowing T-shirt was a color match to the teeth he showed in a wide grin. He was much younger than the other, though his dark hair had been powdered white with saw dust. He found a wood chair, dusting the seat with his hand. Offering it to Sturge, he sought another for Isaac. To both, Sturge shook his head.

Sturge ran a hand over the piece of wood the old man had been sanding. It had been turned nicely. The old man pulled another piece of wood out from a stack. He showed Sturge how they fitted together as a piece. Watching Sturge, he showed him how the two pieces, when slotted, would hold together without nails, that even when you shook them violently, as he demonstrated, first to Sturge, then to Isaac, they held firmly. Grinning, he looked at them both through teary eyes, then at his work.

The old man smoothed the joint with a gnarled hand. All of them watched him caress the wood in the way he might the knee of a young girl. Two of his fingers were missing. When Sturge pulled himself back to the door where Isaac stood, the two men shook his hand again. Then they shook Isaac's. Each time they shook hands they did it the two ways. Now all four of them were *compadres*.

Though the sander and the lathe had been running when Sturge entered, and Isaac may have missed something that was said between the men, he believed nothing was. Heading back along the street, Sturge picked up his story.

"Anyway, there he is, holding up the skeletal remains of his fish. Pablo asks his guests: 'So, tell me, what is this? Is this art or is this garbage?' There was some discussion. What would Pablo like to hear? Most had it as art. Pablo had done it after all. One or two said it couldn't be art as anyone with a little patience could do it and the head and tail wouldn't keep. The little Malagan, black eyed and with that shit-eating grin, called into the kitchen. He wanted someone to bring out the garbage can. Everybody waited. When it came, it was pretty full and it took the cook and a flunky to deliver it. They set it next to Pablo. Still holding the fish carcass by the tail, Picasso turns and drops it into the can. He orders the cook, the flunky and the garbage out of the room. Everyone waits for him to say something.

"Instead he takes a sip of wine and returns to eating the rest of his meal. It would have ended there had not one of the guests who had argued for it being garbage spoke up. 'See?' he said. 'Pablo thinks it's garbage.'

"Pablo fixes him with those eyes. "You are blind," he says. 'It is art, of course.'

"The guest is taken aback, tries to recover. 'But Pablo,' he says, 'Why the garbage? Why put it in the garbage?' And Pablo replies, 'What makes you think that was garbage?'"

During the course of the story a little boy ran out to Sturge as they passed.. He had been sitting on a doorsill with another boy, somewhat older. They had been trying to make a plastic top spin in the dust. He took Sturge's hand and the three of them walked the street. He waited for the big man who was his friend to finish the story, then tried to ask four or five questions at once. Sturge spent some time sorting them out, taking each of them and responding to them in a way that made it seem the world depended on the boy knowing where they were going, why, how long they'd likely stay and whether he would like to see almost all of a dead snake that might once have been a rattler.

At the corner, Sturge found the popsicle vendor. With Sturge and Isaac there, the vendor allowed the boy to dig for his own in the cool smoke of the ice well. He spent some time searching for and finally locating one of the last purple ones for himself. There were many orange ones left and one of those would be all right for his brother.

As the boy started to run back with his two popsicles, Sturge stopped him.

"Look at this," he said to Isaac. "Goddamned, would you look that this?" Indicating to Isaac that he should stay where he was, he turned the boy and his two popsicles to a three-quarter view. Behind him the last of the evening sun swept the alley like a brush fire. The boy stood in blue and purple shadows, some of them the hue and value of one of the popsicles, some the complement of the other. Like Daumier's silhouette of the washer woman climbing the sunlit stairs, the figure was charged with vibrating lights.

The phenomenon would be over in seconds, Isaac knew, long before Isaac could get home and bring back his camera. Even if he made it at a dead run, the light would change before he got back. Though he was tempted to try, he knew he'd come back to a sappy little boy on a cobblestone street holding two popsicles, both running down his arms and dripping on his shoes.

Isaac swore, as he'd done thousands of times before, to carry his camera wherever he went.

"What I'm saying about this Heinrich Guerber and this ass Warhol and the rest of the SoHo pack," Sturge told him, "is that Picasso, Duchamp and dozens of others got there first, said it, and, with the exception of Duchamp who got fixated on urinals, left it. How many times can you say that life is an arm pit and art is dead?"

"Not many," Isaac said. "But that isn't what worries me. I'm worried about — I don't know. I guess it's the clout these guys are amassing. Shock and squeal seem to go down pretty good among those who can't find beauty."

"Isaac, look at it this way: Guerber and his goosey set are in business. They're a concession. They got a territory, the cultural capital of our country and several others, those who still look to New York for answers. They've cornered the market on bullshit. A handful of guys, post-grads from Yale with some money men behind them. Modernism had been neatly expropriated and put on the American map. But face it, it was running short of steam. That's when these guys took over. They already had the press, academia and I.M. Pei. It didn't take much to convince city powers that every town with a population over six needs a contemporary art museum. They had Pei to build 'em and Rauschenberg and Pollock to fill 'em."

"But what are you supposed to do? How can you ignore this stuff?" Isaac asked. "Look at what this Guerber is doing, for Christ sake."

"He's got some press. Next year you won't remember him." Sturge said.

"Yeah. But they'll have someone else, another clown."

"It's got to be got through, Isaac. Doing this stuff takes as much talent as getting the clap, so everybody's in line for instant success. It suits us, for the moment anyway. America maintains a great passion for what's chic and quick. Like the Hula Hoop. You don't need a lot of emotional or intellectual investment. And the times are ripe for anything that can be done in ten minutes. Who needs Vermeer?"

Isaac asked: "What makes it so? What is it about these times?"

"Beats me. It's a product of the war, maybe, or capitalism run amok, or a grab for power. Maybe Tocqueville had it right. Saw it coming. Who the hell knows? Maybe it's the moonwalk, Nixon or Rosemary Woods. But forget 'em. These creeps aren't doing anything your grandchildren will remember. They're not doing anything at all."

"Tell that to anyone who values Cezanne. And when Guerber's through with Cezanne, where does he go?"

"If it's alphabetical, to Degas," Sturge said. "Isaac, you worry too much. All of this stuff is a dead end. You got to wait them out. It's politics, sociology, it's every cliché in the books, but it ain't art. Who was that?"

"Who was what?" Isaac asked.

"Joyce Carey. *The Horse's Mouth.* Remember? 'Like farting Anny Laurie through a keyhole. It's clever, but is it art?'"

"He didn't say that. He said, 'It may be clever, but is it worth the trouble?'"

"Same thing. If the guy could write," Sturge said, "he'd have put it my way."

Isaac could not explain it. He was not sure if he understood himself why he considered the post-modernists and the nose-picking art they proclaimed as dangerous. Maybe it was because they weren't so much reflecting the world as leading it. If Sturge were right, they'd hang themselves on their own overblown rhetoric. Everyone was entitled to make a fool out of himself. The question was how long they'd be permitted to make a fool out of everybody else.

It wasn't even art that worried him. Sturge was right, or would come to be right, on that score. Whatever they had begun with the Dadaists, art would survive it, as it had always survived, beginning with the painting of the bison on the cave wall in Altamira. No. It wasn't art he was talking about.

It had the makings of a new kind of war, this thing they were doing in the name of art, and he couldn't get a handle on it. The old war the Modernists had mounted was within the rules of engagement. It was still spectator art. The abstractionists were not out to destroy the existing order, but to take a place within it, even if they wanted to sit at the head of the table. However they may have flailed, they weren't seeking to erase reality, but to enhance it. They were only extending what the Impressionists began when they stormed the bastions of French salon a hundred years back.

The Impressionists sought inclusion and the abstractionists — those anyway who did not make wallpaper, who did not get caught up in little exercises in defining art for other artists — were not much different. The important ones sought to define reality in different terms. They had not lost the sense of beauty, harmony, design, the weight of history. They were still painting, feeling their way into and out of their canvases. And those who sculpted, saw their forms in this new way. You could see by the work, when it was good, that their new vision was as old as nature and did not forsake it.

What had begun with Warhol ten years back was something quite different. He was a shoe salesman, wanted everybody to be a machine. The wanting part was what was different. He wasn't out to define the human condition, he wanted to change it into something else. He wasn't an artist. He was a practicing pathologist. He wanted to turn the word in on itself. When he and his bunch won over the show-biz set, they could make a pretty good run at it.

But art, Isaac knew, would survive him. It would do so by speaking the truth — as ugly as that truth might be — and finding beauty, as ugly as it might appear. But Isaac could not figure the rest of it.

If art would survive the attacks against it, as surely it would, what was the problem? Why couldn't he pass off the movement that Heinrich and his SoHo colleagues had mounted as easily as Sturge. Heinrich would bring his New Art school, its banality and its considerable resources to the Instituto. Isaac would be an indirect beneficiary. What the hell did he care? He'd rather students understand that art was quite apart from this stuff, but he wasn't a dedicated teacher. In truth, he wasn't a teacher anymore than he'd been a journalist. He didn't believe art could be taught, not in any full sense. He was a factory worker while he got on with his painting. He had been a songwriter for much the same reason.

If he was an artist, as he expected he was, he had nothing to fear from Heinrich. He did not know why he felt otherwise.

Entering the school grounds was not the reason Isaac put on the corduroy jacket he'd carried on his shoulder until then. It wasn't entirely that he needed to be in uniform. With the sun low and falling it was considerably cooler.

For the last couple of blocks Isaac and Sturge had joined a crowd heading for the same place. He had begun to feel underdressed. Some of the arrivals, Isaac noted, had violated the obligatory sandal rule. While no one he could see was wearing a tie — it hadn't come to that yet — some wore, and there was no mistaking it, shoes. He consoled himself into believing that those who did were only New Yorkers. New York was a geographical affliction even the long-term expats couldn't shake.

"Why did you leave the States?" Isaac asked.

"The service," Sturge replied.

"The armed service? The draft?"

"No. I mean the service. Waitresses, waiters. You can't get served in the place."

Isaac laughed.

"No, I'm serious. It's what's wrong with the place. Nobody wants to work for anything except money."

"Is there a better reason?"

"A lot better reason. Money ought to be the least of it. Ever notice how everyone's kind of waiting around in America? Work's a pay check. It'll get them through another week while they're waiting to get famous or marry well. Go anywhere. You can tell a lot by the hired help. The waitress is not really a waitress and she wants you to know that. The waiting on you is a kind of charity she

110

bestows on you. She'll make sure you know that as well. She's going to be a screen star some day, or marry somebody rich, and this business of serving the likes of you and taking your money is an awkward time of her life, and has nothing to do with who she really is.

"It needs to be got through," Sturge continued. "She'll deal out your hamburger, all right, but don't expect courtesy or anything bordering on efficiency. She doesn't give a shit, and you'll be sure to know it. Only in America is waiting on others a source of embarrassment. But don't get me started on the States. It's sick and will be a long time getting better."

"All right," Isaac said.

"What do you mean, 'all right'?"

"I won't get you going."

"Of course you'll get me going. You already have. Look: the country's gone blind to all this stuff. We don't see the claptrap anymore. We quit looking at the mess we made out of the people, the places we live and work, the slab and glass cities we built — and continue to build — on the cheap. We owe our architecture to the Germans and they've got us living like Bulgarian Communists in our bleak little developments, in our two-car garage with its attached living space. I'm talking consequences, Isaac. Who can live like that?

"Little suburbia with its clot of shacks: Forest Shadows, Timberwood Mill, Oak Creek, whatever. All named for what we tore done, carved up or paved over. The woods have been reduced to a single, lifeless twig. It's impaled mid-lawn and tethered for a hurricane. The rest is asphalt. Ask the dog. He's been reduced to shitting in the driveway.

"Isaac, you can't live like that without consequences. We've grown numb to life in the free world's longest commute. What you get in the end are waitresses who can't pour coffee, and you get a six-hour film of the Empire State Building."

It was clear they were early and the lecture and reception wouldn't start for awhile. The had left on Isaac's timetable and would have to wait while everybody caught up. The theater had not

111

yet opened and those who gathered mingled in front of the gallery. Though the double doors to it stood open, no one would have ventured inside. The day's heat was still held within it. The building was construction-block modern and didn't have the engineering advantages of Spanish colonial architecture.

But he was wrong. Chairman Duckworth emerged from the gallery and, seeing them, headed over. He crossed the courtyard on short, thick legs. Only then did Isaac remember about the student show. Duckworth wanted to show off to Heinrich his progressive students and how he, for one, was already shaping them in the name of New Art. Four of them were participating in an installation — a series of embalmed and very dead crows impaled on wooden dowels set in concrete blocks.

Since it had sculptural overtones, Isaac was asked to allow some of his "more progressive" students to participate. When he denied having any, he himself was asked to help "hang" the show.

In attire, as in life, Duckworth, Isaac noted, sought consensus. He wore a string tie and a Navajo clip, thereby affirming his place along side both the cowboy and his nemesis. His corduroy jacket was as threadbare as Isaac's own. He also opted for socks, clearly visible within his sandals.

"Could have used you, Isaac. Really could have used you this afternoon."

"Sorry. I just, well. . .I just forgot." This was not a lie, though Isaac doubted he'd have come if he remembered.

"That happens," Duckworth said. "Let's not worry about it. But please remember, these are important times for the school, for all of us." He gave a sidelong glance toward Sturge. "We've all got to chip in. Do what's right. Glad I caught you. I wanted to get a read-by on this." He pulled a paper folded lengthwise from his jacket pocket and opened it. It was the introduction Isaac had written for him. As he sought the best light, the paper rattled a little more than it needed to. Isaac had attributed Duckworth's heavy perspiration to exertions in a hot gallery. He wondered now how much of it was from nervousness.

There were some editing changes, text shifted, some words

scratched out, replaced, scratched out again. "Let me go through it while we're here and —"

"You remember Sturge," Issac said. "Sturgeon Boswell."

Sturge held out a hand and Duckworth shook it without much conviction. He made some appropriate sounds, but they took a decided second to the paper he was holding.

"Sturge!" It was Spencer. Somehow he'd appeared over the shoulder of Duckworth. He had ironed his Hawaiian shirt and closed it at the throat with a cloth tie. Although his jacket was corduroy, Isaac could see, as Spencer circled around to squeeze Sturge's hand, that he had forsaken sandals for heavy black brogans. Though the workboots had undergone some polish, there may have been a little too much of them showing. His slacks had been cut high enough to keep them out of water. "My God, old man. Thought you'd succumbed to jungle rot. Good to have you back. When did you make it out?"

"Some time back," Sturge replied. "Haven't had a chance to get over here. Wasn't at all sure you'd let me in. Heard about the resurrection of fine art. Thought I'd bear witness."

"Well you might. Seminal. A seminal event. We're making history here. Damned if The New Yorker isn't threatening a feature. Just got off the phone." He turned to Isaac. "This man here, Isaac, has had a place in our history. An important place. Shaped the curriculum. Made do when we had very little. Tough times. One of the best instructors money can buy. Goes and runs off into the jungles."

"Not entirely my idea, as you'll recall," Sturge told him.

"Well, it's all the same, isn't it? Life ends where it began. Am I wrong?" He saw some people and made as though he wanted to move towards them. "Listen, Sturge, come by. We need to get caught up." To Duckworth, leaning towards him and lowering his voice, he said, "If you got the keys, open the theater. If you don't, go get the Goddamned things. Nobody wants to look at dead birds."

Duckworth excused himself, started away. Spencer caught his arm. "Lester, almost forgot. I'll introduce the guest. Got some things I want to say." To Sturge and Isaac, still holding the chairman's arm, "Lester here is my number one man. Couldn't do without him. A peach. An administrative peach. Can money buy a man like this?"

Heinrich's arrival that night was a dramatic one. Isaac guessed he had some practice in making entrances. Whether he had waited out the peak moment or had been genuinely late came to the same thing. By the time he entered the theater, those already there had ample opportunity to find their seats, fuss and fumble with their jackets and sweaters and determine how the crease in their trousers was holding up. They had time to tire of searching for conversational gambits with those near them, those who were not inventive enough to ask questions of their own. They had time to check their watches more than once and to consider whether the central figure in the program would indeed show up. The mimeoed program was not nearly long enough. They had time to memorize it.

He brought Memori down the aisle as though to give her away to marriage. All that was lacking was the processional, maybe French horns.

The bride, had she been one, was dressed in black, a silk dress cut high on the neck. The fabric, which gathered and fell from a wide black belt, drifted against and traced the contours of her long legs as she moved. She wore a single strand of pearls which, against the black dress, appeared only a shade less luminescent than the long and canted neck that rose out of it. The neck carried a fine head. Her hair, done high on it, was loose enough to allow long strands of it to fall and break at the shoulders.

It was an image that had taken, Isaac guessed, a good part of the afternoon to create. She carried it easily as though she were in bathrobe heading for the shower.

Heinrich, by contrast, was in virginal white. He wore a three piece suit, all white, as were his shoes and matching tie. Only the handkerchief at his lapel and his shirt, both of blue denim, took the edge off formality.

They came late, but they came smiling. By the time the cou-

114

ple had moved half the way to the stage they were walking to the beat of Heinrich's leather heels on the wooden floor. Beyond them no one moved. No one coughed. No one whispered.

San Miguel was a long way from anywhere where people would likely dress like this. The deprivation contributed to the impact. It took a moment to swallow the visual effect and to determine whether something should be done about it. It took considering whether one should remain seated or rise to applaud. It would have been a foolish, small-town thing to do. It would have been absolutely wrong, impossibly gauche, yet even those who wore shoes that night were tempted, just for a moment, to do so. Thinking, then quickly discarding the thought, may have accounted for the absolute silence that prevailed for the few seconds it took the honored couple to arrive at the front row and find their folding chairs. Only then did those there find something more to discuss with their neighbors.

Spencer was the act that had to follow this. He wasn't up to it. In introducing Heinrich he tried but failed to overcome the disadvantage dealt him. Recognizing where the attention lay and that the audience cared as little for what he'd come to say as they had for Duckworth's impaled birds, he cut the first forteen minutes off his sixteen minute speech and cursed his decision to supplant the chairman.

Nevertheless, Heinrich was gracious in the tributes he paid to his host and in the introduction extended him. He was all talc and white suit and he disdained the podium and spoke in front of it.

It was not his only concession to democracy. He was folksy, warm and exhibited early on an ability to win over his audience with local understanding and just the right dash of deprecating humor. In two or three minutes he was able to confirm what his audience knew all along, that it was wise and cultured and had no equal. They were pleased that he so readily acknowledged it.

When he came to tell them how he, his foundation and his school were bent to the task of altering the fabric of American life, of erasing the boundaries between art and non-art, of merging the painting with sociology, of celebrating the fall of craftsmanship and the rise of technology, they were ready for it.

The audience was not to be taken as a neophyte in any of this. The speaker had been right about their cultural understanding and wisdom. And they wanted him to understand that.

They applauded as one the part where he told them that art could no longer afford being burdened by its history. He said this with a good deal of conviction, and the pause after he said it was clearly an opening for the audience to fill, which they did with enthusiasm.

So, when the slide show began with some of what was going on in the better venues of SoHo, the audience was primed, pumped and overflowing. Mexico had come to Manhattan.

It could be said that the crowd did not flinch from the pornographic images, though there seemed to be overly much of his slide collection devoted to them. They knew that art and pornography were one and had steeled themselves to seeing such things in public. Even the whips and chains and other variants did not deter them from this sophistication.

They had an image of themselves and they wanted the German who everyone was talking about to understand that he was not addressing some born-again Baptist convention in Des Moines. They were left-leaning political progressives. The speaker and those around them were to be made to see that there was not a provincial bone in their bodies.

This wasn't easy. As listeners there was a limit to what they could express. They made the best of it by strongly nodding their agreement to certain statements; this, for the benefit of those behind them. When possible they used chuckles and nudges and facial expressions and sidelong glances. Occasionally explosive applause conveyed their liberation from social convention. All of it made clear to the speaker and their neighbors that culture and high art were not beyond them. Some, more practiced in showmanship, relied on it to overcome the strict limits of expression of one seated in a chair and compelled to keep quiet. These, the more animated, were the younger members of the crowd. It was

116

not without effort, but they too were able to convey by sign and action something about themselves. Watching them was to gain the unmistakable impression that they had been more politically active than they probably were. They were still playing out the remains of the Sixties and there were certain imperatives in their behavior.

You could tell their orientation by how they dressed and reacted to the speaker. It was not difficult to imagine that they had marched and picketed and done some horse and laid most everything in sight. They knew where things came down and where this speaker was coming from.

These were the ones who were still waiting for the revolution, though it seemed increasingly unlikely that it would occur in quite the way they had in mind. Their inability to ignite a war in their own country made accepting one in Southeast Asia all the more difficult. In that revolution they had lost friends to Canada and Sweden and knew of some American working people who had died in it. They themselves had suffered prolonged stays in universities within graduate programs that didn't interest them much. Others had been burdened with unwanted marriages and children. Its only blessing was that it could be used as fodder in the domestic war they felt obliged to stir. Whether or not the revolution was stillborn, they were to be perceived as being on the right and proper side of it.

They knew about corporate greed and the military - industrial complex and civil rights and free speech and about nuclear annihilation. They knew there was an underclass and that some people in cities slept in boxes and bought food by selling their bodies or robbing banks. Knowing these things they had come to Mexico. They were determined people and intended to stay until their parents money ran out.

When these more radical ideas and the less extreme ones held by the rest of the audience were illustrated in Heinrich's slides, when they were shown installation and performance pieces that appeared to be supportive of their political position, they stood and applauded roundly. It's what would be expected of the culturally advantaged.

117

In truth they found some of the references oblique — pictures of a man confined to a locker for four hours, another being shot in the arm by a friend with a rifle standing a few feet away, still another urinating into the camera — but they did not let on.

When it came to the series of slides that depicted Heinrich in his smock and tie laying great, thick globs of paint over a framed, three-by-four foot landscape, circa 1885, of John Twachtman, they were even ready for this. Sure, they were cultured and wise and heretofore had quietly liked this American Impressionist and certainly saw nothing wrong with the painting that was being decimated. But it was, when you thought about it, about the style and subject matter, a pretty picture, terribly bourgeois. The coloration, the close values and the all too pleasing attention to structure. When you thought about it, it violated all the rules they'd come so recently to accept. Where was the two dimensionality, after all, the integrity of the picture plane. That was the word, wasn't it? Integrity. Where was that? The whole idea of painting, they knew, was suspect. Wasn't this what the German meant? When you think about it, it was perfect! How better to say it! Painting over history. It was beautiful. Getting it was an epiphany. They wondered if everyone else in the audience got it. Looking around, it was hard to say.

Then there were the pictures of his studio. The scene! Clearly it was a cavernous place, a warehouse that had been fixed up. There was a hardwood floor. You could see it beneath all the splattered paint. And look at that easel! What they wouldn't give for that. You can see him bending down, dipping his thick brush into a can of. . . what? You can't see it really. Wait. Sure! It's house paint! Of course. It would have to be house paint. Beautiful.

Then the best part. Laying that heavy paint across the landscape in thick stripes, the paint dripping on the gold frame. Gold frame! Can you believe it? He had a steady hand. Give him that. And the stripes were even. Maybe he'd ruled them and hadn't showed a slide of that. He ought to have, really. It would have made it better. Integrity, right? But it was still beautiful, the reference to Mondrian. When you think about it, about the message. How better could you make it?

The audience knew well and deeply respected Heinrich's celebrity. They had come on an otherwise good drinking night because of it. They knew he was among a handful of artists who could speak to the world and they listened attentively. They also knew that he was rich. Though the audience was left-leaning and therefore didn't like money, it maintained a great deal of respect for those who made a lot of it. For a good many, the older folks, mostly, this not liking money was a quandary. They had some. They wondered if this was all right. It was not like they had a lot. Certainly they didn't have as much as the speaker.

They had been visiting friends in town and had devoted a large part of their visit convincing them in subtle and not so subtle ways that they lived well where they came from and they did so because they had money.

They knew, these older folks from out of town, that they ought to like what this artist was doing on behalf of his art — if that was what it was on behalf of — but that they were not supposed to like it just because he had money. And that was all right with them. They were willing to do that. What worried them was whether their friends would regard them similarly, would judge them on some basis other than money. It wouldn't be fair, not after they'd spent so much of their lives in pursuit of it. It wouldn't be fair to change the rules mid-stream. Was this what this German dandy was driving at?

Who the hell knew. And that's exactly why they hadn't wanted to come. Who needed all this stuff? They were on vacation, visiting friends. They could have had a few drinks. Or had dinner early. But, no. They'd been invited, and as guests couldn't really refuse. How are you going to tell somebody you don't give a shit about an art lecture?

The close of the lecture released a flood of invective that Sturge had dammed up during it. And he wasn't afraid of being overheard as they followed the crowd out past the sculpture studio to the courtyard in front of the gallery where a table holding some magnums of champagne had been set up.

"The bloody American!" Sturge said to Isaac and the half dozen people within earshot.

"But he's German," Isaac corrected.

"They're the worst kind."

Isaac was hoping to leave. Sturge was just warming up, seeing Heinrich's political performance as a vindication of what he'd been saying on the way in. Isaac was only half listening as he declined, than accepted, a glass of champagne from one of the trays making the rounds. He was dividing his attention between what Sturge was saying, and looking for, while very badly not wanting to find, Memori.

His depression had begun at low tide and was steadily sinking. It came less from the lecture than from what proceeded it: the image of Memori and her handsome friend as they walked down the aisle to their seats. He remembered her spectacular smile. She had held it so effortlessly as she advanced past Isaac who, like everyone else, had turned to watch the procession. She did not alter it when she saw him in the aisle seat. She smiled and her eyes swept past him and beyond. He had truly hoped he'd been snubbed, but doubted it.

She had looked right through him for the worst of reasons: she didn't see him.

As Sturge re-established his argument against what he saw as a lunatic fringe, Isaac took stock of his own depleted inventory. He was not wearing a three-piece, white linen suit. His hair, while plentiful, could not be groomed in a swept back manner. Groomed was not a word you'd use when it came to describing the state of Isaac's hair. Having a will of its own, it could not in fact be properly combed. In a bathroom mirror and within moments after he'd get the coiled part in the front to lie still, it would spring to life, often with comic effect.

His art had never appeared in any publication larger than a small town newspaper and that had less to do with the news worthiness of his painting than to an editor's need to fill space on a slow day in the women's section. It also helped that Isaac worked there.

Recently, he earned slightly more than he spent. But this fell a good deal short of funding a foundation, a school of New Art, or a black silk dress for his girlfriend, had he had one.

On the rare occasions when he was compelled to speak publicly, he did not rivet his audience's attention. He did not even nail it loosely. He had, he knew, the distracting quality of wanting to say something very badly, getting a good start in heading for it, then forgetting why he'd come.

Sturge had stopped talking and was looking at him.

"What?"

"You've been fading on me, Isaac. I've been wasting my considerable intellectual prowess. Also you look like hell."

"Sorry. I was just getting ready to head back, I think."

"Ah, I'd forgotten. The disappointed contender." He had told Sturge about meeting Memori at the party and the bullfight promise and his later encounter with her under the arcades. He now saw it as a mistake. He had painted a much too optimistic picture, even though it was based on how he felt at the time. He could see now how foolish he looked.

"No," Isaac said, "It's not that. It's, I don't know, the whole thing, I guess."

"And this girl being a vital part of the whole thing, right? Isaac, you look ready to cut off an ear. Cheer up. She may come to her senses, cast away her wealth and her budding Mark Twain for an apron and life in small town Mexico tending to a depleted sculptor."

"Thanks."

"Want me to tell you about women?"

"Think I could stop you?"

"'You never know,' is what we, who know women, say about them," Sturge said.

"That's certainly a hefty piece of philosophy."

"You'll see. I won't disappoint you. Hefty it may not be. But truthful it is. Not only is it truthful, it's as exhaustive as one can go in the study. Women make absolutely no sense, which is why it is not impossible that Miss America, that spectacular woman over there, may be completely out of her mind, an impairment that might lead her to you and away from wealth, fame and beautiful dresses."

Isaac followed his gaze to Memori. She and Heinrich were contained in a group on the stone terrace. The two were talking to one another animatedly, seemingly to the exclusion of those around them.

Hoffstedder came up, bowed to Sturge, then Isaac.

"I see you found him, Isaac. The S. Boswell mystery is solved. No?"

The life drawing instructor was in his tie, which would be expected, and a blue blazer and shoes, which were not. Heinrich, Isaac thought, was bringing out the worst in everybody. The shifting sands of fashion were about to bury the corduroy, sock and sandal rule.

"Give me the Austrian view, Hoffstedder," Sturge said. "How does European civilization view tonight's talk?"

"We don't think so much that civilization is in danger. About SoHo we don't think much at all. When we look at history, which we do more than occasionally, we don't believe it began the day before yesterday."

"Thank God," Sturge laughed. "One among us. You see, Isaac? All is not lost. Isaac believes it's all over but the body count. He's taken to suicidal measures to see to it that he's not around when art dies and we all become lunatics. He's entering a bullfight tomorrow."

"You would do such a thing?" Hoffstedder asked.

"Not normally. I can't even remember why I agreed to it," Isaac told him.

"That's part of the suicidal behavior," Sturge said. "Isaac is bent on drinking himself into oblivion."

"Before you go and destroy yourself," Hoffstedder said to Isaac, "make sure you pick up your money. They bought a nice painting."

122

"What painting?"

"You didn't know? I brought some new work to the gallery this morning. Big argument they were having over *Girls at the Park*. Between themselves."

"Who are you talking about?"

"The German and his girlfriend. They were in the middle of the argument when I came in. The girlfriend loved, the German hated. He was very mad about her liking such a thing as this painting of yours. For a while they didn't notice I'd come in. In the end he marches out, almost running into me."

"The girl," Isaac said, "What did she do?"

"She stayed. Bought the painting."

When Isaac searched the two out again in the crowd, he couldn't find them. They'd left the terrace and the group they had been with. He could see them nowhere else. He doubted they would have gone into the gallery.

Hoffstedder's news and the couple's apparent absence revived Isaac. As he joined his two friends in condemning the sad state of cultural affairs, he did so while keeping an eye on the entrance. When it became clear that they had not exited the gallery because they had not entered it, Isaac took heart in the growing prospect that they had left the reception well before the guests of honor were expected to leave such a thing, and that they had done so because of a continuing argument between them that involved, in no small measure, Isaac. In truth, the prospect wasn't all that strong, and a part of Isaac knew that. It knew that there were eighteen million more likely reasons for them departing a dreary reception early, but Isaac was in no mood to count the ways. Preferring hope to reason, Isaac's conversation took wings, never had he been so buoyant.

Chapter 11

Sturge and he left late the next morning and took the road that climbed to the ridge out of town. Above the water works it hooked sharply to the left and traversed the hill, past the new hotel built by the Cantinflas organization and out beyond some tree-hidden homes that were set back off gated driveways. The road hooked and climbed again, the town below them; La Parroquia, a bleached and miniature castle commanding a tiny hillside domain.

It was a cobblestone climb, mostly, and Sturge's Deucheveaux roared and hopped like a power lawnmower. The floorboard between Issac's boots — he had forsaken sandals for the occasion — had rusted away and alternately there were a rush of blurred roadway and billows of dust. They could not have talked if they wanted to.

Where the road wove through a series of tight turns near the ridge, Sturge pulled out a leather-covered flask from the pouch on his door. He pulled from it, downshifting with his free hand, and passed it to Isaac. He yelled something to him.

"What?"

"El Presidente, *torero*. The milk of bulls."

It was smooth, warming, and cleared the dust from his throat. The last fifty yards of the climb to the ridge and to where the road was paved was the worst. The rains had done the most damage there and it was a long climb for the trucks that brought the sand

and cobbles for repair. It was easier just to leave the road to the elements and let the cars fight the ruts.

Sturge took it flat out in second gear, the doors flapping, the tin shell that contained them heaving and pitching as though on bed springs. Isaac had to keep one hand on the roof.

Sturge was the proud owner of what may have been the only Deucheveaux extant in Mexico. The rusted body was held in place by ropes and struts and electrical cords that crisscrossed the interior. Riding in it was like taxiing across a plowed field in a Piper Cub. When they made the ridge and the paved road that led along the plateau, the engine noise eased to the angry whine of a buzz saw, and they could talk above it.

"It's best not to think about it," Sturge said.

"I suppose."

"These things are done all the time and they're nothing. They use cows that are very small and it's all a game.

"Except they're going to use bulls," Isaac told him.

"It's only a matther of anatomy."

"Sure," Isaac said.

The road headed straight out into the sun and to either side was farmland, rich, black, and apart from some distant farmhouses and the occasional cluster of corrugated shacks, there was nothing to indicate anyone lived in the area. Cattle grazed in the new grass that sprang from the ditch at the side of the road that had been wetted by recent rains. Occasionally an animal would cross in front of them and they would slow, sometimes to a stop. Sometimes a steer, separated from the herd, would stand on the narrow road and watch the Deucheveaux approach, curious. If there were enough room, Sturge would sweep behind it, not slowing.

"It will be easier when I have a cape," Isaac cautioned. They had just cut within inches of the flank of a Hereford struck numb with panic, eyes rolling crazily in the white of his face. They had made it with two wheels just off the road, clinging to the lip of the ditch. The Mexican roadbuilder was not a strong proponent for shoulders. It was enough that the road was paved and went the distance, more or less.

"They never move backwards," Sturge said through the tangle of his beard. "When they panic they'll jump forward. Except at night. In the headlights they'll do anything."

"Never?"

"Well, seldom."

"If we hit one," Isaac said, "we'll be a giant cloud of rust."

Sturge pulled again from his flask of El Presidente. When a clanking sound started up in the engine compartment, Isaac thought they'd thrown a rod and waited for Sturge to pull over. Instead, he didn't appear to notice. After a while it faded, then went away.

"That's something I've never tried, you know?" Sturge said. "I've liked the color, the music, the wine and the way the women dress, but I've never considered it really. Never thought about how it would be to fight one of the damn things. When you think about it, it's kind of romantic, man and beast and all that. You know anything about it? Or were you putting everyone on?

"I've seen a lot of them and I'm big on theory. That's what got me into this fine mess in the first place."

"Better have some more of this. You can always plead alcoholism. Tell me about the theory."

"It's really quite simple," Isaac said. "Forget the red of the cape. Movement is the thing. The bull goes for that. If you stand still and move the cloth, the bull takes the cape and not the guy who's holding it. The hard part is not in the theory, but in the feet."

"The feet?" Sturge asked.

"Making them so they won't run. When the bull charges, it's hard to make them stand still. It goes against self-preservation. You only know whether it's possible, whether you can do it, they tell me, when you're there, when the bull is coming at you. A guy doesn't know anything about what he'll do until the time comes. That's what provides the high comedy."

"As in tragedy?"

"No. Not in these things, usually. As you say, the bulls are small and relatively harmless, something I'm banking on anyway.

126

It's more funny than anything else. At least for those watching. It's when the bull gets big that it isn't funny. You've been to the fights. Ever see an *espontaneo*?

"No."

"I was in the Army in Fort Huachuca for a while. Dismal. Flat in the middle of the desert. It's where they sent you before they got Vietnam going nicely. Out of boot camp the First Sargeant asks me what I did. I told him I was a journalist. He asked me if that meant I knew how to type. When I said yes, he put down 'typist' and sent me to the desert. Something about radio communications. Damn little chance of any interference. You could be AWOL for three days and the First Sargeant could still see you out the Orderly Room window. I spent as much time as I could in Nogales. It was off the bullfight circuit by a long shot. Mostly tourist stuff. But once in a while you saw a good fight.

"I had a *barrera* seat one Sunday," Isaac continued. "and this young Mexican I'm sitting next to is squirming in his seat through the first three bulls. He can't sit still. He's got his shirt off and he's twisting it in his hands, playing with it, and all the while he's moving like he's sitting on an ant hill. I'm thinking he's got palsy.

"The fourth bull comes out, circles, and is engaged across the ring, first by the *banderillos*, then by the matador. I don't remember who he was, but he headlined the cartel and had drawn a pretty fair animal. That's when this guy next to me makes the move.

"He steps up over the rail and jumps. Now, it's a pretty fair jump. You've got to go over the alley that circles the ring, the *callejon*. I've heard of guys breaking their legs. But this guy does better than that. He hits hard and sprawls headlong on the sand. Then he's up trying to unravel his shirt. That's when you could see he'd been planning this for a long time. It wasn't a shirt at all, but he had rigged a muleta on a piece of dowel.

"With the bull engaged across the plaza it was the worst time to make his move. The bull saw him immediately and had the distance to gather all his speed. That's when the feet began.

"It wasn't that the guy was running. He wasn't doing that. His legs were straight, tense, but they were vibrating like pistons on a short stroke and he couldn't stand ground. Without running, his feet were carrying him all over the place. As the bull closed, the *espontaneo* shook the *muleta*, but it didn't matter.

"The bull carried him the five yards or so to the *barrera* and slammed him into the planks. It was right below me and his head went back and I could hear the neck snap. It was the worst time, with a bull unsubdued, wild, at full speed, and he was dead on impact. The bull worried him for a while, getting his horns under him, throwing him like a rag doll. He was thrown a couple of times like that before the *banderillos* could bring the bull off. But everyone knew it didn't matter. Everyone who saw him hit the *barrera* knew it was over."

"Was it?" Sturge asked.

"It was as over as it gets. He was on his back, his belly open. His head on that broken neck was turned so he was almost face down in the sand. They were pulling him back by his hands, dragging him to cover before the bull would come again. Pulling him back like that had lifted the upper part of his body off the ground, but his head would not come with it. It lolled backwards and dragged in the sand. That's when I noticed his feet."

"What do you mean?"

"They were still going, still vibrating like they'd been when he stood on them for the last time. Incredible. Dead as he was, his feet were still going.

"So they hoist him up," Isaac continued, "and start running with him down the alley. They had to carry him the length of the sunny side to get him underneath, into the infirmary. There was no rush, of course, but those who carried the kid wanted to show the crowd how things were done in an emergency. Somebody ran behind them and carried his head, kept it from dangling, kept it from swinging from side to side on the flesh of his neck. As they carried him out, the sunny-side section jeered and whistled and stamped their feet."

"Nobody likes a coward, right?"

"Sure. There was that. But mainly he had ruined a perfectly good bull. The bull now knew what the game was all about. He had

128

sentido. He knew what to do and would remember. He knew the *muleta* was nothing but a trick. It was the first time he confronted man on foot and he had come out on top. He was a killer and would have to be dispatched quickly. Those in the sunny side had paid a day's wages to see the fight. They had not come as the tourists on the shady side. They did not come to tell their friends in Virginia of the primitive horrors of Mexico."

"So," Sturge said, "they were mad because of what the bull had become."

"That's right."

"Mad knowing that there are millions of kids in the streets of Mexico, but how many fighting bulls?"

"You've got it," Isaac said.

"And today we are going to find out about your feet, right?"

"I hope not. My hope is that the bulls will be small enough that it won't matter, so that I can show off for everybody, and you can take some pictures of me executing some marvelous things with the cape. I'll sweep the crowd off their feet."

"And," Sturge replied, "in the process you'll come to wrest the fashionable *señorita* from her loutish boyfriend, right? Isaac, I can't help but note a renewed sense of vigor since your depression last night, a lusting after challenge, a certain glibness of tongue. I've notice this increasingly since we began this trip. Could it be the El Presidente, amigo? Or is it love?"

They passed a small adobe church just off the road. In the shade of the west wall was a line of peasants, squatting, leaning back against it, smoking. They were men and older boys. Under a tree were the women. They were not in a neat line, but were clustered in small groups. The only ones in the sun were the young children. They had been playing, but had stopped. They and everyone had stopped when they heard the Deucheveaux coming. When it passed them, some of the men smiled, white teeth against the burl of their faces. They were shaking their heads. A few of the children waved.

"This thing," Sturge began, "this thing about the feet. It's no different from anything else, is it? War brings it out, climbing mountains, standing up to the guy who has it in his tiny mind to beat your brains out. It's all the same, isn't it?"

"I guess it's the same," Isaac said. "Except, maybe, the bullfight has a kind of purity to it. The other things you're talking about don't have that. In war the cowards and the heroes are all mixed up. People become one or the other by virtue of things that are totally out of their control. And the weapons tend to act as intermediaries, buffers, removing them, distancing them from what really happens. Then there's the politics. Who's the hero in Vietnam? The guy acting on an order to take out a Vietcong village or the guy who refuses the draft and heads for Toronto? Is it the guy who shoots or the guy who doesn't? With the mountain, one ascends gradually. With each step up you can control it. You don't have to look down. As for the guy who wants to pound on your head? He is human. Even if he's something of a Neanderthal, he's not going to kill you if he can help it. Murder charges aside, chances are he's operating on some basic sense of morality. But with the bull there's none of that. It's a distilled version of the others. It's the best test of the feet."

"You got any idea of where we are?" Sturge asked.

"Sanchez said the turn was somewhere after the church. It's a road off to the right. There's supposed to be a sign."

They nearly missed it. The sign was whitewashed on a rock just off the dirt road. They had to circle back. The French machinery they were riding in made the U-turn with pavement to spare. Dust quickly filled the interior as they headed down the dirt road. The rock had said 40 kilometers.

"Under your seat," Sturge said. "There's a painting. Slide it out."

It was a small, stretched canvas and had lain face down and was coated with dust and grease. That and the dust that filled the car's interior made seeing the painting impossible.

"There's a rag under there too. You won't damage it. Take my word for it."

Isaac wiped it down until the image was revealed. It was a slick portrait of a tousled-haired boy with huge opalescent eyes. At the

130

corner of one, a brilliantly highlighted tear was working its way onto his puffy cheek. The boy's face was decidedly sad. Whatever else were his troubles, the draftsman had contributed to it. The boy was suffering a distinct lopsidedness. The obvious strain on him was telling. The tear no doubt was a product of it.

"It's called 'The Street Urchin'," Sturge said.

"Jesus."

"Now lay it over the abyss at your feet." The dust in the interior slowed and began to settle. He could make out Sturge again.

"Name's Pisano. Does mostly clowns now."

"A natural transition," Isaac said. He accepted the flask again, wiped the lip and took another pull. He tried not to think about Memori and whether she would be there when they'd made the balance of the 40 k's. He had dressed with her in mind. Besides the boots, he wore his buff-colored slacks which he'd pressed under the mattress last night. He'd shopped for a shirt that morning. When he found a bleached cotton one that seemed roomy enough, he tried it on over the shirt he was wearing. When the sleeves reached his wrists, he settled on it. It had lain in a box and the creases hadn't forgotten. They described the underpinnings of a tick-tac-toe game. He looked for them to dissolve in time for the party.

"He was out of L.A., this Pisano," Sturge continued. "Sold encyclopedias, roof coating for mobile homes and typewriter repair courses. Got into selling correspondence art. Turned in his suit and tie for a beard and Levi jacket and was doing fine; nothing big, you understand, but making a living. You know the pitch: why work when you can become a world-famous artist in two weekends. Three and they'll throw in brain surgery.

"Anyway, he got to painting in his garage. Turning out things like that at your feet. Formula stuff for furniture chains. Ever see how they work?" Isaac said he hadn't.

"I'd watch him sometimes," Sturge continued. "Line up maybe thirty canvases. Mix a big batch of umber and a little thalo and lay in all the hair on each. Come back with the ochre and pick up the highlights on all of it. Lay in the flesh tones, middle value.

131

Come back with the highs, then the lows. A pip of Titanium, one each, on the pupil and the tear and you had it, thirty noses, thirty smiles, sixty billiard-size eyeballs. Hang on."

It was a cattle crossing and they took it without slowing. They left the ground and nosed in on the other side, pitching some of the roadway over the windshield as the rear end slammed down behind them. Sturge had not let off the accelerator.

"He'd get maybe five bucks a pop. That's a hundred fifty for an hour's work once a week. He was happy enough and the chain got sixty bucks framed. Since the frame was molded plastic, the chain was doing all right too. For Pisano it was fun money, you know. They'd pay in cash and nobody declared anything. Once they asked if he could do little girls. The next batch he made the hair longer."

The road worked its way around an arroyo, then climbed a low hill. From the crest the road snaked out ahead of them, dipped, and was lost for a while, then emerged in the distance as a straight, thin thread. It culminated in some trees and in what appeared to be an outcropping of rocks. It's where the ranch house and out-buildings would be, Isaac guessed. They had another twenty kilometers.

Clearly, they were the only car on the road. The dust from theirs would be visible for miles. They were either late or early or had the wrong day. It would be better if they were not all waiting out in front watching the arrival of Sturge's Deucheveaux.

"So one day," Sturge continued, "this guy's in Laguna and passing a gallery. Sure as hell there's one of his god-awful urchins in the window, but with another signature. Now, he knew the quality of what he was doing and was amazed that anyone would stoop to rip him off. It was like mugging a mother of three working the Juarez city dump. Curious, he goes in, and an old woman with a tidy bun of gray hobbles out of the back. She could maybe win a Norman Rockwell contest.

"She serves him up some herb tea and pitches him. She tells him that the perfectly marvelous painting he has inquired about was done by a quadriplegic, black woman with terminal diabetes.

She painted with her teeth, it seemed, and was self- taught. It was hard, the woman explained, to find a teacher for such a thing. Though fading rapidly, the artist remained prolific — prolific, at least, for one who painted with, and didn't even own, her own teeth. She had been discovered by Victor Mature's dentist who occasioned on her while vacationing in the Ozarks. She had been working with her gums and, apparently, bleeding badly. He fitted her with specially constructed choppers.

"The little old lady tells the guy that she was surprised he hadn't heard the artist's name, since she had become internationally known and coveted by a number of prominent art authorities, Eva Gabor among them. And all of it accounts for the price of twelve hundred which includes shipping. It would be a little less if he took it with him.

"So, when he carried the story back to the furniture chain, they were quick to agree they had not been fair with him, though they cautioned him against any legal action, since it would likely attract the IRS. To show where their heart was, they offered to double his price per canvas, if he would do something other than urchins. They already had plenty."

"Hence, the clowns," Isaac said. "I wondered who was doing all the Goddamned clowns."

"The clowns didn't come right away. He sort of grew into those. He's the guy who does the bug-eyed little boy holding hands with the bug-eye little girl. He's also got a Cocker Spaniel."

"The one with the tear?"

"That's the one."

The road ended in a cobblestone drive that swept under a stone arch. The drive circled around a garden of cactus and pepper trees and delivered them to the front of the house. It was a sprawling citadel of stone and adobe and ceramic tile and had been there forever, long enough anyway to have been enveloped into the terrain as though it were wrought from it. It sat amid the greenery that contained it as though it were a consequence of nature, something a volatile earth begot long before there was man to inhabit the results.

Parked off the drive was a long string of late-model cars, sev-

133

eral pickups and a jeep. Sturge pulled behind a Mercedes and turned off the key. The Deuxcheveaux was not prepared to end it there. The engine continued to run, lurching, belching, rattling deeply within its bowels, then catching again. It died reluctantly.

"Dieseling," Sturge announced, unfolding his legs and passing them through the door. "It's the one drawback, car like this."

Isaac had to wait for him to unwire the passenger door and lean it against the fender.

It was the first time in a long time that Isaac was not among the first at a party. Sanchez greeted them at the door and led them across the foyer of polished stone, down two steps into a vast living room where his guests, perhaps seventy-five in all, were already gathered. They were scattered in disparate groups around the room, some seated in sling leather chairs, but leaning forward, animated, quietly engaged; others stood or sat in the several furniture groupings containing them, sprawling leather sofas and plush chairs amid some low carved oak tables. About midway into the room, near a long, countersunk window was a grand piano on which an hors d'oeuvres tray bloomed. It was presided over by a covey of *criadas*. Hung on the wall to the right of it was mounted the massive head of a fighting bull. The glass eyes followed Isaac.

Within, it was cool enough for a fire and one had been set in a great stone fireplace across the room. Above the mantel was a large painting in a massive antique frame. As they approached, Isaac could see that it depicted a crowd fleeing an inferno in oranges and purples that colored the sky behind them. They were carrying their dead and wounded. It was cheerless enough to have been a Goya. Isaac glanced back to the mounted bull. It still watched him.

Rafael and Maria were seated in a group below the painting. Beyond, towards an alcove on the left Heinrich and Memori were talking to several people. The others, all strangers to him, were Hispanic. As Old Man Sanchez approached each group for introductions, they fell silent and rose as though on signal.

There followed a hopeless mix of names as he and Sturge were introduced to everyone in the room. There was something

134

uncomfortably formal about the way the men greeted Isaac. By turns they extended their hands and shook Isaac's firmly, tipping slightly forward at the waist as they did so, unsmiling. Even Rafael was distant. Isaac made reference to his friends from Morelia and their late night drinking. He nodded, his expression remained grave.

As Sanchez led the two closer to the group that contained Memori, a thin man with hollow cheeks stepped out of a crowd. Those he was talking to fell silent and turned to watch the greeting. Sanchez had called him Jaime Something. The Mexican stepped forward and clapped Isaac on both shoulders. He wore the tragic look of Manolete in his eyes. Like the trophy's, he did not move them from Isaac's. A muscle quivered at his jaw line.

"*Suerte, patron.*" he said. He shook Isaac's hand and held his eyes with his own in a grip not unlike it. Isaac did not know what to say. After a moment he was allowed to pass. When the Mexican turned away, Isaac noted the *coleta*, the small pigtail that identified him as a matador. He guessed that it was real, not the fake one braided on before a fight. Someone began to finger a guitar across the room. If there was a certain tension among the guests, the music eased it. Conversation rose.

A woman, her face flushed and damp, crossed toward them. She wore an apron and sought a few words with Sanchez. Through the door from which she had come Isaac could make out some hanging copper kettles and the brickwork of a country kitchen. There was the smell of a roast. Lamb, maybe. Isaac tried not to dally with the symbolic content of that possibility.

Sturge and he relieved a passing *criada* of two tall drinks from her tray. Isaac's tasted of fresh fruit, salt and *tequila*.

Near the guitarist some laughter erupted. An old man rose and began to sing a gypsy flamenco song in throaty tones. The guitar moved in behind him and caught up. There was some syncopated clapping from those nearby. Isaac drained his glass much too quickly.

"This crowd," Sturge said to Isaac, "it's taking you very seri-

135

ously. Are you sure you've told me everything about the party that began all this?"

"I think so. I was hoping it was my imagination."

"I don't think so. You're looking a lot like the guest of honor, or maybe the day's entertainment, Isaac."

"It's not what I had in mind."

Sturge nodded toward the old man. He was still engaged with the cook. "He's the one to watch. These Spaniards get pretty crafty once they reach seventy. I think he's got you billed as *Numero Uno* or something. Are you sure you haven't fought before?"

"I need another drink."

Isaac caught the eye of the *criada* and she made her way over. But just as she extended the tray, Sanchez finished with the cook.

"It will be a mistake, my friend," he told Isaac. "One drink stirs the blood, but two . . ah. It makes for false courage. It would not be sensible. It would not be a good thing, another drink."

"This is very true," Sturge said, retrieving a drink for himself.

"Even if it did not dim the faculties," said Sanchez, "there would be some who would see you. You wouldn't want that. It would not be proper."

"Look," Isaac began. "I hope you —"

"Please," he said, moving Isaac and Sturge to the group that was being entertained by Heinrich. The German wore crisply pleated olive slacks and an embroidered peasant shirt open to a tanned and hairy chest. Again, as in Rafael's party, they had to wait for him to finish his story. There was some polite laughter, but this time most had already turned their attention to Sanchez and the two Americans who had come up behind Heinrich.

After Sanchez introduced Sturge as an artist, Heinrich bent toward him and, still holding his hand, had him repeat his name.

"Ah, yes," he told Sturge, as though trying to remember something. "Sturge Boswell. Should I know you?"

"Of course you should," Sturge told him. "I'm Isaac's landlord. I've been basking in the glow of his considerable popularity."

"Yes, I've heard he's the celebrated one today." Heinrich turned to Isaac, "So, I am to learn of the fighting bull. And you, I understand, shall be my teacher. Is that not what it is to be?"

"I'm not sure about any of this," Isaac told him. He wanted to go home. Of that he was sure.

"Don't be fooled by his modesty, Heinrich," Sturge said. "As a teacher of the bulls, Isaac has no peer. His fame in this regard probably hasn't reached SoHo yet, but you shouldn't judge by that. Very little of what's important does."

"Well, your friend's encounter with the bull — It's Sturge, isn't it? — your friend's encounter will be watched with a good deal of interest. But let me warn both of you: My sentiments, I fear, will be with the bull. You can understand that, I think. What doesn't escape us in SoHo is a sense of charity and fair play."

"Yes," said Sturge, "I noticed the charity you applied to the Twachtman last night."

"In the interest, only, of bringing life to it." Heinrich's well practiced smile did not fade. "As an artist, you ought to understand something about the subject."

"I've been trying to learn. I attended your lecture last night for just that reason. Great stuff: New Art and the decadence of history. I came away choosing to be a landlord."

"A wise decision," said Heinrich. He was enjoying his humor and turned to find Memori. She had been talking to a graying, severe woman seated in a straight back chair near the fire. At his call she excused herself and turned to them.

This time Memori wore white, a lace dress she wore low on the shoulders. It was full at the sleeves, layered and brought to the waist with some ribbon. From there it fell to her feet. It was an antique dress and open to an afternoon breeze. The white of it carried a hint of its age. The slight discoloration provided it with a warmth it may not have originally had. The skin on her shoulders and above her small and veiled breasts was bathed in a delicate hue. It seemed to emanate upwards without quite reaching the pale surface.

She greeted Isaac first, her hand reaching for his.

"Thank you for the painting," she said.

"But you bought it?" It was said before he could edit it. He

137

didn't mean the way it sounded. He wondered for a moment if the gallery had taken to giving his work away. In his long and tangled history with commerce worse things had happened.

"The money I paid for it doesn't make it mine. It only gives me the right to hang it, to enjoy it. I'm grateful, Isaac."

Renoir would have rejected her as a model, but he'd have been wrong. She wore her thinness well. The bones within her face and shoulders seemed hollow, like those of a bird that migrates for long distances, and though angular, were not sharp. The dance, Isaac guessed, had rounded her. There was a suppleness to her. She would bend to the wind. Only her eyes wore the hint of hurt or fear, and Isaac could see this was more illusion than anything else. The narrow face made the eyes seem wider. The bones that rose high on her cheeks made them seem more liquid, more vulnerable. There was a young-girl quality about her and she was careful in the way she made up her face not to destroy the effect.

Sturge and she were in stark contrast. Massive, thick-boned, towering above her he took her extended hand. In order to hear her, he had to bend and lean in. He looked off balance, a giant about to topple and bury her. It may have been that he was showing his drinks. They had clearly lubricated his tongue.

"Isaac told me of your vast beauty, your charm, but they were words that pall against reality."

"I'm flattered Isaac would describe me at all."

She turned to him again. "You've not left town after all."

"That's beginning to look like an enormous mistake."

"Please, Memori, you must understand Isaac," Sturge told her. "He's being reticent. So as to make all the greater an impression with his glorious cape work. It is in the heart of Isaac, this thing with the bulls." Sturge was picking up the formal cadence the men whom Isaac had been introduced to had used. "Today you will see the things that you have never seen before."

"I'm sure," Sanchez said, "there is some truth in what you say." This, too, was said gravely, but there was something unsettled in the way he held his mouth. He turned to Memori "It is a pity, you know, that your friend Heinrich here will not also experience this thing of the heart. It would relieve him of some prejudices, I think."

"Very true. And think of the romance of it." Sturge and the old man were working as a team. "A beautiful woman, two courageous matadors and a brave bull. *Mano-a-mano*. Think of the weighty implications."

"No," Sanchez said. "It would be wrong. My German friend does not approve of the thing at all. Even when it is, as he has said, a fair match and there is no punishment to the animal."

"A pity," said Sturge.

"Yes," said Sanchez. "Clearly out of the question." But they waited, looking to Heinrich. He sipped his drink and swallowed. He was still smiling.

"I'm afraid I don't know one thing about it. I would not know what to do with all the traditions."

"It isn't important," the old man said. "You are my guest and you have been invited to watch. It isn't a matter of being cowardly. It isn't that at all."

Heinrich, stung, looked to Memori for support, but she was looking at her glass.

"I wouldn't want," Sanchez continued drolly, "my German friend to do anything he doesn't want to do. It will be a rewarding education just to see these animals, to see how they react to Isaac here. And, Isaac, please do not be concerned. I have only two young animals and they are all but harmless. And Jaime —" He called the name again to the group by the piano and the man who had the sad eyes of Manolete detached himself and crossed over.

"Please know, Jaime, that your responsibility today is to Isaac here. I want you to understand that. It is his first time with the bulls and you must keep him out of trouble." Sanchez put his hand on Jaime's shoulder and turned to Isaac. "Jaime knows about the bulls, Isaac. He is a veteran of the *corrida*. Last week, Jaime, was it not two ears in Hermosilla?"

"No, *Padrino*. It was the one."

"Ah, well. The provincials. There's no accounting, sometimes."

"This other one," Jaime said to Sanchez. "The one who does not understand about the bullfight. He will not also be fighting today?"

"No," Sanchez said. "That's my friend Heinrich here. He will not be fighting today. Today, he tells me, he would rather watch. So there will be only the one."

"And not the two?" Jaime seemed uncomfortable with that. He looked to Heinrich expecting to be contested.

"No," Sanchez said. "But perhaps you could show Heinrich how the cape works. This could be done before the fight, before the bulls come out." He turned to Heinrich. "It will be a part of the education, if you like. Only if you like."

"Well, yes, of course. I would like to. I would like that."

"Good. And Jaime will tell you, of course, when the bull will come so that you can get out of the way, so that you can watch from behind the barrera, so that there is no danger in any of it for you."

"Well, look—" Heinrich began, but Sanchez cut him short with an upraised hand.

"Please," the old man said, "you were invited here as my guest and you need only to watch. Nothing else is important. If, after you see the animal, and you would like to try the things Jaime will teach you with the cape, that is, of course, entirely up to you. It would be better for the learning, but I would not encourage it. No. If you feel strongly about —"

"Look. I don't feel strongly about any of this," Heinrich snapped.

"Please," the old man said. "Please do not be insulted. It is quite enough that you have honored me, to come here as my guest. And to have brought this beautiful woman to my home so that we can all share her smile. That is enough. Now, my friend, it is time for another drink. After, the sun will be better. It will be better for Isaac when there is a little shade to define the animal and his movement. And later, Isaac, when we return for dinner, you will be able to join us in the drinking. Please know. It is not out of cruelty, this. It is for the sake of your health. Is this not right, Jaime?"

"Yes, *Padrino*, it is right."

"Yes," said Sturge, taking a fresh drink from a young *criada* hovering near. "We all believe in your unflinching courage, Isaac, and I, for one, will drink to it. It's a small thing to do for art."

Chapter 12

Either the bullring was not close enough to the house or Sanchez was deferring to the women who had dressed rather more elaborately, Isaac noticed, then what he figured the occasion warranted. At Sanchez's suggestion they would all go to the ring in a caravan.

The guests fanned out to the cars. Some of the younger women had brought hats. They adjusted them against the sun. Memori's was white, the wide brim shading her face like a forgotten movie star of the Thirties. She was seated into the Mercedes by Heinrich, who, after pushing some of her dress aside, closed the door carefully.

Sanchez pulled the jeep around to the front of the line of cars. As he drove past he waved to them like Patton liberating Paris. It was a good, bright day for the bulls and he couldn't be happier.

Sturge and Isaac headed for their car just behind Heinrich's Mercedes. Seeing them he bowed deferentially, sweeping his hand like d'Artagnan in an invitation to pass. He too was enjoying the day. He would not have to do anything dangerous. Like a duchess, Memori offered a little wave from behind the window.

Isaac had to wait in the Deucheveaux for Sturge to secure and tie shut the passenger door. Heinrich came over as Sturge took his seat behind the wheel.

"You are safe to follow us in such a thing?" He put his face on level with Sturge's window, mock concern masking a smile that worked to erase it.

"It goes best at very high speeds," Sturge told him. "If you don't go too slow, it will be all right. It will want to race and I'll have to hold it back." Sturge looked to be serious.

The caravan took a dirt road off the circular drive. It took them alongside the house and down an incline through the corrals. There was a barn, a stone tack house which was almost hidden in cactus and century plant, and some outbuildings. Below them was a long ragged line of willows and scrub oak that fought for purchase on the banks of a nearly dry river bed.

The cars came to a stop at the bridge that spanned it. The wooden planking did not look like it could support two at once. It took waiting for the car in front to clear it, and there was the repeated rattle of the same loose planks as each car went over them. Sturge waited for Heinrich's Mercedes with its New York plates to cross. When it was clear of the bridge, he revved his engine to a high pitched whine and popped the clutch. It took the bridge in a bound and a couple of skips. He had to break hard on the other side.

"Sorry," Sturge said. "Damn thing never liked water or anything that crosses it. You got to take it all at once, before she gets thinking about it. That and dieseling. Small things, really, but if you're going to put your money into a car like this, you got to consider the down side." Again, Isaac could not tell if he were joking.

They hugged the shady side of the creek for a few hundred yards before they came to the bull ring. The fence enclosing the plaza had not held on to much of its paint and took advantage of a flat piece of land below an outcropping of rocks.

The ring was reduced in scale, but otherwise was a pretty fair replica of a *plaza de toros*, far more elaborate than one would expect of a *ganadería*.

On the west side wooden bleachers rose in tiers of varicolored planks. An overhang and backdrop shaded the benches against an afternoon sun. Across from that and on some rocks that climbed to the height of the fence some ranch hands were clustered.

As the caravan pulled up to park, the men stood on the rocks and cheered. Some wore battered cowboy hats, the rim cupped and set low to the eyes. Others shielded their eyes from the sun with their hands. They were drinking from bottles as deep brown as their skin. Their teeth, when they smiled, were brilliant against it.

Near them some children were at play by a cluster of sheds. They too stopped to watch the caravan pull up. On the roof of a low cement outbuilding and overlooking the children some of the women where gathered. They had baskets of food and wine and were sorting it out on blankets. One woman squatted at the base of an oil drum that had been cut open and vented. She fed sticks to a fire within it. Unlike the men, the women were busy with the food and did not have time to acknowledge the line of cars.

Beyond the ring and for miles was flat open country. In the distance was the foreshortened greening, the sparse stubble, from the recent rains. From the long view it looked like a great expanse of lawn. There wasn't a bull in sight.

As Isaac and Sturge came to the ring, the straight chain that had been the caravan wavered and dissolved. The cars fanned off to park on both sides of the road. Sturge took his own and nosed it up against the fence. This time when he turned off the ignition it stopped.

"Is there anything left in the flask?" Isaac asked.

"It is not done, *torero*," Sturge said gravely, while handing it to Isaac. "It is just not expected."

"Go to hell," Isaac told him.

In order not to be seen, Isaac had to scrunch down below the dash to drink from the flask. He felt like a teenager in a drive-in restaurant. As Sturge worked the wire on the passenger door, he took several successive swallows. He screwed on the cap and re-placed the flask in the pouch on Sturge's side. By the time he straightened, Sturge had the door off and Jaime stood with him. Doubtless Jaime had seen him with the flask.

"We have some time before the bulls," he said evenly. He waited as though to say something else, and then said, "You can show me what you know about the cape."

"It is not the cape that worries me," Isaac told him. But Jaime did not smile. The sad eyes continued to fix his. Isaac considered how good he would have been at the Inquisition. He waited for Isaac to get out of the car, then said:

"If the cape is right, the bull will not concern you."

"Yes," Isaac replied, wondering why he submitted to all this.

A narrow walkway had been excavated beneath the bleachers and the three of them walked into it in a single file. It led into the ring and served as a sort of *arrastradero*, a tunnel — had it been otherwise — through which the cuadrilla, the troupe of bull fighters, would emerge.

As he started to follow Jaime out into the sun and into the smoothly raked arena, Sturge stopped him. He clamped both hands on Isaac's shoulders and narrowed his eyes, his face, a grim mask.

"*Suerte, matador*," he said. Anyone watching the performance would have thought he was serious.

"Go to hell," Isaac told him again.

Sturge left the two and turned back to the bleachers. He was carrying the camera.

"Whatever happens," Isaac called to him, "for Christ's sake take some pictures. I'm not going through this again."

Without looking back Sturge raised his hand

Isaac took his place next to Jaime. He was still not ready to move out.

"Where are the animals?" Isaac asked. He felt that if he could see what he was up against he would be all right. It might quiet the pace his heart had set. But Jaime had lowered his head and closed his eyes. It took a moment for Isaac to realize that he was in prayer. When he had finished and had crossed himself, Isaac asked again about the bulls.

"They are in the pen just on the other side."

"I would like to see them, to see what I'm in for," Isaac said.

"No."

"No?"

"It isn't done, my friend," Jaime said, squinting into the sun outside. "Not in these things."

"I'm tired of hearing what isn't done. I don't care about that."

"Yes," said Jaime.

"How about running for one's life. Is that done?"

Just as Isaac spoke, Jaime had started to move out onto the sand. He stopped, put a hand to Isaac's chest.

"Please. We are going out now. You should know that this is not a time for the jokes. It is important that there be nothing funny in the things that are about to happen. Even if others laugh at the way you do things or don't do things. You should not make this to look funny."

"I have never been more serious in my life," Isaac told him.

"You know of the *corrida*. Sr. Sanchez tells me that you know this business with the bulls, that you understand. This thing we do today, it is not the same as that, but for today you must think of it as the same. Today I would like you to think of it that way."

"I feel like I'm being set up for something, that this is some kind of fiesta to roast a gringo, a stupid one."

"No. It is not what you think. Now, walk together with me."

There were six or seven men in the ring. Some of them were the same ranch hands who had been sitting on the wall when they drove up, but now they did not wear their hats. All of them, all but the old man and Heinrich who stood near ring center, were working capes in slow graceful *veronicas*, checking for the wind. When Jaime and he emerged, as one they folded their capes against their chests and stepped back to the *barrera*.

As the two came out there was a scattering of applause from the seats behind them. But the sun, when Isaac turned, was just above the overhang and the crowd was in darkness. He could not see whether they were taking this lightly, as a joke. He tried for a smile and waved, but there was no laughter and nobody called his name. Sure, it was a clumsy wave and the smile did not come off right, but it should have been enough for someone to laugh, maybe, or shout down encouragement or make a joke.

146

The whole thing was not going well. From the time he entered the Sanchez's ranch, it had not gone well at all. If there were a joke in the way they were treating him, he had not been let in on it. None of what was happening conformed to any of the *tientas* he had heard or read about.

"Isaac, my good friend," Sanchez called out to him. "You are much too grim. Please, the animals are as I told you. They are not the dangerous ones. They are not killers. You will not die today on the sand."

"That's good news. Your guests are treating me otherwise. It is like they have come to a funeral, or to the thing that will lead to a funeral."

"When the bulls come, you will feel better."

"Yes."

"It is always better when you have something to do."

"Sure."

Jaime handed him one of two capes he had brought out with him. Isaac watched him as he unfurled his, laying most of it on the sand in front of him. He watched him grip it, careful to make good handles of the cloth. He watched him bring the handles chest high and how he brought the cloth out and away. Jaime tried a *veroni-ca*. He did it first to the right, then to his left.

Isaac followed, gripping the cloth as one would hold the handlebars of a bike. He went through his own pattern of *veronicas*, the cape billowing outward from his legs. He worked it first one way, then the other, his following hand brought down hard to the crotch.

He had learned the movements from a friend in college who had studied in Tijuana as a *novillero*. Isaac had begun with a cape. Later, in a variety of circumstances, he had practiced with anything that looked like one, a beach towel, a robe, a rain coat. Once, in France and with a group of his friends cheering from a sidewalk cafe, he had fought rush hour traffic with his raincoat. It was in Orleans at the central traffic circle beneath the equestrian statue of Jeanne d'Arc and he had drawn a small crowd. It was a heady experience. Though he was grazed by a Peugeot he'd worked too close-

147

ly, he was not moved far off the mark and he managed to follow through nicely.

Working with the cape was the easiest of all of it and, like riding a bike or ice skating, it was something you remembered. When there was no bull, one could look very practiced. When there wasn't an unpredictable animal bent on erasing you from earth, one could almost look like he knew what he was doing.

Jaime nodded. "All right. He will go past you with that, if you do not panic or make some foolish tricks. Don't let him take the cape from you, and when you make the *remate*, when you pull the cape from his sight, do it quickly and cleanly so that the bull will not find it again. That is the hardest part. These are young animals and they will cling to you like gnats."

"You'll be around, right?"

"Yes. But it is not good to think of that. With a bull, you are as alone as you get in life. The bull does not care that I am near. It doesn't matter to him."

Jaime called for another cape and one of the *mozos* brought it and handed it to Heinrich. With his grin in place, the German began to emulate Isaac's veronica. Jaime took him back to the beginning. He showed him why you don't hold the cape like you were changing a table cloth. By yanking it out of his hand, he showed how the bull would take it from him. He showed him how to grip it and then how to create the airpocket that moved the cape out and away from your legs. He demonstrated how to stand in profile to the bull and how to remain in place, or appear to, even if you were moved by the bull.

He showed what Heinrich should do once the bull got by him, how one had to recover and work the other side.

Heinrich was not clumsy. He learned quickly. And he liked the way he looked when he made the right movements. He liked it that Memori was there to see him, and the guests. He liked the idea of playing with the cape without having to worry about the size and disposition of what ever would come out of the *toril* in the next few minutes.

"Marvelous," Heinrich said. "And if I bring the cape like so, yank it from his view, there is nothing left of the cape for the bull to see. And that is what you call the *remate*, the finish. Is that not what you call it?"

"Yes," Jaime said.

"And he will stop, the bull? He will not be able to see a target and he will stop?"

"That is what he is supposed to do."

"Sometimes he does not?" Heinrich asked.

"Sometimes he does nothing he is supposed to do."

"So, if he has a mind not to stop, what is that I am to do with him?"

"That is the training part," Jaime told him.

"You have to train him to stop?"

"It is up to you."

"Yes?" Heinrich wanted to understand.

"Either you are in control and you train him to do the things you want, or he trains you to do the things he wants. It is a contest. It is a matter of the stronger of the trainers."

"Marvelous," said Heinrich.

"Yes," said Jaime.

"Enough," said the old man. "The bulls are restless."

The gates to the *arrastradero* through which they entered were closed behind them. The four of them squeezed into the *burladero* near it. The wooden shield was one of four set equidistantly around the ring. It allowed a man to slide through it while a bull of greater girth could not. The old man slid behind the first. Nodding to Isaac, then to Heinrich, he left the bullfighter and his two guests and moved out down the alley and took his place beside two older men Isaac had not seen before. Isaac, looking across Heinrich, saw that Jaime had draped his cape across the plank in front of him. He did the same. After a moment Jaime leaned across Heinrich to speak.

"Isaac, I will work him for a while. Don't watch me. Watch the horns. Watch what he does with them. It will tell you something about his intentions."

The *toril*, the tunnel through which the bull would come, was

149

to the left of Isaac. When Jaime nodded, two of the ranch hands pulled open the two gates to it, quickly closing themselves off into the alley as they did. The bull, once he came out, could only go into the ring. He'd have to jump the fence to get into the *callejon*. The two ranch hands waited.

The bull they waited for did not want to come out.

The man closest to Isaac looked into the dark tunnel. He was a young man who wore a white dress shirt that was torn on one shoulder. His sleeves were rolled to the elbows. He reached over the gate and pounded on it with the heel of his hand. He yelled and pounded on the wood some more. He swung the gate just enough so that he could see in. He was careful, as it was not unlike peering into the barrel of a loaded cannon. It was dark against the light outside and he had to shade his eyes. Once, he jumped back, thinking he saw something coming.

He borrowed a cape from one of those acting as *banderilleros* and flung it over the top of the gate. He yelled and pounded on the wood some more.

The bull did not want to come out.

Isaac wished he had not listened to Sanchez and Jaime and had gone ahead and carried Sturge's flask. If one deserved a drink, he did. He was not sure how he got into all this, how he got trapped into the game that was being played. He had expected that there would be several others fighting and that they would all have been permitted to be drunk. Under these conditions he could have managed a pass or two. But this was something else. He had been hustled into a game of machismo and escape was out of the question. The rules for this particular one had been laid out from the beginning. It was evident by the way the men at the party greeted him. By Heinrich's presence. By Memori's. By how Sanchez and the others had deferred to him as though he were the guest of honor.

It was not a game he would play as a rule. If you thought about it — and he did now — it was ridiculous, this code of conduct that required him to do things he would rather not do. It was an historic code and most of it — at least the part that compelled Isaac to remain — was written by men. It established what a man did or didn't do in circumstances like the one Isaac found himself. The game was a strong part of many things in Mexico and of the bull-fight particularly. It was not civilized, this game, this honor among men and animals. From a rational viewpoint it was indefensible.

And, what he'd come to admit about himself, was equally indefensible: He believed in it. He believed in the damn rules.

It mattered how men behaved toward one another. It mattered that they adhered to cultural traditions that set the standards for what a man should be, and altogether different standards for what a woman should be. While this differentiation was becoming increasingly unpopular where Isaac came from, he could not shake himself free of the roots that held him. He recognized that his belief was antediluvian. It emanated from a much more complicated time, where manners and customs prevailed and when we still considered ourselves a product of history. It was cumbersome being contained within these rules. It was awkward and often comic when two equally binding rules collided. Today, particularly in his own country, it was much easier. There was a good deal of freedom. You did what you wanted to do. Your thing was what was important. You lived within the standards of Haight Asbury. You wore dandelions in your hair and you shot up and made love to anything that walked. You did what you felt like doing. "I" was the pronoun of choice.

That he still believed in the romance of more formal times — a condition that no doubt led him to Mexico — had trapped him. Even as an artist, who had a great latitude in these matters, he felt compelled to play by unfashionable rules. They demanded that he acquit himself somehow. He could not lean past the grinning Heinrich and tell Jaime he changed his mind, that what he wanted to do was to sit in Sturge's Deucheveaux and drink from his flask.

He did not like it that he believed in this thing. He did not like it that there was something in this whole silly business with the bulls that somehow mattered in life. It had to do with promises made and something else. It was hard to work out exactly what that

151

was. Maybe it was how he would come to think about his actions later. Maybe there was a kind of morality in it, this thing between men and animals. Even though it had been a long time since Hemingway had been read seriously, maybe some of what he said about these things still mattered.

As he stood behind the *burladero*, Isaac knew he would not tell them all to go to hell. He was pretty sure he knew that. He was also pretty sure he would do the best he could with what he had. What he had wasn't much. Of that he was real sure. But whatever was to come, he was in no hurry for it.

Neither, apparently, was the bull.

The bull did not want to come out and face him and Isaac knew exactly how he felt.

When it finally emerged, Isaac was elated. It was the smallest, least dangerous looking single animal this side of Walt Disney. It, too, didn't look like it belonged.

It had bolted out of the dark of the *toril* and stopped not more than ten feet from Isaac. It stood trembling, sniffing the air. It blinked at the sun. There was some laughter from the crowd and then some applause. The bull shied from the noise and stood again a few feet away, head cocked, listening. He was still blind in the sun and could not make out anything. When Jaime slid out from the *burladero*, it turned abruptly and trotted out across the ring.

Jaime had to track it. Someone in the crowd shouted down, *"Todo es toro!"*

"My, yes," Heinrich told Isaac. "So this is one of the killers you have described to me. This is the beast who knows no fear."

Each time Jaime approached, the animal would bolt, trot a few yards and stop. They had circumnavigated the ring this way, the guests cheering, whistling, clapping. Someone had started to chant, "To-ro! To-ro! To-ro!" Others picked it up.

The animal had allowed himself to be chased back to the *toril*, but the way he had entered the ring had been closed to him. It was a discovery that visibly troubled him. And you could see that he wanted some time to figure out what they had done with the opening. But the man with the cape would not let him alone. It was not, apparently, an accident that he kept following him.

It was only because the man was so insistent and would not go away that he turned to face him. The bull had acclimated himself to the sunlight by now. He decided to see what it was this man had in mind.

It would have been easy for Jaime to make a comedy out of the bull's reluctance to fight. Instead he tried to preserve what little dignity remained. He took the bull's first charge with a slow, graceful pass. But the bull broke again and Jaime had to chase it. It would stop, turn, and he would have to coax it all over again. He would charge only when all his other options had been closed. But each time it would break out of the cloth. Jaime could not link two passes together. He brought the bull, one pass at a time, back to the front of the stands.

There it stood hesitant, uncertain, facing Jaime, but wanting badly to go somewhere else. It lowered its head, pawed the ground, looked up. It turned and looked across the plaza, as though he could see something beyond the far *barrera*, something in the fields, and that if he watched that and not the man who was bothering him, the fellow would get bored and go away.

Jaime folded his cloth and waited until the bull faced him again. He waited as the bull fidgeted, backed up a little, snorted into the dust and pawed some more. He waited until the bull looked like it would charge again. Then, and deliberately, he turned his back to it and walked directly away, toward Isaac and Heinrich. He walked slowly, with his back straight. He did not look back. The bull blinked but stood.

"It is *manso*, but the fear will go when the anger comes," he told Isaac, sliding in beside Heinrich. "You will need to chase him some more until he loses the fear."

The bull, small enough to be embarrassing, looked even smaller, more defenseless as he approached it. It was confused, hesitant, and did not seem to like any of this, though it lowered its horns.

When Isaac brought the cape forward, it almost charged. But

there was something off to the right that distracted him. It was frightened of that and divided his attention between it and the cape that moved in front of him. The bull did not like any of it, and with its head lowered for a charge, it edged backward a foot at a time. Isaac in turn shuffled forward, keeping both feet on the ground, bringing the cape within inches of the lowered muzzle. The horns were small but sharp and the bull swung them from side to side. But something was wrong. It did not want to charge the cape. Looking as though it would spring forward at any moment, it edged backward in the sand like a crab scuttling for a rock.

This time, when Isaac brought the cape forward, brought it to nearly touch the lowered muzzle, he shook it. The bull started a charge, but was not sure enough about it and stopped, trembling.

Whatever else made it unsure, it had made a decision concerning the cape. It would stand ground. It was no longer worried about what had distracted it earlier. The cape was its adversary and, since there was no ignoring it, he elected to deal with it, to find out what it was trying to do, while not altogether discarding the possibility that if he continued to threaten it, it would retreat.

Isaac tried rocking the cape in front of it. He tried yelling. When he stamped his foot hard, the bull jumped, actually leaving the ground, startled by the sound. Behind Isaac was more laughter.

He had not noticed Jaime until he spoke. He was just off to the left and behind him. "Let him have that ground," he told Isaac. "Face him from the other side."

Isaac moved back and came at him from another angle. This time when he brought his cloth forward and shook it, the bull charged. Isaac planted his feet and took the bull at a safe distance, well away from his legs. The trick with the cloth worked and Isaac was grateful to the books he had read. Miraculously, the bull turned and came back for more.

On the second pass the bull cut closer than Isaac wanted it to. Had it hooked, the left horn might have caught him. But owing to some other miracle, it swept past him. It was a straight, clean charge and Isaac, it could be said, held ground. This time the bull did not return but trotted out to the *barrera*. There it turned and followed the curve of the planks. Isaac had to head it off and the bull slowed, then stopped, curious to see what the man had in mind.

They were in front of the bleachers again. He caught a glimpse of Heinrich, his forearms draped across the planks in front of him, grinning.

As Isaac started toward the animal, he felt a looseness in his walk, something that was not right, a clumsiness. When he looked down to his right boot, he was startled to see his footed sock extending out of his shoe. This he knew was impossible, an illusion created by a bright sun, maybe, or the fear, but he could not blink it back to reality, make it appear otherwise. It took him a moment to put it together, why his foot, enclosed as it was in a bright yellow sock, was on top and not within his boot. It had not made any sense until he remembered feeling a hoof graze his boot on the last pass. It did not seem possible, but it had opened up the leather, had split the boot cleanly across the instep like a razor. The hoof had not touched his foot.

At first he thought to ignore it. But when he took a step, his boot folded under him.

He tried kicking his heel into the sand then sliding his foot back inside that way, but it wouldn't go. With his eye on the bull, he tried stepping on the edge of the sole with his other foot. While holding it in place, he tried pushing his exposed foot back inside, folding his toes so that they would fit within. It almost worked. The trouble was that he could not get his foot back far enough and holding his toes like that was bringing on a cramp. Finally, he had to bend down and stuff his foot inside. When he stood, there was applause.

Isaac had come to regret the decision he'd made that morning. He had dressed for Memori after her stunning appearance the night before. His slacks and new shirt — even with the vertical creases — would certainly show he'd made an effort. His boots would be an improvement over sandals and more appropriate for a fight. What he wore within them wouldn't show and, since it was hard to find socks in his drawer that had not suffered the *criada's* mixed-wash policy, he settled on one of the dyed-yellow pair. His mother's frequent admonitions for wearing underclothes that you wouldn't mind being taken to the hospital in came to haunt him.

The boot would not stay in place. On his second step, the sole buckled and folded under him and there was the bright yellow sock again. The laughter was growing. He stuffed his foot back within the boot. In order to keep it there he had to slide his foot along the ground. Moving toward the bull that way made him feel like Festus shuffling after Marshal Dillon.

The bull had been watching Isaac with increasing interest. He did not know exactly what to make of whatever Isaac was doing, but it gave him time to consider his own problems. He was puzzled by what had happened. He had charged at movement many times and had not made contact. He had charged at the right place, but there was nothing for his horns. When he should have felt impact, there was only cloth. He had not seen man on foot before and suspected the worst. He suspected that whatever his enemy was doing, his sock had something to do with it. He would wait for him to get closer to see what it meant, to see how he'd come to deal with it.

Isaac's first pass was safe and clumsy. He had been thinking about his boot, worrying whether, if he were forced to move quickly, he could do so without tripping over it. Before he could recover fully, the bull had turned and was back on him from the other side. Its size allowed it to turn quickly. Isaac barely got the cloth open when it came in again. He was a little off balance. The bull started to move past him, then stopped, its flank against Isaac's legs. It was warm and he could feel it breathing. The bull leaned against him as though seeking companionship.

He did not remember reading what he was supposed to do next in such a circumstance. The books had not talked about a bull going half the way through a pass, stopping and then leaning on you. They had left that out.

Before he could assess it further, the bull began to circle him. Turning in on him and around his legs, it picked up speed. Isaac was the axis around which it rotated, winding in around him. The crotch-high horns now took on a more malevolent look. There was no room to make passes now. He had all he could do to keep the cape in front of the concentric horns as they tightened around him. But he could not turn faster than the bull. He was losing ground to a horn that seemed bent on emasculating him. The cape was of no use to him. It was tangled in the second horn and wrapped partially around Isaac's waist. He was in the vortex of a maelstrom with all his lines fouled, pirouetting against disaster. Just as things were at their blackest, the cape came free.

This good fortune permitted him to make the first of two cowardly moves. He made them in rapid succession. He dropped the cape across the bull's face and ran like hell.

It was a cowardly piece of prudence he'd seen used in desperate circumstances before. It was not a crowd pleaser. It was reserved for those few times when humiliation had to supplant a more unpleasant alternative. In Isaac's case it was the prospect of living out his life as a boy soprano.

It was prudent and would have served him well had it not been for the speed at which the bull shook the cape free and the condition of his boot. On his third stride in his sprint for the nearest *burladero* the sole folded, and he sprawled in the sand. With the bull close behind him and gaining, his fall may have saved him. Falling headlong was something the bull hadn't expected. And it was too late to change his course.

The bull fell over and landed directly on Isaac. There was a moment, while both wrestled for footing in a tangle of flesh and fur, that the one was indistinguishable from the other.

It was not what Hemingway had in mind when he'd written his treatise on the bullfight and described the moment of truth when the matador and bull became one. For Hemingway the phenomenon occurs in the third act when the torrero goes over the lowered horns to plunge his sword to the hilt. In that moment, the writer noted, they seem bonded. It is not clear who or what will survive the encounter.

The outcome in Isaac's case was similarly ambiguous. The bull and he were clearly inseparable and for a while it seemed doubtful either one of them would walk away.

Isaac, it turned out, was the more resourceful. Long since abandoning any remaining dignity, he scrambled out from under the beast. He did not take time to right himself. He headed for the *barrera* on all fours, his elevated ass prickling with the thought of those sharpened horns. It was not a race he could win, Isaac feared.

But the bull wasn't chasing him. Some miracle had intervened to turn it away. It was heading for another cape and a man prepared to take its fury. It wasn't until he could get to his feet, to stand upright with one yellow sock on the sand, the boot that would normally encase it encircling the calf of his leg, that he was able to recognize his savior. He would have preferred the horns.

Heinrich took the bull's first charge with considerable and surprising grace. If the German were uncertain, fearful, he concealed it. He did everything right with the pass, except that he took too much time with it. He was too intent on making everything come out the way Jaime had shown him. He was not watching the bull.

When it turned to come back, Heinrich was still watching how his cape looked in follow-through. It wasn't until the bull started toward him that Heinrich recognized the need to do something else. He turned toward the bull and in so doing, into the cape, wrapping most of it around him. What remained was only a small part of the cloth and he had to work with that. The bull graciously waited for him.

It was a conspiracy and the Goddamned bull was in on it. It waited for Heinrich to hoist what was left of the *capote*. It charged that. It tipped its horns away from his legs so as not to harm him and slid by. It was a *chicuelina*, or close enough to be considered so. Isaac had seen it done many times by skilled matadors, the cape used in large part as a shroud. It was impossible for it to happen by accident. It took the full cooperation of the animal. It took a conspiracy.

Had the bull come back again, it would have taken Heinrich

easily. It would have shown how phenomenally lucky he was the first time. The bull would have taken him with his horns. He would have taken him wrapped up like an enchilada.

The bull, of course, did nothing of the kind. It trotted out a few feet toward the *medios*, stopped, turned and waited for the grinning Heinrich to unravel himself. The guests were on their feet, cheering.

Heinrich, buoyed, loving all of it, elected to do what Jaime had done earlier. He turned his back on the bull just as it seemed ready to charge again. He acknowledged the crowd with his grin. He walked away from the animal just as he'd seen Jaime do, his back straight, head thrown back in arrogance, dragging the cape behind him. He did not look at the bull, and as he approached the *burladero* which shielded Isaac, he stopped to wave at the crowd. He was grinning even more.

Anyone who knew about bull fighting knew the stunt, as he undertook it, was impossible. The animal had not been fixed in place and could have charged at any time. It snorted at the retreating figure, it twisted its horns angrily, it pawed at the sand, and despite Isaac's most fervent prayers, stood ground. Like it was rehearsed, the Goddamned bull stood transfixed. It stood waiting until Heinrich, still waving, could slide safely in next to Isaac.

"Marvelous experience, Isaac, my man! Simply marvelous! Can't say when I last had such fun!"

Isaac groaned.

Heinrich had turned fully around and faced the crowd. When he hoisted a peace sign, the crowd thundered its approval. They thought Heinrich was indicating he should be awarded two ears. So enthusiastic were some, they'd have given their own.

"And you must forgive me," Heinrich said. He had to talk over the crowd, both arms extended now, two peace signs. He was either Nixon accepting the Republican nomination or he wanted four ears. Either way the crowd was behind him.

"It was not so good for you. You must forgive me," he told Isaac, still favoring the audience with his boyish smile. "I wouldn't have interceded like that, but with all your little difficulties, it seemed for the best. Wouldn't you agree?" Someone handed him a bouquet of wild flowers. He waved that.

He continued with Isaac: "Weren't injured out there, were you? It was hard sometimes to tell you from the animal you were fighting. A very complicated thing you did. Didn't know there was such a maneuver."

"Yes," Isaac said. "It's a matter of technique. It takes total concentration."

"Of course," the German replied. "Things appear differently sometimes. It looked to me that maybe the bull was getting the better part of your technique."

"Yes, it looks like that for a while, just before I do some brilliant things with the cape. You really ought to have waited."

But Heinrich wasn't listening. He was yelling up to Memori:

"Marvelous! Marvelous experience! Hadn't realized! Can't wait for the next! Dedicated to you, my love! Hear me? To you!"

Jaime brought over a roll of adhesive tape, handed it to Isaac, pointed to his boot and walked off. Isaac tried standing on one foot while wrapping the other. Sturge called to him from the *arrastradero*. Isaac limped over.

"Get in here and sit, for Christ sake. I'll wrap it."

"You weren't impressed then," Isaac said, "with my first showing."

"Drink this and shut up."

Isaac took several successive swallows from the flask and then said:

"As a *mano-a-mano*, how do you like it so far?"

"On a scale of one to ten?"

"All right. It could have gone more smoothly," Isaac said.

"Did you know at one point the bull was sitting on your face?"

"Really?"

"I'm serious," Sturge said.

"That's not easy," Isaac replied. "It's hard to get a bull to do such a thing."

"That's probably true."

"Tell me," Isaac said. "Would you say the crowd is with me? That they cheered me as one?"

"I would say they are partisan."

"And Memori?"

"There's a sympathy factor, maybe," Sturge said. "But it's hard to remain seriously committed to a matador who allows the bull to sit on his face. I mean, there's that."

"Yes," Isaac said, dismally. "There's that."

"Cheer up. It has to get better." Sturge had finished wrapping the boot in place. Isaac walked on it a little. It seemed to hold. He took another swallow of El Presidente and passed it back.

"Sturge. You ever wonder why all the classic assholes in the world always win?"

"No," Sturge told him.

"What kind of answer's that? What do you mean 'no?'"

"I mean, no. They don't always win. It only seems like they always win."

"What's the difference?" Isaac asked.

"Between what?"

"Winning and looking like you won."

"I don't know," Sturge replied. "But right now you're not doing either.

"True."

"You've had some bad luck."

"Right," Isaac said.

"With the boot."

"Sure."

"And wearing yellow socks," Sturge added.

"And allowing the bull to sit on my face."

"It isn't done."

"Yes," said Isaac.

Chapter 13

The second bull did not wait for encouragement from the men at the gate. It drove into the planks before they had it fully open. There was a cracking sound of splintered wood and the young man in the white shirt sleeves was shoved back into the *calle-jon* as the animal thundered out of the *toril*.

Jaime was out and waiting for it. He flung his cape upward, unfurling it high over his head. But something else caught its eye and it skidded and turned toward the *burladero* containing Isaac and Heinrich. It gathered momentum in its run and slammed its weight into the boards. Isaac could feel the concussion in his back teeth. He could feel the impact of it through the planks. He could feel it in the ground beneath him. The bull continued to drive into the wood barrier as though to get through to Isaac, working his horns one way, then the other, seeking out purchase in the way the planks were laid.

It was black and sweat-stained and wore the Sanchez's colors on a barbed *divisa* that had been stabbed high on its shoulder. When it moved away from the barrier and headed toward Jaime, Issac could see the full size of it. It was not yet three years old, an adolescent animal, not fully grown, but big, big enough to display a full set of muscles that churned, rippled beneath the hide as it moved. Its neck was thick and set solidly into its shoulders. The hump of muscles rising from the neck swelled with anger.

This one was not at all like the first. It was a fair-size fighting bull and wore the colors to prove it.

It gathered speed and drove at Jaime. He made a careful pass, legs splayed, leaning out in a *veronica*. The bull followed the cape around in a wide arc and, skidding some, contained himself to drive in again.

The second pass was better and there was some beauty in it. The third and fourth were beautifully executed and linked together in a sinuous, controlled composition. There was a casual economy of movement that made what he was doing look exceedingly easy. It was not labored or obvious and that could only come from experience. He brought it through twice more and ended with a flourishing *serpentina*, the cape floating out around him.

That was the best of it. He tried working the animal in other parts of the ring, but without much success. It had established a *querencia* near the boards across from Isaac. It was a territory in which he felt more comfortable. It wanted to fight from there. Instead, Jaime turned it away and brought it out across the middle of the ring and stopped it. He did all this as though he were parking a car. He returned to where Isaac and Heinrich stood.

Only then, with the bull stilled, did Isaac come to understand the game old man Sanchez had laid out, had planned from the start when Heinrich had first insulted him over bullfighting when they were at Rafael's. The two animals had been selected carefully.

This, the second, was a dangerous *novillo*. Though young it could very well have been lethal, had it not been for the way its horns were hung. It would have a been a perfect animal otherwise and in time would have been used in a *corrida*, if not for that. The horns were rooted firmly. They were thick set and spaced nicely. But they were curved downwards, sweeping radically down across its face. Even with the defect, they would be damaging. They could be used to batter, mostly. And with the force of his nearly fully developed frame behind the impact, there would be no question how it would feel. The development of the neck was the product of how he'd learned to use the horns in mock combat with his siblings. He had not, Isaac guessed, given up much ground.

He may not have known his limitations. He did not carry them in his gait and in the confident way he took the *barerra*, then Jaime. He had the bearings of a killer. He did not know, yet, that he would have considerable difficulty penetrating with his horns. Though they could wound, the way they were hung made killing with them difficult.

The old man had planned it perfectly. This was never to have been a *tienta*. He did not use cows because he had these two bulls in mind from the start. They would illustrate his point. The *manso*, the first, the tiny, timid beast that had made a fool of Isaac and a hero of Heinrich, was probably not of Sanchez's stock. It had few traits of the fighting bull and none of the esteemed ranch. Sanchez had probably trucked it in from somewhere, hoping that Heinrich, seeing its size and demeanor, would commit himself.

Even if he did not, it would be a visual lesson. Heinrich would be made to truly see a fighting bull. The contrast would make it clear. And if he did commit himself to fighting an animal, he would come to understand what a fighting bull was from best vantage point of the study: he would see the bull as it was meant to be seen, from its own terrain, not from a distant seat in the shady side. He would not be able to watch what this bull did while sipping a cold Carta Blanca and making snide remarks to his girlfriend.

And because of the set of the horns, a condition Heinrich would probably not recognize or fully appreciate, he would probably not be killed if he were foolish enough to go in against it. It would be a mistake, but he wouldn't lose his life over it. He would learn and the education wouldn't cost more than he could afford to pay.

It was a perfect plan and Isaac saw the whole thing. What wasn't going perfectly, so far at least, was his part in it. Sanchez and Jaime had not expected him to be quite such a fool. The comic aspect of his performance was, by contrast, bringing far too much credence to whatever good fortune was keeping Heinrich on his feet. The guests, who had no doubt been primed by Sanchez when he had invited them to this radically modified *tienta*, expected a little more from Isaac. They had expected to see a contest, not a comic opera.

Isaac had never been good at handling expectations. Early on in life he fell short of several. He had been born a distant third to parents who had taken great precautions to end it at two. Like those before him, he was male, despite the odds for an improvement. When the name "Veronica" had to be abandoned, he was named for a wealthy Jewish friend of his father's. He bore the name without resentment, believing, as his father had told him, that the man would one day die and leave something to the family. The expectation was only half realized.

To spare his family further disappointment he made himself scarce by running with a pack of neighborhood kids similarly disenfranchised. He took on the practice not long after he learned to dress himself and could turn the handle of the front door. It was not a permanent exile and since it had been, in a sense, voluntary, he was permitted meals, a bed out of the rain and other amenities. He was treated kindly and fairly. He was not beaten or otherwise abused. The meals were hot and on time and often he was grateful for them.

He had not disliked his family and kept from them as many embarrassments as he could. When he was around, he found them cheerful and self-contained. He'd probably still be eating meals there had he not revealed his intention to become an artist. There were limits to a forgiving nature.

Similarly, Isaac felt that the crowd behind him had reached theirs. But this time he was ready. If not decisively so, he was as ready as he'd get. The humiliating effort with the first animal and the cumulative effects of the El Presidente had made him so. Sort of. Glancing at Heinrich's stricken face as he slid out to meet Jaime, reinforced him. Sort of. He would make some Goddamned passes on this Goddamned bull. Maybe.

"He is all right, this animal," Jaime said to him. "It hooks slightly to the left, but it does not matter."

"OK."

"If you make things simple for yourself, it will be all right."

"OK." Isaac wanted to go out, but Jaime was not through:

"You've seen the horns."

"Yes."

"He knows about them."

"What?" Isaac had been looking at the bull. He was looking at the head, the swollen hump and the massive chest. He was wondering why it wasn't breathing as hard as he was.

"He knows about the horns," Jaime said. "He doesn't act it, but he knows. He has worked them all his life and he knows how to use what he has. He's strong and he's smart. God didn't give him some things, so He gave him other things to make up for what he didn't get."

"OK."

"This one will not sit on your head and then walk away. He will damage you, if you let him. Do not let the bull do all the thinking. And, my friend . . ."

"Yes?"

"*Suerte!*"

It was a long walk to the bull. It stood beyond the medios and was not watching him. It was looking at something off to his left. Its chest, he could see now, was heaving, but it was breathing easily through his nose.

Isaac hoped that he would not be noticed for a while longer, until he got closer, so he kept his cape folded in front of him as he walked kicking the bottom edge with each stride. He did not want the bull to take him with a head of steam, if he could help it. It would be better if he got closer.

But at fifteen yards the animal sensed him, turned his head, and started toward him. Isaac planted his feet and waited. The bull was coming hard, head low. Isaac would not take him carefully. He would make the first pass a good one and take him as he came. He would not move his feet. He would stand firm whether the bull went for the cape or not. He would watch the horns and stand there, whatever the bull had in his tiny mind.

The bull thundered past. It slid under the cape, expelling the warmth of its body like a Greyhound bus. The flank of the animal grazed his thighs, but it was not enough to move him more than an inch or two. His feet remained as they were.

The elation of the successful pass consumed him. For that moment he was on uppers or in love. He wanted to shout and laugh at the same time. The split second of the bull's passing was strung out, attenuated, the curved horns moving at the last possible instant to the cape, driving through, pulling with it miles of undulating, blackened hide. The books had been right about it. It was like a freight train on a straight track. There was the euphoria of standing next to it as it went by. It took forever, and not long enough.

Either Isaac had not brought the edge of the cape around, or the bull had too much momentum and could not turn in the radius it had needed. When it did turn, it had lost him. It wanted him, but could not immediately find him.

Isaac ran toward the animal, closing off the distance between them. He took the bull on its right side, sparing himself the hook if it used it, but the pass was less successful. He had gone too far into its terrain and hadn't expected it to come out so quickly. Though what he did with the cape was awkward, Isaac kept the bull in the cloth. When it turned he brought the bull through the other side. He kept the cape out in front and brought the animal back for the opposite *veronica*. Then he did it again. And again.

Once, the cape caught on a down-turned horn and Isaac felt the force of it in the sockets of his arms. But he held it and by-God brought the bull back through once more. These last passes were not good. He lost his footing and had to sidestep the driving horns more than once. He was worried that the bull would continue to come, that he could not make him stop, that he and the bull were caught in a dance from which neither could extract himself. He worried that he'd get confused, as the bull charged first on one side then on the other. He worried he'd lose track of what to do with the cape. He worried that the animal had gained control of him and was only humoring him with the passes, tiring him, weakening him for the moment when it would take him. The passes were designed to weaken and punish the bull, not the fighter, or so he read. He doubted this particular animal knew that.

His hope rested on the *remate*, the pass which, if he could execute it right, would end the dance and give him a break.

This time when the horns swept past his legs, he yanked hard on the cape, pulling it from the horns, gathering it to him, folding it to his chest. He did not have the strength to do it twice. He could not do any more passes. He could not do anything but stand there with the folded cape and wait and pray that what he'd read about, what he'd seen many times and what he'd practiced in rush hour traffic really worked.

The bull threw its head toward the vanishing tail of the cape, but it was too late. Its momentum carried it forward out of play. It faltered and stopped. It turned to find Isaac. Turned its enormous head. A furious eye in a blood-streaked sea of white sought him out and found him. It lowered its head for a charge. Isaac stood frozen, cape folded, waiting.

The bull was no more than three feet away.

The theory was that the bull saw, all right, but badly. It saw movement mostly and that, to the side of him. The bull had mostly peripheral vision only to work with, and if one stood directly in front of it and was careful not to move, one would not be seen, or if seen, not excite.

That's how the theory went.

It allowed for a lot of things that looked more difficult than they were. Once a bull was properly stopped and even though facing him, the matador could turn his back to the animal. He could walk away with disdain. He would not have to look to see if it followed. It was not foolproof, of course, and depended on whether the bull was fixed in place, truly halted. But mostly it worked. When the matador walked away, he would use his ears. If he were smart and wanted to live, he would listen, first for falling hooves behind him and, failing that, to the crowd. If the crowd screamed, he would know to dive.

This limitation about the bull's vision allows for stunts or *adornos* that are not regarded very highly by the classic fighters. One of them is for a *torero* to kneel in front of a bull and put his head to the horn. It is called the *teléfono* and is popular with those

168

in the crowd who do not know the bull cannot see him anyway. And with those who don't care that the matador has stooped to tricks that have nothing to do with the bullfight.

It is important for one to be close to the animal for a lot of these maneuvers to work at all, as close as Isaac now was to his bull. But the proximity was also the danger. If the bull isn't fixed or doesn't know about the theory and charges anyway, it makes it vastly more difficult to prevent a tragedy. The problem is to get the cape open in time. If the bull decided to charge Isaac, it wouldn't take him long to cover three feet. Even if Isaac had the strength, there was very little time or space to do anything defensive.

Fortunately, the bull was not yet convinced of its target. He sensed Isaac was there, but there was no movement to confirm it. It puzzled him a little and he decided to wait. Tense, poised on the brink of a charge, he would wait for the slightest movement. He could smell this man. Feel him. He only needed to find him.

And the bull told him that. It told Isaac clearly that it knew that he was there and dared him to move. And Isaac answered: he didn't stir.

As frightened as he was, as tired as he was, Isaac saw the moment for what it was. He saw the intimacy of it, the beauty. He acknowledged it with the same rush of euphoria he had experienced with his first pass.

For Isaac, there was no question about what happened.

He had heard about it many times, this thing between man and beast. In the *corrida* it especially happens, though it is reported to occur far more often than it actually does. It's the ability to talk to an animal and hear it reply. It's a rare ability and in the plaza the great ones were said to have it and having it permitted them, in part at least, to be great. Manolete, it was said, had it. Dominguin, but to a lesser extent. A Mexican, Joselito Huerta, had it, but didn't know what to do with it. Arruza had it when he was on the back of his horse. He had more of it when he was fighting on the ground.

El Cordobés, the handsome and flamboyant Spaniard, had that and little else. He abused it in the things he did with the ani-

169

mals, but it permitted him to survive some impossible stunts. You would watch him in a fight and despise him for what he did. You would come to see him, prepared for that. But despite yourself, you would get caught up in what he did and you would be on your feet with the rest. He was a magician, not unlike Nijinsky who, in another discipline, could retain a leap for minutes, or long enough to make you think so. Cordobés, too, was a magician and by talking to the animals and listening to what they had to say, he knew what to expect of them.

Isaac had been allowed a glimpse of how that was. He was grateful for the bull and for the conditions that permitted it to speak and allow Isaac to hear. He doubted it would ever happen again in his life. It had come because he had not thought about it. It had come because he was exhausted and afraid. It had come because there was nothing left for him to do but listen.

And when the bull told him what he would do when he moved, he could swear it came in words. It was not his interpretation of visual signs. It was a knowing, and the knowing came in words. It was not the El Presidente that made it seem so. The Goddamned bull talked to him.

And Jaime had heard it. He came out and took the bull from him.

When the bull turned toward Jaime's cape, the spell between it and Isaac was broken. Only then did he hear the crowd. They were standing and cheering and he turned to see what Jaime was doing with his bull. But he had only pulled it away. He stood near it with his cape folded.

When Isaac turned back, he heard somebody call his name from the bleachers. Someone else called and yelled something he couldn't understand. Then a third started up with the chant: "To-rer-o! To-rer-o!. . . " and others began to pick it up. Even those on the wall, those who ought to know better, were chanting. As he approached the *burladero* and Heinrich, someone reached over the fence and hit him hard on the shoulder. It was one of the Mexican workers, his face crinkled in a grin. "*Torero*," he said reverently.

It was not true, of course, and all of them knew it was as far from reality as things get, but it was offered in the spirit of a good drinking day, as a tribute to the gringo who had not yet killed himself, who had acquitted himself, sort of, of the disaster of the first bull. Isaac knew that, but could not help smile. It crawled up and took over his face and he could not help it.

Heinrich was smiling too, but it was not working quite right. As Isaac slid in next to him he could see that the smile was placed a little too high on one side. Heinrich said something to him but Isaac could not hear above the crowd. Isaac lay the cape across the *barrera* and spent a long time adjusting how it lay. His legs had begun to quake underneath him and he didn't trust walking on them just then. The muscles in them were jumping on him and he took his time smoothing and re-smoothing the cloth. He had to wait for them to quell.

By the time he slid out into the alley the fear and what he'd done with it was coming on him like a main-line rush. It swept him like coke, every vein, vessel within him distended and he could feel the sting of it behind his eyes. He leaned against the wall content to stay with it. He resisted the something that was trying to pull him out of himself. It was Sturge.

He was saying something, grinning through the black thicket of his beard. He held out the flask, this time in full view, and Isaac looked at it as though it had to do with something long ago. Sturge had filled it, somehow, and he tipped it too soon in bringing it to his lips. Tequila ran down the front of him. He took some long swallows and felt it drain down him like hot oil. He could trace the warmth of it to the pit of his stomach. And further. He could feel it in his bloodstream. He could feel it sweep him. He could feel the heat of it in his finger tips as he capped the flask. The looseness in his knees stilled.

It was Heinrich's turn. Isaac would not have to go out again. He had done what he had to do and he could relax. He looked beyond Sturge and into the stands. Memori, her face shaded by the floppy brim of her hat, was in a *barrera* seat just off to the right. She was looking at something just to the left of Isaac and behind him. The crowd had stilled. All of them were looking at the same spot.

Sturge, who had quit talking, also was looking in that direction. Following his gaze, Isaac turned to see that everyone was watching Heinrich. He had not yet gone out.

Jaime had left the bull and was facing the German over the *barrera*. Jaime was doing all the talking. He was watching the bull and talking to Heinrich who listened, head down, nodding. Once Jaime looked over at Isaac, then spoke to Heinrich again. The bull waited, working at the sand with a hoof. A silvery strand of saliva hung from his mouth and caught the sun like a jewel.

Sanchez came over and the two of them talked to Heinrich. The older men who had been with Sanchez crowded in. Isaac could only see the back of Heinrich's head. He could see that he was still nodding.

Heinrich turned to the crowd and appealed to it, smiling upwards, shrugging his shoulders, arms outstretched, a Christ figure.

"He's not going, the shit," Sturge said.

"What?"

"Heinrich. He's not going out."

Someone behind him called out in falsetto, "*Mamarracho!*" The whistles began first from the men on the wall. They carried to the stands and those there joined in them. It was not polite, of course, but they were not guests now. It was a bullfight. At least that was what they were pretending it was. They had it that this was a *mano-a-mano* between two Anglos and that the girl with the white hat was at stake, maybe, or, if not directly so, a party to the outcome.

Though many in the crowd knew better, they only knew it as individuals, and they knew it intellectually. Normally, these were reasonable people. They knew they had been invited to the ranch and to something of a *tienta* and to dinner after. They could see the two men knew nothing of the *corrida*. If you asked them individually, they would tell you it didn't matter what was done, whether one refused to go out and face the bull or not.

But the things that had happened had turned them from individuals into a crowd. They had become a single idea, an expression. There were no longer parts to it. It worked as a whole. It didn't like

172

it that the German was afraid and had appealed to them as individuals, acting like a Christ as though they owed it to him to be forgiving, as though they cared.

The rational side of the crowd was lost to what the afternoon had become. They did not like it that they had cheered the German earlier when the thing that he did was not dangerous, but was only good in comparison. It had been good only when one put alongside the comedy of the other, the one who had made an ass of himself

When that one redeemed himself, sort of, a contest was made. One this good had not been expected. It was shaping up nicely and the crowd knew how important its role was. They had the ability to heighten the contest, to make the thing they were watching more important than it was. That's why they whistled, jeered and stomped their feet in unison, the bleachers reverberating with the protest.

From the crowd's standpoint it was not fair about the German. They had cheered Isaac with him in mind. Isaac had not done all that much. Not even for a gringo. They had given him far more enthusiasm than what was called for. But they knew by doing so they could turn the screws on Heinrich. By cheering Isaac, they had paid the price of admission. Now, just when they had made something of the day, that German son of a bitch took it from them.

Those who knew better understood that this was a casual thing, that neither of the men had faced a bull before and were not technically required to do anything more than what they'd already done.

In the face of that understanding they jeered and hurled insults at Heinrich, who had turned away and did not risk looking at them again. There was a redness at the back of his neck just above the collar of his embroidered shirt. They wanted him out with the bull and thought to shame him. But Heinrich shook his head.

When Jaime approached Isaac, he already knew what he had in mind.

"You need to cape him some more," he said.

173

"Yes," Isaac answered.

Isaac knew the tradition would require that, that the *machismo* thing would be in play. What Jaime was asking him to do was expected. Isaac could understand it. He could even understand why Heinrich, who had not subscribed to any of it, would not risk himself.

"You need to make him pass you a few more times." Jaime said to him gently.

"OK."

"It will be over then. It will be over once you make a few passes."

"Sure." Isaac was thinking "No" and "Go to hell," while he was telling Jaime he would go out again. But still he hadn't moved.

"Cape him some, then let me take him. It will be all right then," Jaime said.

Isaac took the cape Jaime handed to him. He passed Heinrich in the alley. Their eyes didn't meet. He slid into the *burladero*, then stepped out to get the feel of the cape again. One of the *peones* stood between him and the bull. Isaac gripped the cape and moved it to his right, to his left. It seemed heavier than it had been before.

Chapter 14

A piece of the tape that was holding Isaac's boot together had come unraveled. He bent over and ripped it off. When he stood again, Jaime was still next to him.

"You know about him, don't you?"

"The bull?" Isaac asked.

"You know that he is waiting for you. That he wants you more than anybody."

"I suppose."

"Remember, in the thing he does, he is much smarter than you." Jaime had not taken his eye off the bull. "He wants to show you that. He does not like it that you were lucky the first time."

"How do I tell him I'm sorry?"

Jaime ignored him. "You need only to make a showing. Make a few passes and let me have him. They'll be satisfied with that. Keep clear of him."

"I will try my best." It wasn't so much fear that consumed Isaac this time as overwhelming fatigue. He had come down from his high all at once. He had brought the audience with him.

There was a kind of inevitability to what happened next. Most of those watching the fight could see it coming. Those who couldn't would see the inevitability of it later, once the accident came to pass. Then, after the fact, they would shake or nod their heads in recognition, understanding how there was no other outcome possible.

But those who knew in advance, and this included the bull, deprived the moment of any dramatic uncertainty. The only suspense was to see how it would happen and, when it finally did, how bad it would be.

No one had to wait long. The bull did not rush Isaac this time. It waited him out. Waited for him to close the distance between them, waited while Isaac tried to get him to charge, waited for him to shake the cape. It waited while he yelled, while he passed the cape to the other side and shook it there. It waited while he backed off and came again at another angle, until he got careless, until he brought the cape in front of him, until he least expected him to charge.

That's when Isaac saw it coming. He saw the bull had no intention of taking the cape, that it didn't matter that Isaac had moved it clear of himself. The bull had no intention of doing anything other than driving square through Isaac.

The down-curving horns hit him chest high and he was on his back. There had been a lot of other things before he was on his back, but they had happened in such rapid succession they were hard to single out. Anyway, none of what happened after the initial blow was equal to it. What he knew was that he was on his back and that he couldn't breathe and that the bull was trying to work his horns into his stomach. It was working at opening Isaac's stomach the way one worked with the old fashioned can openers. It was clumsy, it was not efficient, but if you kept pumping and digging and prying into the top of the can long enough you'll get the lid open and the spaghetti and meat balls delivered. This was not how Issac wanted to lose his life.

There was a theory covering his current predicament and lying there Isaac considered it. He knew that if he lay still, the bull — if it knew the theory — would soon tire of mauling him, that he would be attracted by the cape that Jaime or one of the *peones* would be throwing at his face. He felt sure that Jaime would have covered the distance at a run. And he knew that if he moved, the bull would continue with him, that the moving excited him further. He knew that if he were moving, the bull would ignore Jaime's cape when it was thrown in front of him, preferring to continue

176

with the man he had felled. He was supposed to lie still and cover his head and wait. He knew that.

This defensive action was based on pretty good science, one upon which still another theory was constructed. But Isaac's respect for science and its theories was diminished by the facts as he saw them. This bull, in the next thrust or two, would disembowel him. There was nothing theoretical about the intent or capabilities of the animal. Isaac had great respect for those who thought up theories. They knew much more about bulls than he. His quarrel was that the theory did not go far enough. It did not cover the exigencies of the stomach.

Contrary to everything he knew about, had read or been told, Isaac reached out and gripped the two horns. It was a stupid thing to do. There is no way a man can wrestle a bull the size of the one bent on exposing Isaac's innards. There is no way one could even hope to deflect it. It was a stupid thing to do, and it may have saved his life.

The bull lifted his head. Isaac, holding the horns, was picked up and deposited on his feet.

Standing there presented some new considerations. None of them could be defined as theoretical. This was fine with him. What he had a need to do was quite clearly objective: he wanted to get from where he was to a safe place. Though the literature was generous and offered wealth of comment about what a bull could or would do to a man standing in front it, it offered only two possibilities to Isaac. Neither was promising. If he let go of the horns and ran, he would never make it to the *barrera*. If he held on, and at the bull's pleasure, he'd be whipped and thrashed like a flag in a high wind.

He caught sight of Jaime coming up on his left. Still holding the horns, he shuffled to the right. He pushed off, hoping the bull would find Jaime the more attractive target.

He had hoped to push the bull's head in the matador's direction. It was impossible, of course. Impossible to believe that he could turn the head or that at that instant the bull would turn of its own to see Jaime. It was impossible that the bull would do all those things and enable Isaac to reach the *barrera*. But it did all the impossible things and Isaac was over the planks hardly touching wood.

The *mozo* who had called him a matador was there and handed him his cape. Isaac looked at it. He did not remember what it was for. Then he was behind the *burladero* again. There, it occurred to him that he had not been breathing, and quite consciously he took his first breath since the spill. The whole episode of being hit, down, worrying about the horns, being lifted up, running, the whole thing had taken hours. He didn't know he was capable of holding his breath that long.

He did the next stupid thing without thinking. He started across the plaza. His intentions, though vague, were plausible enough. He wanted to return to where he'd begun this nightmare, to the *arrastre*, to Sturge and his flask. He had finished with the bull and had done what was expected of him and needed to return to his own *querencia*. All he wanted was a drink. He had forgotten that you could walk around the ring, that if you were not interested in facing a bull, you could walk the alley that circumscribed it. That's what *callejones* are for.

Even with the mistake, his timing was only slightly off. Sanchez had already driven in the jeep. The doors to the *toril* were open. Sanchez was helping the *peones* near the barrera off to his left to herd the bull around the ring and into the tunnel. If Isaac had waited the few minutes it would take Sanchez and Jaime and the others to corral the bull, he could have crossed the ring without incident.

Instead, and in shock, he started out across the sand. The bull looked up from Jaime's cape. It looked away from the approaching jeep. It saw Isaac and started off to meet him half way. It was in no hurry. It's head was still high. It carried itself effortlessly. Unlike Isaac, it did not know it had been in a fight.

Realizing only then were he was, Isaac stopped. Curiously the bull slowed and also stopped. There was fifteen feet of sand separating the two. Jaime had moved in behind the bull, but kept his cape closed. Sanchez stopped the jeep.

What Isaac had done was not irreversible. He had only to wait there for Jaime to take the bull, to move him off, so he could get back behind the *barrera*. But Jaime was making no move to open his cape, to intercede, to shout or otherwise do what a bullfighter was paid to do. And Sanchez, who sat quietly behind the wheel, was making no move to drive the jeep between Isaac and the bull, as anyone who knew these things were dangerous ought to do. Both the men and the bull were looking at Isaac.

With a sinking stomach he remembered why. He did not want to believe it, but he knew exactly why everyone was being so deferential: he was carrying the cape. By where he was and what he carried he was telling everyone that he wasn't through, that he wanted to fight the bull some more. This is why everyone was waiting. The American wanted to make a heroic gesture and they were obliged to let him try.

He had seen it, now that he thought about it, dozens of times. A matador, badly gored, would shake off his *banderilleros* in order to return to the bull. He would fight off his men if they tried to carry him out. He would fight with his fists if necessary to wrest clear of them, so he could limp to the bull. Even if it took holding a *cornada*, holding back the lethal flow of dark blood as it pumps from a thigh wound, holding it with one hand while moving the bull into the *muleta* with the other, he would come to finish what he had started. He would want to continue with the bull. It was his bull and he had the responsibility for it. Sometimes, if he could not dispatch the bull quickly, it was not clear which of them would die first.

It was *machismo ultimo* in the best sense of those words and was what the bullfight was based on. It was how the rules of conduct were written, things were done.

But *machismo* had nothing to do with why Isaac found himself ring center facing the bull that floored him. Standing there, cape at hand, was nothing but a piece of very bad luck.

It wasn't at all what it looked like.

The bull lowered its horns for a charge, but lifted its head again. Slowly.

As before, the blood-streaked eye found him and held him.

179

The bull looked at him for a long time before it spoke. It told him exactly what it intended to do to him once he opened his cape. It told him clearly. And Isaac believed he knew what he was talking about.

Instead, and with his cape folded, Isaac turned. He put his back to the bull. He took the bull at his word and walked away. He walked slowly across the sand toward Sturge and the figure beyond and just above him, the girl in the white hat. It was something he knew the bull would let him do, maybe. He felt that the bull would let him retreat if he did not face him again, maybe. It wasn't a contract, of course, but it was a good deal more than a notion. Preferring certainty, he took what he could get. He prayed he had it right.

As Isaac walked he listened for the bull behind him. He did not look back, even when he heard the falling hooves, the crowd scream. Even when the scream died and in the quiet he could hear the snort of the animal just behind his legs, he didn't look back. He walked a step at a time and the bull followed. It had closed the distance, first to match Isaac's progress and then to slow it.

The bull, so close behind him, was a gravitational force and the mass of it pulling at him made forward momentum difficult. Walking ahead of it was like wading through a bad dream.

It was a long way across the plaza and the bull followed Isaac as though on a short leash. It was a silent procession, the American with one taped foot and the fighting bull that followed him. In honor of the two, no one moved.

It was how cowardly things can sometimes look heroic.

When Isaac slid into the burladero, the bull turned. It did not alter the funereal pace that had been set. It turned in the silence and walked out of the plaza the way it had come.

The ranch hand in the torn white shirt slammed the gates behind it. The noise of that resounded like a clap of thunder. It took another moment before the crowd was ready to react to what it had seen. By then Isaac was already uncapping Sturge's flask.

Before he could get it to his lips a crowd of workers who had spilled into the *callejon* began to wrestle him. He was pulled off his feet.

He tried to fight them, tried to save Sturge's flask, but there were too many and he was too weak. Someone came under his legs. He was lifted upwards, almost dropped, then others came to support the first. They wanted a *vuelta*, to give him a tour of the ring.

On the shoulders of two men he could see the stands. Those there were on their feet. They were making as though they were shouting, waving, yelling out to him, but the sound, for some reason, had not yet reached him. Memori was there. Her hat was off and she was mouthing something to him. She was excited and she was trying to tell him something, but he was turned away.

Those who carried him sought to bring him down the *callejon* and out into the ring, as they might a matador who had done something important. But the effort soon dissolved. Those who had lifted him to their shoulders, reconsidered. They were, after all, looking a little foolish. The man they carried was not in a bloodied suit of lights and he was not hoisting the severed ear of a dead bull. The gringo had done nothing, really. When you thought about it and were not caught up with the cheering and the pretending that what he had done was worth remembering, you were not sure you wanted to carry him, or to be seen carrying him, if it were the wrong thing to do. And when it was considered in the light of a real bullfight, what he had done did not stand up. The two supporting Isaac and the others supporting them allowed him to slide off. Isaac was permitted to tuck his shirt in, to straighten, to walk back. By the time he heard the noise of the crowd it had calmed some.

Sturge was there, grinning.

"It wasn't bad. They wanted you to die, but still it wasn't bad."

The crowd had quit clapping. The handkerchiefs, those few he had seen flutter, were no longer in sight. Most of those who moved down toward the exit were guests of a ranch party again. They were heading for their cars so they could return to the house. Memori had left her place in the bleachers. Neither she nor Heinrich were in sight. A dozen kids had taken control of the plaza and were noisily fighting one another for any residual moments of attention.

"Are you OK?" Sturge asked. "I thought you were really hurt until you came out again."

"Me too."

"What made you come out again?"

"Made me come out?" Isaac was not paying attention. He had been thinking why it was he could not find Memori. He realized Heinrich could not have stayed. He could not have faced dinner and the party after what he'd done, or hadn't done. He and Memori would have gone back. Not seeing her was bothering him much more than it should have. It took away a lot of what had happened. He felt depleted. He remembered that she had been trying to tell him something from the stands.

"Heinrich left?" Isaac asked.

"It was a great parting. You ought to have seen it."

"Did Memori say anything?"

"She had a lot to say."

"I mean to me. Did she say anything to you about me before she left."

"She didn't leave."

"She didn't leave?"

"Are you hard of hearing?"

"You mean she's here?"

"Sanchez wanted to get to the house before his guests, Sturge said. "He took her in the jeep."

"What about Heinrich?"

"You really don't hear so well. I told you. He left. Went back alone. They had a great and public fight. He was trying to get her to come with him. She wanted to stay. They had a good row. He's standing down here shouting up. She's up there shouting back. Great theater. When he couldn't get her to leave, he stormed off. There was considerable applause for his going, or for Memori's part in it, or maybe it was directed toward you. About the same time you, in your wisdom, had come out again to collect your bull."

"You're kidding."

"About your coming out again? I wish I were. It doesn't speak well for your judgment."

"I mean about Memori."

"Isaac, you know how these things work. There's a great precedent in all of this. Ask anyone. What else are pretty women for?"

"You *are* serious." The grin crawled up and overtook Isaac and he couldn't keep it down. It was a foolish grin and it swept his face. Sturge saw it.

"For Christ sake, I said she'd be at the house. I didn't say she was going to marry you."

"Did you take the pictures?"

"What?"

"The camera," Isaac said. "Did you get me with the bull?"

"Yes."

"Good."

"I got you with the first one," Sturge said. "I was too worried to get you with the second."

183

Chapter 15

Isaac woke to the ticking of a clock he couldn't see and to a throat raw with snoring. He was lying on his back in a strange bed and he was alone. Being alone wasn't unusual, but a ticking clock was. He tried to piece his world together from the dark within which he found himself, but there were few clues. He didn't own a clock and the room was too quiet for it to be his own. Also it smelled of furniture polish.

His first clue came when he attempted to turn on his side. The pain in his chest was sharp and it startled him. He took in a half breath against it and the noise he made seemed to come from someone else. He lay quietly in order to collect himself. Wherever he was and however he came to be there would take sorting out little by little.

He started with the pain, testing his limbs one by one. He did not own a piece of anatomy that did not hurt. He postulated some events that could account for how he felt. He had fallen from somewhere: the roof of a house, a tree, a cliff. Whatever was left of his cognitive abilities did not respond to any of these possibilities. He tried some others: he'd been crushed under a large boulder, had been buried in the collapse of a tall building, had been hit by a truck.

The last thought was close enough. His central nervous system began to fire. He got from truck to bull to Memori to Sanchez to dinner and to here in an expanding progression of synapsed nerve impulses that scrolled through the day and got him to his bed, on his back, in the dark, alone, tasting the socks of an infantry division and feeling like he'd been hit by that truck, feeling like it had been a large one, carrying a load, maybe of black walnut, downhill, with the brakes gone.

The next thought overrode everything that came before it. Memori was waiting for him in a room nearby. That she was waiting for him to come to her bed got him to sit up in the darkness in his own. It hurt him to do so, of course, but not all that much.

That's why, he remembered now, except for what remained of his boots, he was dressed. They had agreed. He was to wait until the family and those of the guests who were staying over had gone to bed, and when it was safe he would come to her room. He had not meant to fall asleep. He had really not meant to do that, but the dinner party had been a good one and he had had far too much too drink. Now he had no idea how long he had slept. If the curtains were open, it couldn't have been long. There was no sign of dawn and the party had gone on late.

It had been a triumph in every respect. All of them had been even more deferential than before. They had asked questions of him and talked about what they'd seen him do. When he deprecated his part in it all, they did not want to hear it. He was accused of being modest. He was given drinks and he and Memori were escorted from one group to another by the old man, who presented them as a couple, as belonging together. And the drinks made him believe it, as it made him believe that he had done something in the ring that he could be proud of. They spoke to him as though he were one of them and that what he'd done was something most Americans would not have understood or wanted to do, but that he had done it, they said, in a way men here or at the ranch, or in San Miguel, or — hell— in all Mexico would appreciate. How Isaac had performed was a credit to the rest of Latin America and the homeland, Spain. And would he drink to that? They did not take the compliment to a pan-global dimension, which Isaac by then was quite prepared to accept. In fact, by the time the evening drew to a close, he had become a little miffed that the deed would not recieve world-wide adulation.

Much of the time Isaac and Memori were left together. She had greeted him at the door when he and Sturge arrived from the

185

ring. She and Sanchez were together and she held out both of her hands to Isaac and brought her face near to be kissed on both cheeks. After, she kept hold of his hands and made him look at the way her upper lip was shaded against the fullness of her lower lip, even in a wide smile you could see that, and how the lips did not match up, not perfectly. If you looked for it you could see the slight scar that had drawn the upper lip slightly and provided it, even behind the broad and beautiful smile, that hurt look he'd seen earlier.

"You were wonderful," she said, "I didn't think you would go back after what the bull had done. I was — we all were — so worried. I thought you might have been hurt. I didn't expect you'd go back to it."

"It wasn't what I expected either."

"You will feel it, Isaac," Sanchez said. "But not until later. Later it will hurt a little. Now you are too happy, am I right?" He spoke as the proprietor for all that had been.

"You'll hate me," Memori said, "but the best part was when your boot was torn. You looked lost. You looked so miserable with everyone laughing." She laughed herself, recalling it, but she held to his hands. "You looked . . . You looked like — I told you you'll hate me — like a little boy. I wanted to come take you home."

"I wish you had." Looking at her, Isaac held back telling her how much he meant what he said.

"Nonsense," Sanchez said. "Isaac, you must never listen to women in these matters, even when they're as charming as this one."

"Especially," Sturge said, bowing to Memori. "Especially when they're as charming as this one. I'm glad you stayed. Isaac would have been hard to live with if you hadn't." He brought his lips to her hand. "You can ride back with us when the time comes. My car's a step up from what you're used to, but you'll get to sit on Isaac's lap."

"That wouldn't be at all proper, I'm afraid," the old man said. "And absolutely unnecessary. Memori has agreed to stay over so that she can see the ranch in the morning. I hope you'll do the same. We have plenty of room here."

"I'd like that," Isaac said. When Memori released his hands, he felt something drain away, though she still looked up at him, smiling. Fearing he would involuntarily reach for them again, he folded his arms in front of him, winced at the pain in his chest, and let them drop rather conspicuously to his side.

No one had mentioned Heinrich, even as they made arrangements to work around him. Isaac was surprised to find her so calm. She was not looking troubled about his departure, though it was hard to read her. Clearly she had chosen to ignore it, probably the only course open to her. If it had been, as Sturge said, a public row, any reference to it would be both painful and unnecessary.

"I regret I can't stay beyond dinner," Sturge told Sanchez. "The car, you know. She's not used to staying in the country, overnight, I mean. I'll have to get her back."

"A car like that, I can understand," the old man said, drawing them all inside. "French, isn't it?"

"Top of the line," Sturge said, "but very temperamental. Won't take any abuse. Comes from a family who fought in the Resistance. She's out of Bordeaux, car country."

"I'd heard about the wines."

"They do some wine as well."

Isaac swung his feet off the bed and found a floor beneath him, one the darkness in the room kept him from seeing. He stood slowly. The looseness of the joints that supported him made taking his first step a tentative one. The cold floor under him seemed to give way like rubber ice. He found one of his boots on his second step. It was a long way down to pick it up. Sweeping his hands out across the wooden floor, he found the other, the taped one. The socks were inside. He stood. It was longer going up than it had been going down.

He did not know why he had to bring his boots except, maybe, that he was checking out of one room for another. When Sanchez's sister took them to their rooms, she had looked at the dirty tape

187

with disgust. Maybe it would be best to keep them with him. For Señora Sanchez, tidiness, he surmised, took a back seat only to propriety. Without saying a thing, she made it clear fraternization was unthinkable. She was the woman Memori had been talking to when Sturge and he first arrived at the pre-fight reception.

That Memori had gotten her to talk at all was the surprise. Later, as they followed the angular woman through a labyrinth of hallways, Isaac's attempt at small talk failed to rouse whatever good humor might reside behind the chilly facade. She wore her hair in a severe bun. The thin stalk of her neck rose out of a waist-coat that fitted her like a corset. That and her martial bearing as she strode down the hall in serviceable shoes gave her the air of a prison matron at lock up. She only needed a large set of keys on a wire loop. The religious iconography on the walls didn't help. They had passed dozens of tortured renditions of Christ, each bloody account contained within a dark, thick and elaborately molded frame, one or two of carved and intertwining serpents.

They stopped at Memori's room first. He was permitted to shake her hand and bid her goodnight. Her glance did not seal her earlier pledge that they would sleep together, but that might have been risky. The warden, he guessed, wouldn't have missed the slightest hint of sexual possibility. The Old World was alive and well on the Sanchez preserve. Neither the old man or his sister were willing to come to terms with the liberated times.

At the end of the hall, two doors from Memori's room, Isaac was left in his own, and to contemplate a print which was mounted above his bed, Ribera's *Boy with a Club Foot*, circa 1640. He was tired and beyond caring whether this piece of whimsy was also or-chestrated by the old man. He pulled off his boots, turned off the light and felt his way to the bed where he would wait out a more forgiving hour.

Now, standing in the dark holding his boots, Isaac sought the door he had entered. That, he figured, would be easier than find-ing a light. It was dark enough to develop film and he feared knocking into something. He shuffled forward, groping the dark with his free hand. He touched a wall and traced it to a dresser. He

188

tipped, but caught something tall and metallic. He was able to right it and allow it to stand on its own. He was going the wrong way, if he remembered right.

He moved back, still feeling the wall until he came to the door frame, the door and the handle. He turned it. He would not have been surprised if it were locked.

The hall was lit dimly, but it was a large improvement over where he'd been. Hearing no sounds, he stepped out and closed his door quietly. To his left were two doors, the second, Memori's.

At her door he listened and waited for the bravado, which had carried him to this point, to catch up. It had been an unlikely day and his part in it had been unlikelier still. Since it wasn't good judgment, but luck, which got him this far, he thought to take this next step with some circumspection. Had he really won permission to sleep with this beautiful girl? Had she said he would be welcome if he came to her room? Or had he been drunk and hopeful?

It had been after dinner before she finally brought up Heinrich. He remembered how they had found some privacy outside on one of the terraces. The starless sky was washed in India ink. A distant smell of horses hung in the damp air. More proximate was the smell of sage and sweet grass, some jacaranda and the delicate perfume he'd inhaled when he'd greeted Memori at the door. They sat together on a ledge and she looked away.

"He's not all bad, you know."

"Heinrich?"

"He's not, really. When you know him, you see that he's not as sure of himself as he makes out."

"Are you sorry you didn't go back with him today?" Isaac asked.

"No. I'm not sorry about that." Memori was speaking quietly, as though to somebody on the opposite side of her, someone who wasn't present but ought to have been. "I'm sorry about the way it happened. It was going to happen. I'm just sorry about the way it did."

"Why was it going to happen?"

"It had been a long time coming. He's very demanding. You

189

can probably guess that. It's his way. He grew up believing the world was hired help. His parents certainly contributed to the idea. They dote over Heinrich. It's terrible."

She turned to Isaac, looked down, picked at something on the ledge between them. "I knew it, of course. I even loved him for it. The arrogance. The way he took over, commanded. He took on art the same way. He's so positive, so sure. He's convinced a lot of people that he's right."

Isaac said: "He may be, you know."

"You think so?

"No."

"You hate what he's doing," she said.

"I hate it more that he gathers so many around him, that he's so damned popular. There's a climate for this stuff and I hate that."

"He says that he speaks to that . . . climate or whatever it is."

"These are his times, all right," Isaac said. "Maybe he ought to be heard. Who knows? Who's to say he's wrong?"

"I thought that too. I really thought that would, well, excuse it. But you don't know him. He's after something else, I think. He's always talking about the purity thing. He sees what he's doing as pure and honest. All the rest of it, in his words, is 'sentimental shit.' That's what he calls classical music, the dance. We had arguments about it. The last — a big one — was yesterday morning, when I bought your picture."

"He was not happy, I take it," Isaac said.

"Worse than that. He saw it — he sees it — as some kind of personal affront. He sees it as if I had, you know, run off and . . ."

"Slept with someone?"

"Yes." She smoothed her skirt, looked down at her hands. "He sees everything in sexual terms. He was furious. I've never seen him so angry as he was this time. He saw me as a traitor, I guess. And . . . well, he's very destructive."

"Did he . . . does he hit you?"

"He's hit me before. I got over it. It's worse than that. I've got to tell you this. I'm sorry. Isaac, he tore up your painting."

190

"He tore it up."

"Yes.

"He tore up the painting?"

"Yes."

"Why, for Christ sake? I mean, why would he do that to a painting?" But Isaac knew why. How could he not? It just never had been so personal before. He'd read about what Heinrich did to paintings. How long had he been reading about it? Recently, there had been a feature in Time, a sequence of photos: Heinrich overpainting . . . who was it? Last night there were the slides, he'd heard him discuss it. It was in the abstract.

"Your decision to stay today," Isaac asked, "It's part of that, isn't it. It's because of what he did to my painting. You wanted to tell me what he did."

"Yes," she said. "It's partly that. I wanted to explain, but I didn't know — don't know — how. If I hadn't bought your painting it wouldn't be destroyed. He wouldn't have ripped it into pieces. In a way, I did it. I'm responsible for that happening. But there's another part. This one's also hard to explain."

"Try."

"I've stayed because, well, I want to . . . I want you to come to my room tonight."

"You do?" He was incredulous.

"It has nothing to do with what Heinrich did . . . or maybe it has a lot to do with it, I don't know. Mostly, I've stayed because of you. Because of who you are. I think I know that. I think I know who you are."

"How? By what happened today? Memori, you've got to know. I'm a coward. Everything that happened was an accident. I don't usually do these things. I'm not a hero. I was lucky. The bull was in on it."

She laughed, then looked at him for a long time. "You don't always have to go by the rules, you know."

"What do you mean?"

"You're too honest. Don't you know that? There are no rules about that anymore. Nobody tells the truth."

"I can't help it," Isaac said. "I don't think I'm smart enough."

Memori put her hand on his knee, leaned in and kissed him on the cheek. He turned to embrace her, but she held up her hand. "Please, I want to explain this, if I can. I thought about this when we met, that day in the rain. I wanted us to be together then. I don't mean I wanted the sex of it. That's not what I felt, what I feel. That's not the important part.

"You were there, all wet, in the rain," she said. "I watched you trying to get all your bags in out of the wet. I watched you as you tried to move against everyone, to get inside. You didn't get mad or yell or push someone. If you did that, everyone would have seen you. They'd have made room. You just kept at it, trying to move in until someone finally stepped away.

"And today," she continued, "I think you know that they were trying to use you, to get back at Heinrich. But you kept going. You went beyond what they were doing. Beyond Heinrich. You believe in this thing."

"The bullfights? In a way, I guess I do. I believe in life. It's part of that, I think, the ritual, the beauty. You heard what I said at Rafael's the other night."

"But that was talk."

"Yes."

"Heinrich had talked, too," she said, "yet he didn't believe in what he was saying."

"How do you know?"

"He was there today. He was drawn in. He allowed himself to be drawn into something he doesn't care about, something he hates. His arrogance did it."

"You helped him, as I remember. You insisted he come."

"Yes," she said, and in a lower voice, "but he came."

"You knew he couldn't stay," Isaac said. "He couldn't come back to the house, not after what happened. You knew that, I think. They never would have let him forget that he was afraid to go out. They would have done that by not talking about it. By avoiding it, they would make it obvious. It doesn't matter that he did not want any part of the game, that he doesn't subscribe to any

192

of it. They would make it important. He would be made to remember that he didn't go out for the bull. You're doing the same thing. You're punishing him. You're a part of that, a part of the crowd."

"Maybe," she told him evenly, "maybe that's true. But I know Heinrich. We don't matter with him, Isaac. Not even me. He shrugs us off, like the critics. He does exactly what he wants. He doesn't care about anyone else, about *anything* else."

"Maybe," Isaac said, "but it's different down here. They can make you care. They've got a fine old culture. They've had a long time to develop it. They know how to make you feel bad when they need to. They're real good at it. They still got families here, know how to work together. Like this afternoon. They used you. They used you against Heinrich. Used me."

"How?"

"You heard them today. They showed you that they knew he should have gone out, even if he was afraid. Whether important to him or not, they showed you the thing they knew about him. If he came back to the house, they would damage him some more in your eyes. And that would be enough. You'd carry the knowing, and it would come up later sometime in an argument, maybe, or when you thought you'd forgotten about it."

"Is that why you went out even when you were afraid, Isaac, and then you went out again after that?"

"It's how they see things and maybe I agree. Those rules again. Maybe we need them. Maybe we need the structure. Even if you'd gone back to town with him after the fight, they'd have won. Down here they still have rules."

"But you like their way."

"Yes, I want to believe in it, if it's still possible," he said.

"Why?"

"Maybe I'm Victorian. I still believe there ought to be civilization."

"You think all this today was civilized?"

"It's one up over Haight Asbury or SoHo. I don't know, Memori. We can't go back. I'm not saying we can return to the 19th

193

Century. But neither can we abandon humanity, give it up, for what? Expediency? A little money? They still live life here. They believe in something. They haven't yet come to painting over Cezanne. Who's the more civilized?"

"But, Isaac, they're shooting students. They're shooting them in Mexico City."

"I'm not saying we can learn anything from governments. Ours has got us paving over a very large rice paddy in Indo-China. I'm talking people and whatever it is that links them to their past."

"You believe in people," she said

"I think so."

"You're not sure?"

"No."

"That's why I want to sleep with you," she said.

"Because I'm not sure?"

"Yes."

"That gets me to sleep with you?" he asked.

"That and what you did today."

"Because I won?"

"You didn't win, Isaac. We both know that. It's because you did something that was important to you, and I want to do the same."

"You want to fight a bull."

"I'm serious, Isaac. I'm saying that I want to do something important for me."

"Sleep with me?"

"More. I want to leave Heinrich."

"And sleeping with me is going to help you do that?"

"I hope so, but there's more to it. There's you."

"The bullfighter, right? Memori, I told you I was scared, wished I hadn't come. Honest. I'm afraid of bulls, afraid of jealous and powerful boyfriends and, God help me, I'm afraid of you."

"I believe you," she said quietly.

Isaac stood, put a foot on the terrace ledge and looked out into the night. Without a moon the hills and the distant trees along the creek were not fixed in any distinct position. It was a tonal landscape, a Whistlerian study in mauves and grays and greens with values so proximate that one thing was almost another and that thing very close to something else.

For a long time she didn't speak. She stood and put her arms around his neck. "Isaac, it's because I want to give you something."

"And after, you'll walk away."

"I don't want to walk away." She spoke to his shirt and he pulled her as close as they had been under the arcade. She seemed more slender now, even more vulnerable. Though this time she arched her back a little.

An overhead light washed the terrace. The door opened. Sanchez stepped into the blinding illumination. He held both hands out and at shoulder height and shook them like Al Jolson winding up a rendition of "Mammy."

"Please. This is embarrassing, but please. This is not right." Sanchez's had startled them. They stepped back from each other reflexively. He wagged his head as well as his hands.

"I'm sorry," he continued, "I know you are my guests. It was entirely my fault and you must not think you've done anything wrong. I will take responsibility for all of it. It's not your fault you're out here alone, that you're without chaperons. Let's call it an accident. Let's be done with it. Please, let's go inside."

He held the door for the liberated Americans. Memori passed through it first. For what may be the fifteenth time in three months, Isaac forgot where he was. He did not duck as he entered. The lintel caught him just above the bridge of his nose. To no one in particular, he apologized.

Now, boots in hand, Isaac stood before another, this one Memori's, wondering whether he should knock. He didn't wonder long. Hearing what might be someone coming, he quickly stepped inside and closed the door quietly behind him. The room was as dark as his own. The light from the hall had enabled him to do little more than locate the bed before it was eclipsed. He stood listening. The sound in the hall diminished. A door closed distantly.

From the bed Memori breathed steadily through the mouth. A less charitable audience might have accused her of snoring.

Isaac whispered her name, but he couldn't get it high enough out of his chest to be heard. He cleared his throat and tried again. "Memori."

She breathed on, her quiet snore catching once in her throat, then resuming again.

He had slept too long. It was late. Doubtless she thought he had decided not to come. He could leave now, let her sleep and explain in the morning. Or he could crawl into bed with her, if that wouldn't startle her. Maybe he would sleep quietly alongside of her, not moving, until morning, when he would then move close to her and, depending on what she wore, if she wore anything at all, he could . . . Or lying next to her he could wake her just as soon as he got into bed. He would hold her warmth to his and, while everyone slept, they could . . .

"Memori?"

Isaac put his boots down quietly and took off his slacks and his boxer shorts. He was more than slightly aroused. Not wanting to approach her as a picador bearing a lance, he tried to think of other things. He stood on the bare floor in some part of the darkened room holding his clothes and wondering where to put them. When he slipped through the door he had not seen the room or any furniture in it. He needed something on which to drape his slacks. They were his best trousers and he'd be wearing them in the morning. He didn't want them wrinkled. He could feel around for a chair, but didn't want to tumble over something. He would simply line up the creases, fold the slacks and lay them next to his boots. Then he'd find the bed.

But he forgot about his loose change. In Mexico the practice was to carry a lot of it, since the bills of low denomination were oily, damp with the sweat of labor, and clumsy to handle. When he held his trousers by the cuffs, the coins spilled out across the wood floor. One of the heavier coins, maybe a five-peso piece, spurted out from the spill and set off across the room. It did not hit anything and wound its way around him in a long arc. He guessed it went under the bed and out again. It tightened its circle and left off in a metallic drum roll.

"Memori?" She was no longer snoring. "It's me," he said in a whisper. "It's Isaac." Realizing how foolish that sounded — how many others would she be expecting at this hour — he added, "Are you asleep?" That was worse. No one could sleep through the racket he'd made.

Still holding his pants and shorts, he crossed to and felt for the bed. He could not quite make her out. She had been sleeping on the distant side of it. She was only a dark shape and it was hard to tell whether she was looking at him or facing away. He gently pulled down the blanket to get in.

"Memori?"

The figure said something in a calm and deliberate voice. It did not come in a whisper, but neither was it shouted. However it was spoken, the sound struck Isaac like a high power line that had fallen across his shoulders. The voice did not come from Memori. It was several octaves below and a good deal less melodic than what he had been looking to hear. It spoke a language, but the meaning was secondary to the fright. At first he could not put it together. Frozen in place, he could not make any sense of it.

The figure had not moved. Neither had Isaac. The old man had to repeat what he said before it registered:

"It would be better, Isaac, if you slept in your own room."

If there were something he could say in the circumstance, some reasonable explanation for wanting to crawl into the old man's bed while calling out the name of one of his guests, Isaac could not think of it.

He could not, in fact, think of anything. If he spoke he would have to debate his own presence in the room and there weren't many arguments one could offer. He settled for an early and hasty retreat. Without comment Isaac turned and set off in the dark towards the door. He carried his clothes in one hand and his pride in the other. He laid claim to a single hope. It was not terribly promising. If he shut up and got out, maybe Sanchez, in his grogginess, would think he had a dream, a bad one to be sure, but

197

nonetheless a dream. Isaac would be an apparition that the old man would come to dismiss with the light of day, a figment, maybe, of too much to drink. What other explanation could there be?

Sure. Isaac would insist on it. Denial was always the best defense. He would be incredulous the next day when confronted. He would demand an apology if the old man dared accuse him of coming to his room. Coming to his room with a hard on! Can you imagine? Damn right he'd be mad at such a suggestion. What kind of man did he think he was?

Isaac, by good luck, found the door easily, let himself out into the hall. More good fortune found it empty. He closed the door firmly, quietly and with the indignity appropriate to a ghost that had been wronged.

The thought that such behavior was beneath consideration got him back to his own room and into his bed. He was a long while calming down. He spent it going over his story, creating and delivering his lines. His dignity, wasn't that at stake? Weren't we talking about an old man of eighty, maybe, waking from a dream? Just who had come to his room? Could the old man see? He had called out Isaac's name, but that was a guess. A drunken old man had seen a ghost. It was he who had dropped some change on the floor and had gone to bed. An old man and some fitful dreams. How else could it have been? He really ought to watch his drinking.

With that, Isaac almost dropped off to sleep. Had he not recalled where he left his boots, he might have succeeded in doing so. Dawn was painting his room before exhaustion and sleep simultaneously overtook him.

Chapter 16

When Isaac opened his bedroom door in order to track down his boots late that morning, he was delighted to discover that they had been placed neatly side by side in front of it, as though they had been put there to be shined. The good fortune saved him the indignity of walking around in his bare feet and asking about them. The boots were not a subject he'd want to raise. They had been a source of embarrassment once. Revisiting the subject would not help to diminish that.

He had braced himself for a confrontation with Sanchez at breakfast. It would be of his own making this time. He had enough of being used as an unpaid entertainer. He was certain now that he did not have the wrong room last night. He was the butt of a long and elaborate joke. And he'd had enough.

Though he expected that he might face a crowd at the breakfast table, and had readied himself to have it out with Sanchez anyway, the *criada* led him to an interior patio where two settings had been placed. His camera case, which Sturge had left for him, was in one chair. Beneath his plate was a note from Sanchez:

Dear Isaac:

> *I hope you slept well. Please forgive my absence this morning. It is unforgivable, I realize, but I call upon you, my good friend, to understand.*

*I have arranged a car and a picnic lunch for you and Memori.
I've asked my sister Graciella to show you a splendid site. Please
don't disappoint us. Later Juan, my driver, will take you back. My
house, meanwhile, is yours.*

Abrazos,

Alfredo.

Memori and the warden came out just after he'd finished the
letter. They appeared quickly and behind him. Before he had a
chance to stand, Memori bent to kiss him on the cheek.

"Isn't this wonderful?" She turned to model a crisp white peasant blouse she wore off the shoulder, and a full cotton skirt of mut-
ed stripes. The oranges and reds and purples danced against the
greenery of the potted and hanging plants behind her. As she
turned, an edge of lace played at her knees.

"And this," she said excitedly. "What do you think of this?"

She bent from the waist in front of him. Her blouse did not fit
snugly. Her small breasts were clearly visible within the shadows of
the cotton shirt. They were rounded gracefully with bright pink
nipples, but Isaac did not know what to say about them. They were
beautiful, but he did not know why he was being invited to discuss
them. It took a moment to determine that she was referring to her
hair which he now saw had been braided in the traditional way and
put up at the back of her head.

She stood and reached for the warden's hand and brought her
toward the table. The woman still wore her penitentiary grays,
though her face had loosened considerably since last night.

"All of it is courtesy of Graciella," Memori told him. "She
spent ages with my hair, but don't you just love it?"

And he did. He loved all of what he had seen. He stood to
help her with her chair. As she sat he automatically looked down
again for her breasts, but this time the lip of her blouse concealed
them. When he straightened he caught the eye of his chaperon.
She had been watching him and did not care that he knew.

"We're having a picnic, Isaac! Graciella knows this marvelous spot by the river. There's some old ruins and it sounds just beautiful!"

The older woman was still looking at Isaac. When she turned to her other guest, her face softened considerably. She chose to speak to her, as though he were furniture.

"It is too soon for the picnic. Please take some coffee, some juice of the orange or papaya. A roll, maybe. I'm sorry that my brother is gone to business. Especially he wanted to show you the ranch, the pastures and the animals. I hope another time for that."

When she excused herself and before she marched out, her eyes swept over and past Isaac. If he had been suffered, it was very briefly.

"I see you've made a friend," Isaac said, taking his seat across from Memori.

"She's really quite nice. Doesn't like men, I guess."

"The feeling's probably mutual. You moved last night. What happened?"

"Oh, I'm sorry, Isaac. Just after you left Graciella came back with Sr. Sanchez. He was very apologetic. Said the maid had made up an uncomfortable room. Took me off to a wing on the other side of the house. A beautiful room with a sunken tub. Absolutely spectacular."

"I had a spectacular time looking for you," Isaac said.

"I'm so sorry. But there was no way I could get word to you. I know you're disappointed, as I was."

"It was more than disappointing. I almost went to bed with Old Man Sanchez. It was his room, I guess, and in the dark I couldn't see."

"He was in the room when you opened the door?"

"He was in the bed as I was trying to climb into it."

She watched him, holding back her laughter with a hand at the mouth. But she had to wait while a *criada* appeared and served them fresh fruit, coffee and some pan dulce. There was a covered plate of warm tortillas. Isaac found some butter and started with

201

that. Memori waited until the *criada* had gone and until she closed the door leading to the kitchen.

"What did you do?"

"What could I do? He told me to go to my room and I did."

"He had to have known you would come," she said. "Isaac, how do you get into all this trouble? I'm sure that wasn't his room."

"I thought about that this morning."

"It was a guest room, very plain, very austere. I believed him when he said there was a mistake about my staying there. I'm sorry, Isaac, but you've got to admit it is a little funny."

The laughter she tried to stifle indicated that she found it more than just a little. Her laugh was contagious and once Isaac caught it he became as infected with it as she. It took a long time for Isaac to recount the details of the episode in Sanchez's room. It took getting over one detail before you could get to the next. Sometimes he would get to a part of the story and couldn't get the next word out of his mouth. She'd want her to hear it but they already were laughing too much. He had to wait and choke back his mirth, pull it back down so he could talk, but the laughter kept bubbling up, getting in the way. When he got to the part about leaving his boots in the middle of the floor, neither could contain themselves.

They tried not looking at each other and that was a little better. They could eat a little or sip coffee. It would be all right until one glanced at the other. Then they would start up again.

When they had calmed down and had eaten some, Memori could look at him without laughing. She smiled and watched him for a long time.

"Do you know what I just love about you?"

He did not and shook his head, thinking about her use of the word love, and liking that it was applied to him.

"You're hopeless, Isaac. That's what I love. You're a marvelously talented painter. You're sensitive. You're thoughtful. And you're hopeless. You don't belong to this world. You really don't fit, do you?"

"Nice of you to say."

"Oh, I'm sorry," she told him, watching his eyes. "I don't mean it in that way. I mean it in the best way. I mean that you're not a part . . . of what? Of reality, I guess. I don't think you're a part of that, somehow. Your ex-wife, growing up alone . . ."

He remembered now that he had done a good part of the talking the night before. It was unusual for him to be open and he wondered what it was about her that brought him out.

"I will make it up to you," she said. Her eyes did not move away from his. She smiled a little. "I'll begin by making up for last night. I'll begin just as soon as I can."

"I wish we could begin now," he said.

"Soon, Isaac. We will begin soon."

The maid came and refilled their coffees. Again they waited until she left.

"Have you thought about Heinrich?" Though he did not want her to talk about him, he was compelled to find out where he stood with her. He took account of the stages common in his romantic relationships. Insecurity was the stage just before the big fall.

"He called," she said.

"When?"

"This morning." She was going to leave it there.

"What did he say?"

"He wanted to go back."

"To New York?"

"He wanted to pick me up here, so that we could go. He had already packed. He had the suitcases in the car."

"What did you tell him?" Isaac asked.

"I told him no. I told him I didn't want to go back, that we would discuss it later. I told him to wait and he said he would."

Isaac knew that she was reciting the content of their talk and withholding the flavor.

"But he was mad?"

"Yes. But it was better than yesterday. He seemed less mad. More anxious to get me back."

Isaac remained unsatisfied. She spoke of the morning's phone call off-handedly. She didn't seem bothered, though again he found her hard to read. At some point she had been committed to the relationship and now that it was breaking apart she didn't seem all that concerned. Only a few moments ago she was laughing uncontrollably.

"How do you feel about it, about him?" Isaac asked. "I mean, have you changed your mind about wanting to leave him?"

"I haven't changed my mind. Isaac, let's not talk about this. We have a beautiful day ahead and a picnic. I don't want to talk about Heinrich. I want to talk about you and me and I want to laugh some more. When we get back I will tell him what he must know. He's mad now but he will get over it. He'll go back to SoHo alone."

"You're sure?"

"Isaac, you get so serious. I like it better when you're laughing. You worry too much. I haven't changed my mind. I wish I could show you that. I wish that we could go somewhere so that I could show you. I could make it so you wouldn't worry." She put a hand on his wrist and squeezed it. She looked at him, studying something in his eyes. He wanted to kiss her, but she pulled away, taking her hand from his wrist. He started to reach for her when he realized why she had pulled away. The warden stood behind him.

"The car is packed," she said flatly. "When you have finished breakfast, we can leave."

In his room Isaac loaded his last roll of film into the camera. While washing up, he looked at his face. It seemed odd, the mouth a little lopsided. There was something wrong with the way he held it. He had the look of a kid sucking on a piece of forbidden candy, the taste of it in his eyes.

At the front of the house they loaded themselves into a black '39 Plymouth buffed to the color of a wet stone. The driver was an old *mestizo* Isaac had not seen before. He was thin and surprisingly quick for his age. He held the door for Memori, then sprinted around to get Isaac's. He wore a straw fedora and a thin sweater that bound him like a bandage. Graciella opened her own door and took her place in the front next to him.

They crossed the bridge as they had yesterday and took the road out past the plaza, the creek bed on their right. The road was as smooth as fired clay, and it stayed within sight of the creek's tree line as it climbed into the near hills. The buff colored chaparral gave way to a chalky green. The road snaked around boulders sometimes as big a barn. At the crest of the hill Graciella spoke to the windshield in front of her:

"The animals are not to be seen today. It is probably too late. When it warms in the sun they sometimes will pasture beyond the trees out there. They don't like the road, even when no one's on it. It takes a good horse to get into them."

The road ahead lay like a slack rope and they started down it. The rains were contained better here and the vegetation prospered. It could have been a valley in Ireland. The sun reflected off a ribbon of creek water below them. The road down to it was rutted and the vintage car took it leaning one way then the other. Sometimes the grass was high enough beneath it to brush across the bottom of the pan. From the crest down it took them nearly half an hour to reach the creek. They parked near it and carried the blankets and baskets over to a flat rock beneath some willows. The creek ran just below it, shaded by the trees that banked it. The water was thin and still and was the color of weak tea. Rounded rocks lay like *bollillos* on the dappled sand just beneath the surface. Some rose above it and bridged the water between the banks like a pool in a carefully constructed Japanese garden.

But mostly it was the verdancy of the place that lent it its otherworldly quality. There was a deep spring somewhere and green was reflected in and from everything, deep viridian in the shadowy depths, sparked here and there by bright oxide-green sun pools that shimmered and danced on the feathery leaves of the trees and on the grass that lay like moss beneath them.

Sanchez had been right. It was a good place to picnic. The light was spectacular. Isaac could have used ten rolls of film if he'd had them.

Juan brought out some cloth-backed folding chairs and some red wine. Isaac stepped back until he could get a wide-shot in his view finder, then he closed in some with his lens. As the three set up for lunch, he read the figures as color against the greens and blues that shaded them. He moved around and shot the grouping. Once, a piece of the sun caught the bottom of the wine bottle and it glowed like molten metal.

The three of them took lunch at the rock, Juan eating his at the car. They ate corvina and ham with chunks of fresh bread and cheese. At the end they ate from a bowl of fresh cut pineapple and thick slices of watermelon as rich and as red as a Tabuena still-life.

When the wine was gone, Juan brought another bottle from the trunk of the car. Graciella by then had withdrawn herself from conversation. Discreetly, she moved her chair to the river bank a few yards away and opened a book. Juan played the radio quietly, a vocalist lamenting her husband's infidelity. She sought to be heard above an accordion and too many fiddles.

Around the bend and on the opposite side of the creek were the ruins of an old church. Juan thought that the water could be crossed easily at a point just off the path.

If the dutiful chaperon were uncomfortable about their walking off alone, she did not protest, as Isaac thought she might. Either she had softened with the wine, was into a good book, or had relinquished her authority to the sanctity of the church grounds they intended to visit. He didn't dare risk taking a blanket.

Juan was right. At a point just around the bend the river was at its lowest, just above the rocks that would bridge it in a drier season, but if you stayed on top of the rocks, it could be waded. Isaac, carrying his boots, Memori's sandals and his camera, crossed first. The rocks, though submerged, were still negotiable. They had not been underwater long enough to accumulate a layer of moss. They were slippery, but you could still walk them.

When Isaac had crossed, he put the shoes in the dry grass above the lip of the bank and returned with his camera. He had fifteen shots remaining on the roll.

He called across to Memori: "Stay on the tops of the rocks. Don't go off them. The river's pretty deep. Balance, take your time."

He watched her through the viewfinder. He brought her up close, then moved her back as she took her first tentative step. The sun off the still water drew little circular designs that scrolled across her blouse and face as she moved in and out of the shadows.

She paused on each rock, gathering herself in a ballet line, a configuration that seemed to rise from where she stood, moving upwards off the rock, defying gravity. She worked large, fully aware of the camera and Isaac. She was on stage. Her arms, her legs, the cant of her head and torso were united in a composition of counterweights. She was perfectly balanced and did not seem to touch the stone she stood on, and when she drew each foot out of the water, the water closed back without a ripple.

Though the creek ran only inches above rocks, she held her skirt high, not so much to keep it from getting wet as to free her long thin legs from its confines and, no doubt, to show Isaac the shape of them, their singular beauty and how they moved. She wore lace panties cut high in the bikini fashion and she chose, sometimes, to show Isaac and his camera how thin and white they were and how they clung to the triangular dark beneath them. When she allowed her dress to fall, her legs against the reflected sun behind her would be silhouetted within it. She took her time coming across the creek to Isaac and he took pictures of her along the way.

She didn't move in parts or in isolated pieces, but came to him all at once as though the hum of insects around them was the music of Beethoven, maybe, or Chopin, and she was dancing to that. He took pictures of her until there was no more film.

The ballet was in celebration of a promise, the lovemaking that would come. She had choreographed it on the spot. The narrative, though wordless, was a libretto with a single meaning. When she arrived where Isaac stood, they embraced, then kissed deeply. She pulled away and looked at him. Showing herself to him had excited her and she breathed through parted lips. Neither spoke as she turned and headed up the path to find a place where they could lie together.

The path at first was steep and he walked behind her watching the way she moved beneath her skirt. It brought them to a clearing, a ribbed wash of baked earth so blond it could have been a great slab of ivory. They crossed it in their bare feet, hardly picking up dust. With the sun blazing off it they had to move quickly.

The church stood behind a thicket of wild cane and tall grass, and while the adobe walls and part of the tower remained, much of the roof had caved in. The thicketed hill that rose above it contained the stonework of a crumbling aqueduct. Pieces of it stretched off into the distance. A long straight-edge would need to stretch for miles to link them.

There was no reason to speak as they approached the church. Within a shallow portico the tall wooden doors remained, though one, slightly askew, hung by a single hinge. Isaac pushed at the other door and it swung open. He stepped over the threshhold and she followed. It was dark within, or too bright without, and it took a moment to see. The air was thick with the smell of rotted wood. Sunlight fell in a shaft from where the roof opened. It illuminated part of the altar. The dust motes that rose from it licked upwards into a piece of bright sky like an elongated flame.

In his bare feet Isaac walked up the nave, careful not to step on the debris that had fallen from the roof. Memori followed. The pews had been torn out. Straw, shards of tile and splintered pieces of timber remained. He nudged a long piece of 4 x 4 with his foot and the length of it moved like balsa wood. The termites had hollowed it. Midway on its length the straw it had been sitting on quivered and parted. The flattened head of a thick and mottled snake emerged from it, licked at something, curled and dove under the debris again. The long fat train of its body followed it into the hole.

Hoping Memori did not see it, he turned. But she was looking at where it had been.

"Is it a rattlesnake?" she asked.

"I think so."

"Will it come back?"

"No. It won't come back."

But she watched where it had gone, her mouth slightly parted. For a long time she watched the spot in the hay where it had disappeared. Then she looked at Isaac. He took her hand and to-gether they moved up the aisle toward the blaze of dust. There was an altar table and he would lay her on that.

But it too was rotted and would not bear the weight of them. He would have to take her standing. He could not wait any longer. His back to the altar, he turned and kissed her, holding her face hard to his. She opened her mouth a little and breathed from it.

He was in shadow and when he held her away she caught the sun, it swept the blue-black of her hair, the side of her face, a bare shoulder. She waited for him to do what he wanted, and he want-ed to reveal her breasts. He held her arms to her side to show her that she should keep them there. He brought his hands to the blouse at her shoulders and pulled it down to her waist. As he did she pulled her arms free from the sleeves. Her nipples were hard against his palms as he cupped her breasts. Something moved be-hind her. Some wood crumbled beneath a foot.

It was a figure and it stood just off the entrance. It was thin and insubstantial in the shadows, but there was no mistaking that it was moving, and then that it was moving forward. The figure stopped and stood in the center of the nave. Then it dropped to one knee as though it were wounded.

Juan, the driver, bound tightly in his sweater, made the sign of the cross and stood again.

"*Señor,*" he said. "I am sorry."

"What is it that you want?" Isaac called out to him, the adren-alin pounding in his ears.

"I'm sorry." You could see he was not understanding what he was looking at. He was waiting for his eyes to adjust to the dark-ness and his age worked against his doing it quickly. He could see that she was standing, a part of her in the blazing sun. The man she was with, the American who had been with the bulls yesterday, spoke from the inky shadow behind her. They were not praying, as he had first thought. The man was facing her and was not ad-dressing the altar. He could see that now. And she wore her shirt at her waist.

"Juan, you better go back," Isaac told him.

"There is a problem, *Señor*. There is a message that is a problem."

The old man did not come forward, but stood where he was.
"What message?"

"A friend of yours, *Señor*. It is a problem with a friend of yours. He called the house by telephone. The maestro, the foreman, drove it out. He has written it down. It is here. It is to be an emergency. He wants me to say that it is about the police and that you must go back now."

Chapter 17

Sturge's message was cryptic. They were to come at once and to meet him at the hot springs just out of town. They were not to go into town until they talked to him. He would be waiting for them at the entrance of the resort.

When Isaac, Memori and Juan got back to the car, there was no sign of the picnic. Graciella had packed up and gone back to the ranch with the foreman. Juan would drive them directly to Toboada.

Sturge, no doubt, was in trouble with the authorities again. They had thrown him out of the chicory jungle. They probably wanted to drive him out of San Miguel. There were those who wouldn't forget his correspondence with the exiled activist, Siqueiros. That, and his ability to gather a loyal crowd of natives wherever he went, made him politically suspect to those who had nothing better to present to their bureaucratic bosses.

The Deucheveaux was parked beneath the shade of a stand of oak trees just outside the entrance to the swimming area. Sturge was standing next to it. It did not seem possible that the black-bearded man with the wide smile could ever fold himself to a size that would accommodate his automobile.

If he had met Juan for the first time at the ranch, he had made a fast friend. The old man sprang from the Plymouth almost before it stopped and crossed over to where he stood. They shook hands and then shook them again as familiars. Once, Sturge looked over the head of the old man as the two of them talked. He tried to give Juan some money, but the old man shook his head in disgust. When Sturge insisted, he took the bills grudgingly.

Beyond where the buses from town were parked there was a concession stand. Juan headed for that, leaving Sturge to approach the car.

He opened Isaac's door, reached across him and shook Memori's hand, then Isaac's. He stood, looked to each side of him like a cold warrior with a nuclear secret, then bent toward them.

"You got my message," he said to Isaac.

"Sturge, for Christ's sake, of course we got your message. Why do you think we've come? So, what's wrong?"

"Don't worry. It's no problem. You'll be staying here tonight. I've got a reservation. It's in a phony name. You'll be all right here."

"What do you mean? What's wrong with the place I live in?"

"Isaac, I've got to tell you a lot of things, but I don't want you to get too worried about it. I mean, it's a little serious, but it's not all that bad if you're careful."

"Great. But we got to begin somewhere, Sturge. Why don't we quit with the James Bond so you can give it to me up front, then later you can tell me why I shouldn't worry. Has the place burned down?"

"It's been ransacked."

"Well, what could they take? I mean, I don't own much."

"It wasn't burglarized. The police tore it up. There were four of them. They didn't like it. They were embarrassed about it, but they did it by the book."

"When? What book? What were they looking for?"

"Signs of trafficking."

"Drugs?"

"Before dawn," Sturge said. "They spent nearly two hours going through your stuff. They were apologetic. Said the mandate for the search came down from the top. They said that is why they needed to find something."

"There's nothing to find. You know that. I don't do drugs."

"They could see that. But that's not the point. They had to look good. They were sorry. They had to find something. One of them had seen a movie somewhere and tore up your mattress. That's where they said they found it."

"Found what?" Isaac turned to Memori, then back to Sturge, who put his foot on the running board and leaned on one knee like an old-fashioned traffic cop.

"Coke. Some ounces. I don't know. But don't worry about it. They don't want to catch you and you don't want to be caught. They were just doing their job. Tonight you'll stay out here and tomorrow I'll get you on a bus for Guatemala. You'll be all right."

"Guatemala?"

"Antigua's the best of it. You could do worse."

"I could do a lot better. What am I going to do in Antigua?"

"Look, Isaac. These things happen. You don't have a big choice. Not a good one anyway. If they find you, you'll do half your life waiting for trial, the second half running a prison store. You don't want to get found, and that's perfectly all right with them. So go to Guatemala. It's a far better place to learn the language. You can paint. In a couple of months you can come back. These things are forgotten very quickly. Nobody is very serious about them."

Juan approached carrying some beer and some *tortas*. He passed them out. Memori declined. Isaac, wanting to feed his insecurity, looked at his sandwich. It was thick with cold *chorizos* that had been sliced and laid side by side. Each bore the color of the congealed eye of a long dead fish.

"You can eat these?" he asked.

"If you're hungry and not too proud," Sturge said, taking a large bite of his. "The beer will help. It'll kill anything that crawls."

Memori said: "Sturge, is Heinrich . . . is he involved in any of this?"

"I can't imagine it would be anyone else. Looks like he got to the mayor. You and Heinrich met him, I hear. You may know he's roundly despised. Still, the job had to be done. The police had to get real imaginative. They needed to show him how professional they were. They spent the night typing up a two paragraph warrant, or whatever it was. 'Suspect, a major drug trafficker, known in the U.S.A, Mexico and Jamaica.'"

"I've never been to Jamaica," Isaac said.

"Neither have they, apparently. They couldn't get the spelling. It had been erased several times."

"This is a joke," Isaac said. "This is ridiculous. There's no way they can be serious about this. Heinrich did this? I mean, what the hell." Both he and Sturge looked to Memori. She put her hand on Isaac's knee.

"Let me go talk to him," she said. "This is probably something he did last night. He'll be calmer now. I can talk to him, make him change his mind. This is terrible. I'm sorry, Isaac. He has an awful temper. He's lashing out, that's all. I'll talk to him."

"He's done this before?" Isaac asked her, knowing.

"He's done a lot of things before. I didn't think, down here, he'd try anything. Damn his ego anyway. He knows it's the end of it between us."

Isaac ate his sandwich. He had the kind of raging hunger only entrapment could fire. It was odd behavior, he recognized, but he had lived with it all his life. If it weren't for a raging metabolism, he'd be as thick as a stuffed red pepper. He had to think, but to do that he had to sate his hunger first. Sturge and Memori waited until he had finished his torta. Juan had discreetly taken his to the front of the car. He leaned back against the hood, ate and drank his beer.

"Why don't you call him from here, from the hotel," Isaac said at last.

"It won't work," she said. "He'll just hang up. He won't get serious on the phone. I have to see him. He'll demand that."

"Are you sure that's safe?" Isaac remembered that she said he'd hit her. Stable people don't try to put their rivals into the Mexican prison system. Or destroy paintings.

She said: "He must have done all this yesterday, when he went back after the fight. He'll be better now. He gets very mad at first, then he gets better. Isaac, I'm so sorry. But I'll get him to change it, to change what he did. I promise."

"I'll go with you," Isaac said, believing that maybe he would, then doubting it.

"That would be smart," Sturge said. "Isaac, think about it. Once they glom on to you, it's all over. You want to be a hero. Forget it. He's probably got three guys waiting for you now, one in a closet or two under the bed. Stay out here. We'll leave in the morning. I'll get you to Querétaro or San Luis Potosi. They'll be watching buses here. If you don't like Guatemala, I'll get you to Brownsville. The United States is still a step up from jail. I got somebody you can see in San Antonio. They got Mexicans there."

"Will they be waiting for me at the border?" Isaac asked.

"I doubt they'd want to spend a long distance call. As long as you got your papers and a little *mordida* to soften their tiny hearts, you'll be all right. The only thing you don't want to do is be seen around town. Trust me on this. They're dumb, Isaac, but like all of us, not that dumb."

"How about Spencer?" Isaac asked Sturge.

"He'll hold your job for a couple of months."

"I mean, he's got some influence. Can't he get them to call off the dogs?"

"No."

"What do you mean, no. Why don't we talk to him?"

"I did. He doesn't want to get dirty. I was at the school just before I came here. But he'll hold your job. He promised to do that."

"So, what did he say to all this. Did you tell him everything?"

"He likes you," Sturge said. "That's why he's willing to hold your job."

"If he likes me, why isn't he willing to make some phone calls?"

"He doesn't like you that much. Isaac, I don't know where you've been, but you got to start understanding adult life. Heinrich is going to sink a quarter of million into the school. Do I need to tell you that Spencer likes money?"

Isaac could use another sandwich. He took down the last of the beer instead.

"He's willing to wait for you. Unless you're in jail. Then your mother won't wait for you. In two months he'll have Heinrich's money and the new buildings will be under construction. He'll be in a better position to risk, as he so delicately put it, having a pusher on the faculty."

They waited in the car for Sturge to get the Deucheveaux started. It seemed to have thrown a rod again, but Sturge only waved as he swung around them and headed out toward the highway. It took a long time for the clanking sound to diminish.

Juan drove them over the to the resort hotel. Memori made no move to get out.

"You're staying here with me," Isaac said. "You're staying, right?"

"I have to talk to him. This is terrible and I've got to make him understand. He's got to understand what he's doing to you."

"Tomorrow. You can talk to him in the morning. Or you can call. We'll have dinner, a shower. You can call later."

"I told you, Isaac. This won't work on the telephone. And it has to be done now. I'll go with Juan, talk to him and return. It won't take so long. It won't take long at all."

"If you want, I'll go with you."

She smiled, leaned over and kissed him on the lips. But it was as a little girl might kiss her father.

"You're so gallant," she said. "People don't do things like that anymore. Don't you know that?"

"To hell with that. I've given up on people. I don't want to give up on you. I've found you. I don't want to lose you."

This time she didn't kiss him as a daughter. She held him tight around the neck and when she pulled back there were tears in her eyes.

"Please wait for me," she said.

Isaac stepped out of the car and patted Juan's shoulder in passing. It took the Plymouth three reversals to get out from the trees and onto the road. Sturge had made it in a U- turn.

As the car passed him, the reflection of the leaves on Memo-ri's window made it impossible to see her. He waved and smiled but it was as though she were visiting royalty in a motorcade, and all he wanted was a glimpse.

Chapter 18

She answered on the sixth ring and didn't speak right away. ". . . hello?" It was just after ten, yet she sounded like she just got up.

"Memori?" He had been calling since eight. He had called Sturge, but he had been out. Then he remembered the writer whose home Heinrich and she were using. The hotel had his number.

"Yes." She didn't recognize his voice.

"This is Isaac."

"Oh." She appeared on the verge of saying something more.

"Are you all right?"

"Isaac, I'm sorry. Yes, yes, I'm fine. I'm OK. I was just going to call you."

"Are you alone?"

". . . yes."

"Are you sure?"

"Yes," she said softly, "He just went out. I couldn't call you before. I was just getting ready to call you now."

"So, what happened?"

"There's so much to explain," she said. "It was terrible."

"Did he . . . did he hurt you?"

". . .no."

"We'll talk about it when you come over here. When are you coming?"

"I had to send Juan away," she said.

"Then take a cab. They'll all be in the *jardin* now. It's a good time. Tell the driver you want to go to Toboada, the hot springs."

"I can't, Isaac."

"You can't?"

"He'll be coming back. I can't . . . I've got to finish this. He wants to know where you are."

"You told him?"

"No, Isaac. Of course not."

"Why can't you come now, before he comes back? We've got to talk. I've got to leave tomorrow. Why can't you just get a cab and come over? Or tell me somewhere in town we can meet?"

"I can't explain, Isaac. It's just that it's in the middle of everything and I need to get this done. He'll be coming back and I can't talk long right now."

"I can come there. I can meet you."

"It's too early for that. I need to talk to him some more. Please, Isaac. Please understand."

"I'm trying to. Are you asking me to forget about it? To forget about this whole damn thing? I'm not going to do that."

". . . no," she said, "I don't want you to forget about it, about me." She was speaking softly again.

"Is he there now? Put him on the phone. Let me talk to . . . let me talk to him."

"He's not here, Isaac. I'm just tired. This is so hard. I love you, Isaac. But this is so hard."

"Memori, please. Please get a taxi. We've got plans. We've got to figure this all out. Listen, I'll come to the house. Give me half an hour. I'll be there in half an hour."

"No, Isaac! Don't try to come here." She spoke fiercely. There was almost a hiss behind the words.

"Then come here, for Christ sake."

"Isaac, please listen to me. It's so hard, but I'm trying to end this with Heinrich. It takes time. Are you going to Brownsville?"

"Sturge is driving me to San Luis Potosi. He's putting me on the noon bus. Why don't you come early tomorrow morning. Come here to the hotel. We'll have breakfast."

" . . . I can't," Memori said softly. "I just can't. I can meet you in Brownsville."

"How will you get there?"

"Heinrich has some business tomorrow with Spencer. We'll leave the day after."

"You're going to drive back with Heinrich?"

"I'll go as far as Brownsville," she said, " I'll leave him there."

"You mean you're just going to get out of the car? Memori, are you telling me the truth? You'll meet me in Brownsville?"

"I'll meet you. I'll meet you in Brownsville. You need to tell me where. Where will you be?"

"Sturge knows Brownsville. He'll know a place. He'll call you tomorrow. But tonight —"

"Isaac, it can't be tonight." There was the muffled sound from the phone, then she spoke more urgently: "I have to go. Please understand me. Please do that."

"Memori, I love you."

There was the distant rumble of voices, a rubbing sound from the phone as though someone were polishing it with a thick cloth.

"Memori?"

"Yes," she said. "I know." The phone was hung up.

Chapter 19

There was no mistaking the clanking of the Deucheveaux the next morning. You could hear it climbing the hill on the main road, then it slowing for the turnoff to Toboada. As it turned into the drive to the hotel, Isaac was out front waiting for it.

Sturge had strapped Isaac's laden suitcases to the top. The car, already tall for its wheel base, took on a decided lean to the driver's side as it negotiated the oaks. Sturge sought to counter the list by sitting, as best he could, on the passenger side. He rode it like piloting a catamaran in a high wind. He took it in under the portico and brought it to a stop. None of those who had been brought out of the hotel by the commotion would have been surprised if he had dropped anchor. Sturge got out and shook Isaac's hand, but they could not easily talk above the engine noise. They stood, apart from the small group of curiosity seekers and waited while the car shuddered to closure.

"Once you get in it will balance out," he said. "You'll be able to keep the wheels on the ground on that side."

Isaac said. "Also, no one will ever suspect we're trying to be in-conspicuous, that we're running from the law."

"You've never seen what she can do. Full out, I mean, if we get in trouble. She may be a little noisy, but in a high speed chase I'd put her up against anybody."

"I can hardly wait," Isaac said. "I won't ask you if anyone saw you sneaking out of town this morning."

When Isaac was wired in, Sturge crossed in front and slid in behind him.

"You got to learn cop-think, now that you're on the lamb, Isaac. What do you think will come to their mind when they see a good friend of yours heading out of town in this thing?"

"That you've come to pick up a major drug dealer in Toboada."

"Sure. But what else will they think?"

"I give."

"That anyone who reports it will only have to get one of their cars started and give chase. Since I'm already heading out of town, what's the point?"

When Sturge started the car and headed out, the clanking sound faded then stopped. The engine was left to whir like a badly oiled lawnmower.

"Have you ever determined what the problem is?"

"With what?"

"With the car. Why it sometimes sounds like you've thrown a rod."

"That bother you? Isaac, you don't want to worry about the little things. You want to leave a car alone. You don't want to get tampering with it. You open the hood and it's all over. God knows what you'll find. Get fussin' with stuff and she'll never be the same."

The morning was crisp, the air clean and each of them tied their windows up and took in the fresh smell of country, of damp grass and the sometimes not so distant fragrance of cow shit. Isaac told Sturge about last night's call to Memori.

"I noticed she was conspicuously absent this morning. Are you sure she's going to be there, that she'll meet you in Brownsville?"

"Yes."

Sturge didn't say anything for awhile, pretending to concentrate on the road. "I was afraid of that," he said. "I think it's a mistake."

"To meet her? Why? I thought you liked her."

"I do, I guess. That doesn't mean you're making less of a mistake. I've got to tell you something. I was hoping to talk you into getting on a bus heading in the right direction this morning."

"To Guatemala?"

"Yeah, or to anywhere else that isn't the United States."

"To Belize, then. There aren't many options."

"I'm saying, don't go. Don't go to the states."

"They're waiting for me?" Isaac asked.

"You mean about the drugs? No, I don't think so. And if you don't act stupid they won't check around. What's waiting is worse than that. Well, maybe not worse, but similar. Slow death. That's what's waiting for you. You're an artist, Isaac. You can't live up there."

"I'm not going to die, Sturge. I'm just going to Brownsville. Who's to say I won't be back anyway in a couple of months? You said to give it some time and it would be all right again down here. Memori and I could come back."

"You know Memori, of course, better than I. But somehow she doesn't strike me as a camp follower. Not many with her looks are."

"Then we'll stay up there. I'll go to New York. Maybe my luck will change. Nothing's permanent. Maybe, with Memori . . . I don't know."

"Sure. It'll be different, right? You've been reading your own lyrics. You'll become an acclaimed artist, right? The two of you will sit on your porch overlooking your vast acreage. You'll have converted the barn into a studio and once a day you'll trek out to a mailbox. It'll be as pregnant as Memori, with checks and offers for shows and invitations to travel and speak and do interviews with *The New York Times* and the rest of the oppositional press. It'll be great and you'll be generous to your peers. You'll offer sage advice to those who'll come and sit at your knee and ask you how you've come to rival Picasso in popularity."

"And in Guatemala I could do better?" Isaac asked.

"You wouldn't be destroyed."

"Are you talking about the United States or are you talking about Memori?"

"It's pretty much the same thing. And you can throw in Heinrich. That Kraut is more American than I am. Look, Isaac, you're not ready yet. You haven't yet got anything to fight them with. They'll get to you. They'll kill slowly in a way they're good at: they'll ignore you to death. Flat ass ignore you. You're a fine painter, and they don't like that. They'll cripple you, Isaac. Unless you play the system — theirs — they'll cut you off at your knees."

"And so I'm going to get world famous in Antigua?"

"No. But you'll be able to work. You'll be able to paint. What else is there? In our sad trade, that may be the end of it. Ask yourself, my friend, what brought you here? Your divorce? Your failure to excite a masturbatory teenager with some stimulating lyrics? I've seen it, Isaac. What drove you here drove me, and drove a whole lot of others: you wanted to work. You wanted to make pictures. You can't work there."

"You can work anywhere, Sturge. All you need is easel space. It's a big country. Who says there's not a place?"

"I got ten years on you, Isaac. I spent a good part of them in America proving you wrong. I've lived in the woods, in big cities and small; I've lived in suburbia, a desert, the deep South. I've lived in twenty states and whatever California is. Everywhere I went, it was the same thing. Whether I had to drive twenty minutes to get to a crossroad grocery store or whether I was half a block from Central Park, it amounted to the same thing.

"Wherever you go," Sturge continued, "you'll get a pervasive sense of worthlessness. It'll be delivered in a lot of fancy packages, in subtle and not so subtle ways. But the content won't vary. It's America's gift to those who are serious about art and not very serious about money.

"You won't be able to shake it, Isaac. Try ignoring it. Try holing up in your cabin. The day will come when you'll need to get out among 'em, you'll need to declare. Even if you're stronger than that, you still need to go shopping. You'll take coffee or breakfast, maybe, at the local cafe. The quiet will follow you until you find a stool. There'll be a jacket on it. You'll have to wait while the guy seated next to it moves it.

"He'll have a problem with you," Sturge continued. "You don't look like a hippie and you don't look like you work for a living. He'll want to know what you do. It's the first question out of him and, as far as he's concerned, the only one that counts.

"Tell him you do mass murders and he'll ask you what it pays. Tell him you're an artist and he'll name three close relatives and a mentally deficient son who also dabble. He knows what it pays. You'd have gotten more respect bludgeoning old ladies."

"So, I need this guy?" Isaac said.

"Yeah, you need this guy. But you won't know it right away. He's pretty representative of where America comes down, and that's going to get to you. You'll get more lip service somewhere else, but it's all the same. You're a nonentity. Where America is concerned, you're either among the ten or twelve guys getting paid to make art into social theory and fools out of anyone who paints, or you're scratching your ass."

"Maybe. But where is it different?" Isaac asked.

"Almost anywhere else. You know that. You've traveled. Go to Europe, the Far East, Central and South America. Go to Mexico, for Christ's sake. In any of these places you're doing something. You don't need to hide in the closet. You may not make any more money, but you count. You count in a way that money can't. And that — knowing you count for something — will keep you painting."

Sturge turned north on Highway 52. Much like every other country, Mexico ends where through highways begin. In this case you enter a black land thick with the smell of undigested diesel fuel, the two lanes just wide enough to accommodate those who believe it is three. This belief is held mostly by the drivers of buses and an assortment of ungainly rigs which, by virtue of their size and weight, can likely sustain a head on collision without losing much time. The Deucheveaux, lacking speed and substance, was no more a consideration than a swarm of gnats. Sturge waited until a passing bus thundered by, inches from his left shoulder, before continuing:

"Don't get me wrong about America," Sturge said. "You can't beat its hamburgers. Tell me about Memori."

"You tell me," Isaac said. "You've got the answers."

"You're just getting mad. You don't hear me so good. Look, go meet her. Shack up for a few days or a couple of months. Who's counting? Trouble is, I don't see you doing that. Whether you marry her or not, she'll get you married to America. And when she sees what that does to you, she's gonna dump you. And you'll lose another year or two in recovery. Or worse, you'll start writing songs again for pre-pubescent rockers. Or your ex-wife."

"Come on," Isaac said. "I'm meeting a girl in Brownsville. If I wasn't a Goddamned fugitive, we could stay here."

"You know it's more than a meeting in Brownsville. Maybe not for her, but for you. I'm talking about you. You can't afford America, Isaac. Not now. Not for a long time. The cost is too high. It cost you before, it will cost you again. The country's sick and your vaccination didn't take.

"And I'm not talking about the Goddamned war, or Kennedy or the riots in the cities. I don't know what all these things mean. They may be symptoms of what I'm talking about, but I doubt it. We're sicker in a more fundamental way than that. America's one of your rock stars that got his plug pulled. He's still got acne and he's wondering where his world went, why the crowds are gone, why the girls quit dampening their knickers each time he takes the stage.

"Like this 14-year-old wonder, we've never understood our makings. We never understood how phenomenally lucky we were to fight all of our wars — the recent ones anyway — somewhere else. If our cities look like hell — and they do — it's not because of the bombs. We built them that way. It's what we call architecture."

"This has something to do with Memori and my escape from a drug conviction in a clown car?" Isaac asked.

"I'm getting to that. Remember how in the first half of America's evolution we had all the land? In the second half, all the money? Is it a wonder we're material and not a little arrogant? Tocqueville saw it coming. But like our young rocker with money to burn, we got our cork pulled. Unlike his, our bath water is taking a while to drain. That's the sickness, the disease your friend Heinrich so ably reflects in his art."

"Are you being ironic? Heinrich's art?" Isaac asked.

"No. He speaks to these dreary times. There's a place for him. As Spencer would say, 'He's right on the money.'"

Sturge pulled out to pass an open-bed truck full of watermelons. It was a strain for the Deucheveaux. It took on a curious shimmy as it labored past the bed of the truck, then the driver, who watched the French car with some interest, looking over the crook of his bare arm, grinning. He wanted to see whether it would succeed in slipping into the lane in front of him or be flattened by the oncoming beer truck. It was close enough to be entertaining and in appreciation he gave a series of blasts from his horn.

"So you like what he's doing to Cezanne?"

"He's part of the sickness, Isaac. In time you're going to be part of the cure, if they don't get to you and if you're still painting and if you don't become some virago's answer to a middle-age husband."

"Jesus. What the hell has Memori ever done to you, Sturge?"

"You got it wrong, Isaac. I told you. I like her. I'd like her better if she came down here with you and stayed. But I don't see that happening."

"Why not? Why don't you think she'll come back with me in a couple of months? She likes Mexico. I think I've even got her to like the bullfights."

"She won't come," Sturge said.

"Are you a prophet?"

"Just a wiseman. You can't afford her."

"And if I stay up there with her?" Isaac asked.

"You'll deflate. You'll become bogus currency, or nothing at all. They'll prick your ascending balloon. Remember the guy with the cape a couple of days back? You did what you did nicely or with a good deal of luck. But you did it in context, in a place where art and beauty are not separate things and where money doesn't figure into everything. Go to Brownsville, or San Antonio or Chicago or SoHo and tell your art story. Who needs you?"

Isaac said: "So, even if I give you that. Who says I'm trying to change the world? I want to paint. I love a girl and I want to be with her."

"Every time you paint, Isaac, you change the world. Not a lot, but you change it in an important way. Here or anywhere else, they understand that. Where you're going they don't. They're caught up in money and politics, believing that the changes these two things make are permanent and important. Up there it's group-think. Everybody's got a political agenda. Whether they're burning bras or proclaiming Heinrich's New Art, it's done in a crowd. Nothing, not one Goddamned thing of importance, happens that way. Politics is a scam.

"The things that really count," Sturge continued, "are done by individuals — singular. Painters, writers, scientists, philosophers. People who work and think alone. The truth is in their art or in-ventions. Go to a museum. Stand in front of a Turner, Millet, Lautrec, Vermeer, Cassatt, Degas, Gaugin or Monet. What do you see? You see the truth, the beauty of it. But more, you see that this incredible act was performed by a member of the human race, your very own. And you swell up in gratitude and pride. God-damned if you're not a member! This, Isaac, is the only group that counts. You sway it one genius at a time."

Isaac said: "I agree with you, mostly, though I think you're too hard on America. But you're talking to the wrong guy. I'm a for-mer teacher of sculpture. I paint on the side."

"Bullshit," Sturge said. "Look. I got to tell you something, and I'm going to do it for the best of reasons: I don't want to feel guilty. I don't want to find you working for J.C. Penney in a shoe depart-ment with a suburban mortgage and a two-car garage because of something I didn't say, something I should have told you. Here it comes:

"You and Sequieros — and he in a very different way — are the only two artists I've ever known. And we're talkin' 'ever'."

Isaac looked at him. If he were joking, he did not show it.

"Sequieros lost his art to politics," Sturge said, "something Diego Rivera, who was equally political and a far better painter, never did. You're about to lose yours to love. And to do it before you've begun."

"Wait a minute. You're not a painter? You're not an artist? You going to put all this weight on me? Didn't you run off to the jungles to play around with Mayan ladies? What do you want from me?"

"I dabble, Isaac. Like ninety-nine point five percent of those who hold to be artists, I don't qualify. In those ten years, the ones I got over you, I came to learn that. I came to recognize that what I do doesn't matter. The guy in the cafe would have it right. I don't do much more than three of his close relatives and his imbecile son."

"You're feeling sorry for yourself."

"Of course. But what I'm telling you is true, though I'll deny that if you ever bring it up. You qualify, Isaac. Ask me how I know."

"All right. How do you know?"

"By the only way that counts: what you paint. I've seen your work in the gallery. I was impressed but not wedded. Memori bought the one I wanted if I could have afforded it. I've seen some of the stuff you left at school. I was encouraged but still undecided until this morning. The roll of your paintings in your apartment decided it for me, the roll up there," he nodded toward the roof. "I've been studying them since dawn. You've got fifteen paintings. Ten make it. Three of those make it big.

"Your problem, Isaac, is that none of it matters now. It doesn't make a damn right now that in some of your figures in landscape and some of your interiors you're getting light that I'll swear has never been got. I like your looseness. I like the restraint. But it doesn't matter. It won't matter for a long time. It may never matter up there. It won't matter until we've come to see how sick we've been and see a need for getting better. Then your paintings will matter. They'll matter a lot, I think."

Isaac said: "I haven't . . . I don't know what to say about all this. I haven't been thinking, you know, in these terms. If you're right, I haven't been thinking like that."

"You're lucky, Isaac. You don't need to think. You need to paint. The rest of us need to think. So far we're not doing much of it. We're in the Dark Ages, burning books, tearing up paintings, paving over the countryside, feeling sorry for ourselves. Our country's out front in this. They got Warhol and Guerber and Rauschenberg to count the ways. You don't need any of it. You don't need to save the women, or the whales or the rainforest. But stand in the way, you're dead. Find a small and quiet piece of the Old World, Isaac. Shut up and paint pictures. When the Renaissance comes — as it's got to — it will find you and your stack of paintings. Trust me."

They didn't talk for a long time after that. Until they got into Potosi they didn't talk about Isaac's impending trip at all, except to consult one another on a likely place to find the central bus station in such a city. Isaac declined Sturge's invitation to lunch. He had not had breakfast, except for coffee, and a roll he'd largely disdained. But the thought of more tortas made a tight fist in his stomach. If he still needed to feed his insecurity, he was no longer getting any announcements.

At the terminal Sturge and Isaac untied the cases on the roof. The boy working the lot found a pushcart and they put them in that.

"I better buy the ticket," Sturge said. "I don't think anybody's going to be looking for you, but I better buy it anyway."

Isaac pulled out some money and handed it to Sturge.

Sturge said: "You wait here with these." He handed Isaac the roll of paintings and strung the camera around his neck. "I'll get your bags on the bus so you can go directly on."

"OK."

But Sturge did not make a move to go

"You can go anywhere from here, you know," he said at last. "They run on the half hour, mostly. This is a major city so you can get on here and go anywhere you want. It doesn't matter where you go."

"I guess so," Isaac said.

"You don't have to go to Brownsville."

"Yes."

"You don't have to meet Memori."

"Yes."

"But you want me to buy you a ticket to there. You've made up your mind."

"Yes," Isaac said.

When Sturge returned to the parking lot for Isaac, he took the roll of paintings from him and they walked together through the terminal and then out to the wing that held the waiting bus. It was still loading. Sturge wrote the name of a gallery in Houston on the inside of a candy wrapper. He wrote the names of two of his collectors in San Antonio.

"Don't even have time for a *cerveza*," he said, handing Isaac the roll of paintings

"I don't think it will be like you say," Isaac said, "with Memori, I mean. I think it will be all right. She knows some people. I think we'll come back, the two of us."

"Do you have *mordida* money?"

"Yes."

"You'll need it. There are two checkpoints and you'll need to give a little at the first and a little more at the second. You don't want them making phone calls. If you got your papers and you pay a little money you'll be all right."

"Sure," Isaac said.

They shook hands the two ways. As Isaac turned to leave, Sturge called him back.

"Listen," he said. "If you ever tell anybody what I told you, about my not being an artist, I'll kill you. Fair enough?"

"Fair enough."

"And . . . Isaac?"

"What?"

When Sturge clapped him on both shoulders, Isaac feared for a moment that he was going to get kissed. Instead, Sturge held

231

him with his eyes in the near perfect imitation of one man sending another off to face death on the horns of a bull.

"*Suerte*, Matador," he said.

Isaac couldn't tell if he was kidding.

Chapter 20

The orange drink he'd bought from the vendor working the bus was a mistake. He'd wanted bottled water, he'd even take a beer. The old man only had the orange and several bottles of a violet concoction in his rusted tub.

Isaac needed something to slake his thirst, but the orange drink was thick with sugar and tasted in no way like any piece of fruit he'd ever experienced. Now, in addition to being thirsty he had a mouth that felt like he'd been chewing on a roll of fly paper. He would wait for the next stop to find somebody who sold water. In keeping with Mexican bus travel, that was never far off.

Here, if you go by bus, there are several ways to get to your destination. None of them is designed to get you there in a hurry. A second class ticket earns you the right to share your seat with anyone carrying a pig, a cage of chickens or any number of vomiting babies. The bus is obliged to stop for everyone standing at the side of the road, even if he's been waiting to cross it. Likewise, anyone can get off the bus wherever he chooses. It's even possible for one to take a leak and re-board, if you don't mind an audience and you don't dally. Though it's a rocky ride, there is forward movement toward the place for which you bought the ticket, but it comes at a price: how much of your life you can afford to spend and the value you place on your internal organs.

Things would be speeded up some if those waiting for a ride would flag their intention to the driver, but this is not the fashion here, it's not done. Rather it's the custom for those who work the fields, those most likely to save some money on a second class ticket, to look away from an approaching bus, to appear bored and to stand, if they are with others they don't know or want to recognize, separate from one another as though they've collected at the side of the road by accident. Even when the bus rumbles to a stop, they will not immediately move toward it. They will stand facing away. They will look out ahead of it and across the road. They will look at the empty fields and the distance beyond them, as though the bus's stopping was of no concern to them. Even when the brake drums squeal on the approach and there can be heard the cackle of hens caged and strapped to the roof and the crying of babies through windows that can't be closed and the chatter of women who sit spread-legged on aisle seats discussing the effect of garlic on male turgidity, these people standing silently on the side of the road would look out and away as though the noisy busload of humanity did not exist.

The men and the peasant women standing barefoot and apart would look away from one another, away from the bus. Only when the doors opened would they reach down for the bedrolls and bundles at their feet. In some magnificent bronzes Francisco Zuniga captured the feel of these people, how they related to one another. His sculptural groupings of peasant women, the life-size figures inches apart as they stand or squat together on the baked earth, have the distance of empty fields between them.

The first class bus, like the one on which Isaac rode, did not often stop for those at the side of the road, but neither did it advance very quickly. It served every town and the places that could not be called a town or had much in the way of prospects for becoming one. As long as a cluster of shacks was within ten miles on each side of the main route you thought the bus intended to take, a stop was warranted. Hence the first class bus was only a mild improvement over the second, though you saw a lot more countryside.

You can, for some extra money, buy a direct first-class bus ticket. It will have your destination stamped on it and the word

234

"*Directo*" stamped beneath it. This is a ticket purchased almost exclusively by American tourists. Should you be a tourist and want to compare your more prestigious ticket with the regular first class ticket held by other riders, you'll have plenty of opportunity to do so, since you'll both be on the same bus.

As Isaac's wound its way back and forth across Highway 57, two things became apparent: It would take forever to get to Matamoros, the feeder city to Brownsville, and he was sick. None of a variety of soft drinks he bought in the several stops they made was a substitute for water. The thirst, if anything, had increased. His head throbbed, his legs ached. The fist that was his stomach remained clenched. The cords at the back of his neck tightened. They were attached somehow to his eyes which, as a result, were drawn deep into their sockets. The pressure made moving them difficult. They were as dry as prunes. The best he could do was close them and try not to remember the chorizos in yesterday's sandwich.

A figure dropped into the seat beside him like a sack of dry beans. Isaac kept his eyes closed, feigning sleep.

"You gotta be outta your fuckin' skull, man, put up with this shit. Where in the hell are we?"

With some effort, Isaac drew his eyelids upwards a crack and turned his head. He found the hippie he had seen when he got on the bus at Potosi. Then, he had been sleeping, mouth agape near the front. His head had lain back against the window, crushing his black velvet cowboy hat. His bare feet had extended over the arm rest on the aisle seat and those boarding had to move around them. They did so gingerly. His feet had seen a number of miles since they last touched water. He wore his hair at his shoulders and snored. He revealed a surprisingly long set of front teeth as he did so. He was clutching the crotch of his Levi's.

"Tell me, man. Go on. Tell me what I'm doing here, riding this Goddamned thing. Must be outta my fuckin' skull. You know what's goin' on, man? I'm gonna tell you. I'm on vacation, for Christ's sake. You beat that? Outta my fuckin' skull, man.

"Stayin' with a few friends in this commune out of San Angelo.

235

I got no worries, you dig? Grow a little weed, whatever we need. Got this chick, part Cherokee. Likes to make you happy, if you know what I mean. We're talkin' fat city here, y'understand? Name's Bonnet. Kid you not. Who the hell knows why. Old man's a fuckin' Indian. Gotta be outta his fuckin' gourd, y'understand? So Bonnet says Morelia's where it's at. Mexico, man. Got some friends, she says. Good Columbian dope. We can score some, she says. Lay back for a month, two. So I'm sayin' OK, man. Cool. I can dig that. I'm thinking, got me an squaw. I'll get me a couple of chili-beaners on the side. I'll ease up, take life as it comes. Y'understand? You with me? Hey, wow, man. I mean you don't look so good. You sick? Got the revenge? Name's Billy, man."

Isaac took what he hoped to be an expedient and shook the offered hand. He closed his eyes. It didn't help.

"Didn't see you get on, man. Goddamned chili-dips. So many dips, forgot what another white man looks like. Outta my fuckin' skull, comin' down here. You on business? That don't look like no tourist camera."

"I do some painting," Isaac said.

"I seen the roll. Thought maybe you was an architect, some fuckin' thing. Art, man, I can dig that. Bonnet's into that. Never studied or nothin'. You gotta see her stuff. Wild. Shows at Luboff's on 277, across from the Mobil station. Out towards Abilene. Far out stuff. What you call abstract art. She got a small one by the cash register, two others out by the pay telephone. You want to show there, mention you know Billy. They take ten percent, but only when they sell something. It's worth it to get your name around."

For the next two hundred miles and well into the night Isaac learned a good deal about Billy and Bonnet and their disastrous trip to Morelia. He learned how they had met in Santa Fe. They had been holing up in a trailer court. She had dropped some acid and tripped out, believing — according to her boyfriend — that she was a ground squirrel in heat, though Isaac, who was finding it hard to concentrate, could have been wrong on this point. He learned how they behaved in bed the night they met and several nights thereafter. Billy made it clear that he did not like Morelia,

236

Bonnet's friends, Mexico, its people, anyone over the age 25 (present company excepted), police in any country, those who supported the war, Indians, Martin Luther King and "liberated broads."

Conversely, Billy seemed to support the notion of free love (even, apparently, if you had to pay a little), coke, pot, heroin and acid when it was properly cooked (he drew the line at booze), doing nothing of consequence, and being, as he put it, "a full fuckin' -blooded American."

Sometimes, for what seemed like hours, Isaac would drop off, or nearly so, and the monologue would wash over him, mixing with his own thoughts about Memory, her crossing the creek, the way her hair fell. At other times he worried about the coming checkpoints and whether they were waiting for him and how it would be if he were to be pulled out and searched and what they would do after that and how he would try to explain himself, but the words would not come in the right order and he would run from his accusers on aching legs as they talked to one another. Not watching him they would talk and talk and he would slip away and if he were careful they wouldn't see him as they talked and talked some more. They wouldn't see him even though he was too slow, so slow, at getting away, running to the open gate. If he could get his legs going he had a chance. If he could only get to the open gate. With each step the muscles in his legs grew heavier. There was the consuming need for the next step and the one after that, but he could not find the rhythm for running. And they were coming up from behind him, just behind him, and they were talking and talking about an Indian girl who slept with her legs in the air, legs that turned in the sun like Memory's as she moved from rock to flat rock. It was the bull behind him, just behind his legs, matching him step for painful step.

"WHAT!"

The two policemen stood in the aisle of the darkened bus. One was talking to him, but he could not understand the words. The other was holding a flashlight and beating it against the palm

237

of his hand. He could not get it to stay on. It would light, but when he turned the beam towards Isaac's face, it would go off again. The bus was empty. Even Billy was gone.

The policeman who was talking leaned down and shook him by the shoulders, though he was already awake.

He spoke in English: "You go. You get out. You go somewhere." He pointed toward a window. They were not at the border. They were in the country and the bus had pulled off into an empty field. Fifty yards off stood an open tent. A string of lights illuminated a row of wooden tables. A shadowy stream of passengers moved towards the tent. They were in the dark and they were dragging their luggage toward the lighted tent. They had made a line of themselves and the smaller shapes, which were children, clung to the larger shapes.

"Papers," the policeman said. "Papers. All luggage. You go somewhere."

Isaac rose, then nearly fell back. His head seemed to float toward the roof of the bus. It seemed unconnected and bobbled crazily. He was able to control it some, and then to move down the aisle by holding the backs of the chairs on each side. His legs were rubber as he passsed the driver and stepped down the stair well. He started off across the field on stiffened legs. The policeman caught his arm.

"Papers," he said. "You luggage." He was pointed to the bus's open luggage bin.

Only Isaac's cases remained. He pulled them out. He did not try to carry them. He dragged one to the end of the line and then went back for another. When he had them all together, he sat down on one. When he remembered his papers, he stood up to get his wallet out. At first he did not want to believe it was gone. He would not accept that the pocket was empty. Then he wanted it to be somewhere else. He slapped at all his empty pockets and looked at the ground near where he'd been sitting.

He had left it on the bus, he concluded. He had slept and it slipped out of his pocket. It was on the bus seat, with his camera. He had forgotten that. He'd left that as well. And his roll of paint-

238

ings. He had forgotten to bring these things with him when he got out. He had been too sleepy, too sick.

The bus door was shut. When Isaac pounded on it, the driver didn't move. In the dark Isaac could not tell if he were asleep. He hit the door hard several times, this time putting as much strength behind the blows as he could muster.

The driver stirred. The door opened grudgingly.

"Some other things, Señor," Isaac told the driver. "I'm sorry, I need to get some other things."

But there was only his empty seat, and on the floor, nothing. The bus driver was tired. He did not want to talk about it. He yawned and pointed for Isaac to return to the line. It had already moved up into the tent.

His bags stood forlornly in the empty field. One by one he brought them to the end of the line then stood in the thick air waiting for his lightheadedness to clear. Sometime earlier, it had rained briefly. There was the pungent smell of high desert sage. Some crickets sounded in the distance.

Under the tent and in the lights they were opening some of the bags. The two policemen from the bus were there and two others. These last wore short jackets and gray pants. They were older than the policemen.

He looked for Billy. He would know about his paintings, his camera and maybe his wallet. He was not in the line ahead of him and, with a sinking certainty, he knew he'd not be among those who had gone through the check and were now a cluster of shapes near the door of the bus. He knew Goddamned well he'd gotten off the bus several stops back, that he'd gotten off with the paintings, the camera with the roll of film he'd shot of Memori, his papers and any money he might have used to bribe himself across the border.

The last of the line was moving into the lights. It was still possible, maybe, to take a bag or so and walk off into the night. But to where? There was only darkness. And he'd have to go back along the road where, no doubt, there had been those who had waved

239

the bus to the checkpoint. And if he got by them, what would he do without money?

Also, since he could not carry all the bags, they would notice the ones he'd left in the field and come looking for him. They would ask the others on the bus and they would tell of the two gringos who sat together. He would be the one with the boots.

He could not think clearly. He wanted to be at the hotel in Brownsville waiting for Memori, but he didn't know how he was to get through this. He did not have a plan and had no idea how to make one.

The two policemen were talking as Isaac slid his cases into the light. One of the custom officials was going through a bundle of clothes belonging to a young Indian woman. She wore the light, bright colors of a Oaxacan. She had unusually large breasts and the policemen were talking about that. They were laughing and nodding toward her, inviting Isaac to do the same. She held a *rebozo* under her neck with both hands and looked away from Isaac, the police and the official who was going through her things. She had smooth skin drawn tightly across her cheekbones. She had the classic Mayan nose.

She waited under the naked light for the police to finish with their discussion of her breasts and the fruit they could be compared to. The custom official took a long time examining each article. He was pretending to be seriously in search of something. The police wanted an audience and were glad for Isaac's arrival.

The one who contended they looked like large cantaloupes, slapped the table twice, indicating that Isaac should put his cases there. The other had it that they were the size and shape of small watermelons. This one, the younger of the two, drew out his analogy with a gesture using both his hands. His partner nodded and giggled and then elaborated the gesture, making the watermelons considerably larger and the joke, therefore, all the more funny.

The woman stood facing away. She wore no expression. Above her a flying beetle smashed its body repeatedly into a light bulb.

The official had one drooped eye. He pushed away the girl's belongings leaving her to re-pack them. He dragged the first of

Isaac's cases in front of him. He opened the strap, then the case. His good eye found Isaac.

"Papers," he told him.

"What?"

"Pasaporte, papers," he said.

Isaac gestured toward the two policeman, as though they had taken his papers. They were still engaged in their discussion. They were watching the girl. She had abandoned her defensive position in order to gather her things. She did this hurriedly, but there were a lot of clothes to be put back and the bundle tied. They had moved the discussion to speculating on her nipples. They did so watching her breasts move beneath her clothes as she worked. The official, pretending to look at the contents of Isaac's case, was also looking at the girl.

She was nervous and could not tie her bundle into a knot that held. When she meant to move the bundle away, it opened, spilling some of her clothes on the ground. She had to stoop, pick those up and work with the knot again.

Watching her, the official flipped closed the lid of Isaac's case, waving him through. He liked her nervousness and watched her closely. The two policemen had also seen her vulnerability. They did not talk any longer. They watched her as she fumbled with her clothes. The three of them were quiet. The beetle, in some desperate and very private war, whirred and slammed into the bulb above her.

Isaac, with adrenalin singing in his ears, got his case fastened. He wrestled it and the others onto the ground. With two under his arm, he carried them all into the dark. He did this all in the space of time it took for the Indian girl to get her single bundle tied and off the table.

The sun rose with Isaac's fever. Throughout the night he had lost a lot of water at fetid stops at clogged and overflowing toilets along the way. At the rate he was draining, he had not been able to replenish it with the soft drinks. Now, without money, he couldn't even buy these. He wanted to drink the water but dared not take it from any tap. He was losing to dehydration and had begun to feel chilly. As the desert sun rose over the gulf and the heat climbed, Isaac began to shake uncontrollably. He could not get warm.

The bus pulled into still another depot. He had to wait for a man who had taken a small comic book in with him. He was a slow reader. Outside again, a sign told him he was in San Fernando. He did not know how far that was from the border or even if he were going in the right direction. He only wanted to get warm and into the sun before he would have to get back on the bus. He no longer felt thirsty, only a deep chill. He took a seat on the curb behind the idling bus. It was where he could be in the sun. He sat in the engine exhaust and tried not to go to sleep. If he could stay conscious long enough to reach Matamoros and get lucky again at the checkpoint, he could cross the border to the American side. He didn't know what he would tell Immigration there, but he would have put himself, by then, beyond a Mexican jail. Maybe Memori would be at the hotel. He could call her.

The combined air temperature of the desert sun and the heat from the exhaust warmed him enough to make him drowsy. He fought the sleep that wanted to envelop him. He'd be out for hours, he'd guess, and would be sitting on the curb long after the bus had left. Unless he could get on another bus. Maybe he could do that. He could sleep for a while and board another bus. He tried to think whether this was possible. He didn't have any money but he had — didn't he? — the stub of his ticket. Sure. He could sleep and get on another bus. If he could remember where he put his ticket. He'd been careful with it. He'd always been careful with things like that. In his mind's eye he could see it. Sturge had given it to him, and just in case he needed it, in case of some emergency, he had put it carefully in his wallet.

The roar, at first, came from a long way off. And then it was next to him. The heat from the engine blasted across his face. He stood in the thick, hot wind and wondered where he was. He could not get his legs to move right, but by using the side of the bus as support he was able to work his way around to the driver's open

242

window above him, and, hoping he'd been seen and that the driver would wait for him to reach the door and not drive over him, he crossed in front.

The passengers were still re-boarding. They were lined up the length of the bus. Isaac did not have the strength to go to the end of the line, so he leaned against the front fender. Just behind the open door and a man who was asking questions to someone he couldn't see. Until they'd finish no one could board. Isaac leaned against the bus and closed his eyes. He would wait for the two men to quit talking and then for the others to board. He would sleep a little leaning against the fender. He would sleep, listening to the two men talk about a third, someone the man closest to him was looking for. It was a gringo he was looking for and Isaac wondered who that might be and whether it was someone he knew. The man he couldn't see knew the gringo had gotten this far. He wanted to help the other man. He assured the man standing with his back to Isaac that the gringo had gotten off the bus just ten minutes ago.

Isaac still had not put it together when the man who had his back to him spun and grabbed his shoulder. A younger man became a part of it and the two of them pulled him away from the bus. He tried to wrestle away, but his legs were not working. He tried swinging, but the older man caught his arm, then called him by name. Isaac was drained of further resolve. It did not matter what they did with him. He was past caring.

The older man had to support him. The younger man went into the bus to talk to the driver. Isaac concentrated on keeping his legs under him. With some effort he could do that. But he couldn't get them to take his weight. He wanted to sit down, but the older man held him up.

When the younger man came down the stair well, the two of them walked Isaac through the terminal. With each holding an upper arm they walked him faster than he could move his legs. He was half carried, like a puppet on tangled strings. They brought him to a parked car. The older man propped him up against the car and held him there. The young man left and then came back carrying some battered luggage. He put the bags into the trunk

243

and slammed the lid shut. The younger man held his arm while the older man took a seat in the back. The younger man held the top of his head and guided him into the seat next the older one.

Then he got behind the wheel and started the car.

Chapter 21

It wasn't very pretty. Each time the little girl woke him she had to pull him out from under a thick blanket of sleep. She would pull his legs out over the edge of the bed and then bring him upright. She had to do this against what he really wanted to do: fall back and be left alone.

She was twelve, or thirteen maybe, but she was surprisingly strong. When she walked him to the bathroom, he would put much of his weight, more than he ought to, on her shoulders. She did not seem substantial enough to hold him and he feared falling and crushing her beneath him. But she held him. In the bathroom she would seat him before leaving, only to stand outside the door until he was through. She did not mind any of it.

Once she hadn't woken him on time and she had to wash him and then change the sheets. He was placed in an upright chair near the bed until it was made. Sitting there, he had both slept and watched her in her crisp yellow dress. She unfolded each clean sheet and from the foot of the bed snapped it flat. It billowed like a cloud and settled on the mattress. She tucked in the sides working quickly and efficiently. When she had him back in bed and covered, she took his place in the chair.

Sometimes when he woke, she'd be reading. Sometimes she would be sitting at the edge of the bed with a soup spoon, wanting to feed him from a mug of hot soup, or she would have a glass of sugar water for him to drink and some powder she would want him to swallow.

Once she had not been there when he opened his eyes. It was dusk and the room had not been lit. Against the wall where the girl usually sat was a small and varied crowd of people. Straight-back chairs had been brought in and they were sitting on these watching Isaac in silence. The old man who had brought him from the bus was there. There were two others older than he. A woman, the skin of her face crazed like the surface of a 15th Century painting, watched him, her hands in her lap. A gray-haired man next to her, his hands propped on a walking stick in front of him, slept with his head on his chest, snoring quietly. There were two other couples, much younger, one standing behind the other. Nearer the door a very young woman nursed a child. A little boy with one foot on the rung of her chair stood next to her. He too faced Isaac.

The figures were as motionless as a grouping posed for an important family portrait, a *tableau vivant* colored in rich washes of sepia and faltering light. Dignified by the space and atmosphere that defined them, they did not stir. Outside, a long way off, a dog barked.

When Isaac tried to speak, he found that he didn't have the strength. He watched the group from where he lay until there was no more light to see them or until he had closed his eyes.

Once, when she hadn't been there, he woke to the sounds of the house below him. It was before dawn and there was the thrum of distant voices. A radio was on. Doors were slammed. A car was started in the yard below. A child called out to his grandpa and was shushed. There was the smell of tortillas and the sound of them being slapped into shape.

When the cars drove off there was silence, deepened by the throb of a hall clock. Isaac thought to see if he could stand. He needed to find a phone, to talk to somebody, but he could not remember who he would talk to or why. With effort he'd got his legs to the floor, but when he commanded them to take his weight, they rebelled. He could not get them to obey. He sat in someone else's pajamas alone in a strange room and wondered why his legs would not work.

When the little girl turned on the lamp near the door and

246

spoke, he didn't recognize the language. She put a bowl of soup on the bed table and held her hand against his forehead. Her hand was as cool as a silk glove. She had a trace of milk on her upper lip and smelled of buttered toast. She had enough Indian in her to color her skin, but only faintly. Her smile was brightened by it. She looked evenly at him and brushed his hair from his forehead.

"It is better for you?" She was using the familiar pronoun of lovers and of the way children and adults speak to one another. That was why he didn't understand her.

"It is better," he said.

In a single movement she kissed him on the cheek and sat next to him, then shifted closer. She threw her pony tail across her shoulder and out of the way and took up the bowl. When she brought a spoonful of broth to his lips, he shook his head. She smiled and shook her own head. She held the spoon at his lips until he took it.

"Your father. He brought me from the bus? He brought me here?" He had only just remembered about the bus, his wanting to get back on when he had been grabbed. He could not remember why or where he was going. His chest hurt. Maybe he had been in an accident.

"He is my uncle, the one who brought you." She ladled up more soup. She had once painted her fingernails and had not gotten it all off. He took the spoon from her, but she held the bowl.

"Why?" he asked. He remembered something about drugs. There was something about that. There had been a long time on the bus.

"You were too sick," she said.

"But . . . I don't understand." To recall where he was and why he'd been there was too much of a struggle. The effort could not be sustained. It was like commanding his legs to walk when they did not want to. It was easier to sit comfortably alongside the little girl and not think at all, not try to remember anything except the soup which he took a spoonful at a time.

When he had finished, she stood before him and put a hand at the back of his neck and lay him down on the pillow. She

247

brought his legs up under the sheet and pulled the woven blanket to his neck. She kissed him again.

"Where are the rest?" he asked. "Those who were here. Your family. Where are they?" He could not keep his eyes open. He yielded to the counter-weights that sought to close them as they would the lids of a doll that was laid on its back. He wanted to know whether the tableau he had seen had been a dream or whether a Mexican family had really existed, had sat in this room, had really watched him in silence. But the wanting to know didn't last. When he closed his eyes the wanting wasn't as strong as it was when he framed the question. By the time she answered, it didn't matter at all.

She spoke from a great distance.

"They are doing different things," she said. She told him that the men are in the fields and are farming and that the women are at the market. There was a place where the children were but her voice had become a whisper by then, barely stirring the air in which he slept.

"Isaac! Will you get the hell out of bed? You look you've been washed up on a river bank, for Christ's sake."

Sturge strode across the sun-flooded room carrying some clothes. He draped them on the back of the chair and threw open a window. Isaac recognized the shirt and slacks as his own, something he wore a long time ago. The boots, which Sturge had placed in front of the chair, were not.

In the bathroom, Sturge ran some water and emerged, wiping his hands on a towel.

"Breakfast is ready, but they'll only serve humans. Take a bath. And shave for Christ's sake, before you frighten someone. Some of these people still believe in Americans. Don't ruin it."

"What the hell are you doing here?" Isaac could not quite come to terms with what he was seeing. The man in the room clearly belonged to a life he remembered, but it was one he'd lived in a different time and place. It took him a moment to bring the two disparate histories together. That he could do so at all meant he was coming to life.

"I've come to take you away from all this," Sturge said. "Didn't anyone tell you I was coming? Or have you been that far gone."

"You drove from San Miguel?"

"No. I walked backwards. Of course I drove. I've come to save your unworthy ass. Now get out of the sack."

"How did you know I was here?"

"Christ, Isaac. Where have you been? You're here because I got you here. Don't you know about Sanchez? Didn't Roberto tell you?"

"Who's Roberto?"

"Your host, Isaac. He's the one who wrestled you off the bus. If he hadn't gotten to you, you'd be three days into a twenty year prison sentence. He says you didn't have papers, you didn't have money, you didn't have diddly."

"And Sanchez?"

"I stopped off at his ranch on the way back from Potosi. Told him your troubles with the law. He made the calls while I was there. The old man was really steamed. He had the mayor by the balls. You should have heard him."

"Then it's off, the drug stuff?"

"It's off. But he couldn't get the bulletin pulled, or whatever the hell it's called. At the border they were still looking for you. That would take a day or so. That's why he called the ranch here, Roberto. Got him to drive to San Fernando. His orders were to get you off the bus if he had to shoot you. If you tried getting into Texas, they'd have nailed you. They had descriptions of you in Matomoros. They were waiting for you there. You're famous, Isaac. Big-named trafficker. Anyone who busted you would make Chief of Police, or an equestrian statue on *Avenida Independencia*."

"Heinrich did this?"

"Sanchez wanted to turn it around on him. He's a lucky bas- tard."

"What do you mean, turn it around? And where is Memori?"

"Sanchez, as you might have guessed, is one of the political

249

powers in the country. When you made him a friend, you made a good one. Heinrich would never have made it out of the country if it weren't for Memori. Sanchez didn't want to get her involved. They would have interrogated her as well. She's riding with him. I wasn't sure you knew."

"She was going as far as Brownsville with him," Isaac said. "She had told me that. She was going to get out at Brownsville."

"Listen. Get cleaned up. Come downstairs. You all right?"

"I'm a lot better than I was."

"You need help getting into the bath?"

"I can manage, Dad."

Soaking in the deep tub, Isaac realized he had not asked Sturge why he'd come. He could have told him everything on the phone. Isaac could have made it to the border on his own. Why would he drive all this way in order to drive him the few remaining miles to the U.S.?

The mirror was fogged. He took that as a piece of good fortune and shaved the dimly lit image within it by feel. His clothes had been cleaned and pressed and seemed a little larger than they had been when he last wore them. It was as though he'd been in prison a long time and just got sprung.

He put on the infamous yellow socks and tried the boots. Though they were much more highly polished than his own, they fit well. He'd scuff them up soon enough.

"They are my brother's, the boots."

The little girl stood in the doorway. She wore a white cotton dress trimmed in ribbons of faded lavender. One knee sock was a little lower than the other. She had tried to put her hair up on her own. The bun was a little loose and decidedly off- center. She looked like she had been crying.

"I'm sorry," Isaac said. "They were here. I didn't know."

"They're for you, please. It is a gift," she said. She stood in the doorway and made no attempt to come in.

"Your brother may have a different idea."

"It's all right," she said. "He's dead."

"He's dead?"

"Last fall. He was driving tractor for my uncle. It rolled and they didn't find him right away."

"I'm sorry."

It didn't at all look like she was going to cry again, but she stood in the doorway and was quiet for a long time.

"They were mine," she said. "My mother said I could have them. When you came, I saw that your boots were the same."

"But they're . . . they're your brother's boots and it's all, you know, you've got. To remind you, I mean. The boots are all you've got. You ought to keep them."

"It was your size exactly. I could see by the numbers written inside. The numbers were the same. The boots with the bandage and these. It was the same number. It will be all right with my brother. To keep the boots, I mean. I have yours. I'll polish them every day. I'll get a new bandage for the one."

"I'll have to talk to your mother, to see if it is all right with her." When Isaac approached the girl, he could see that she was holding back some tears.

"It will be all right. You can talk to her, if you like. The day you came, and when I saw the numbers on your boots, I told her about you."

"What do you mean? You didn't know me."

She remained at the door, her hands behind her.

"But I did," she said. "I do. You came because of my brother. I told my mother that. She understands how things like that work."

"Is that why you were so nice to me? Why you stayed home from school and took care of me?"

"I was told to do that. I'm the oldest of the daughters. I would have done that if the boots had not been the same. But it would not have been important." She bit at her lower lip and turned her face. Still she did not cry.

"Don't worry. I will remember everything," he said. "I will come back some day, just to see if you're shining my boots and see what kind of tape you've put on them."

"Of course," she said. She had the bright smile again. "Of course you'll come back. I told my mother that, after I saw the

251

boots. I told her that you'd go away, but that you'd come back. When I'm older maybe."

"Sure," he said. "When you're older."

"I'm twelve now, but I'll be thirteen next month."

"There, you see?" he said. "You're already heading in the right direction."

She giggled, then regained her composure. Something more she wanted to say crossed her face and was gone. She held forth an envelope she had been holding behind her back.

"Your friend wanted me to give it to you," she said. "It's not from me."

It was sealed. The envelope bore Isaac's name in feminine script.

"Well, maybe I ought to read it anyway," he said.

"Sure," she said, but she remained where she stood.

"Maybe you better let me read this alone. Then I'll come down and we can talk some more."

"Sure. That's OK. You can read it alone."

"And you'll go downstairs?"

"It won't matter, you know."

"What won't matter?"

"Whatever it says won't matter. You'll go, then you'll come back. It doesn't matter what the letter says. You can read it, but it won't matter."

When she left, Isaac shut the door. He sat on the straight back chair and opened the envelope. Someone knocked on the door.

He crossed the room and opened it. The little girl stood in the hall where she'd been.

"They were waiting," she said.

"What?"

"They were waiting in Matamoros, the police."

"I know."

"They knew about the bus," she said.

"What do you mean?"

"She told her boyfriend. He told the police. That's how they knew."

252

"How do you know?"

"Your friend. He told my uncle this morning. They said not to tell you. It would be better, they said, if you read it in the letter."

"Clearly," Isaac said.

"I tried. They said to keep it a secret and I tried."

"Don't worry."

"I couldn't help it."

"It's OK," Isaac said.

When she left, he closed the door. He crossed to the window and looked down into the yard. Sturge was roping Isaac's suitcases to the roof of the Deucheveaux. The younger of the men who had pulled him from the bus was helping him cinch tight the rope. They were talking animatedly, laughing about something.

Isaac sat on the straight-back chair and unfolded the letter. The sun was bright on the page. He had to wait for his eyes to adjust enough to see that the page had been filled with the same neat script that he had seen on the envelope. But the sun was too bright. He could not keep the writing from flowing together. It was the sun that made his eyes hurt, he figured, and he blinked several times to bring them into focus, but that seemed to make it worse. It was like trying to read something underwater.

Isaac stood. He folded the letter and put it back into the envelope. He waited at the window for a while. When his eyes got better, he tore the envelope in two and dropped the pieces on the chair.

The little girl in the cotton dress was not waiting in the hall as he thought she might. As he passed through the low doorway, Isaac ducked his head beneath the lintel. He did this neatly and quite without thinking.